ENDORSEMENTS

"Nothing beats a real cop telling real stories about the work we do every day on the streets of America. This is a tale of truth . . . and a good yarn to boot."

—**SHERIFF JOE ARPAIO**, *Maricopa County, Phoenix, AZ*

"As a captain for a federal agency charged with protecting federal employees and property from San Luis on the Mexican border to Chinle on the Navajo reservation both before and after 9/11, I find the scenarios Mike puts forth in *Lit Fuse* are gut-level real and make for yet another compelling read."

—**DAVID STADDON,** *former city, state, and federal law enforcement officer*

"The new novel by Mike McPheters, *Lit Fuse*, proves once again that Mike can capture the essence of the ongoing war waged by our law enforcement and military elements against tyranny and the oppression of terrorists who seek to undermine our nation with drugs and assaults on innocent people.

"Mike has always been an example of the intense dedication of our law enforcement officers and portrays that with true concentration and loyalty to the love of country extant in our police and military members."

—**TED LIVINGSTON,** *former Oakland, California, police officer, Sergeant First Class, United States Army (Retired)*

"As a former FBI agent working the border, Mike McPheters has lived where the action is. He's seen the corruption and the costs of criminal behavior, poor enforcement. Who better to write about what really happens?"

—**SHARON HADDOCK,** Deseret News, *Salt Lake City, Utah*

"Mike McPheters has done it again! First it was *Agent Bishop: True Stories from an FBI Agent Moonlighting as a Mormon Bishop*, then *Cartels & Combinations*, now *Lit Fuse*. This final book is the trilogy with a three punch knockout! Mike's intimate knowledge of the ins and outs of the Federal Bureau of Investigation, as a Special Agent for thirty years, along with his experience as an ecclesiastical leader in The Church of Jesus Christ of Latter-day Saints, makes him the right man to write this book. Mike knocks it out of the park with *Lit Fuse*."

—JAMES B. TILLEY, *retired special agent,*
Drug Enforcement Administration

"Ten years after the Sept. 11 terrorist attacks, are we better defended against the possibility of a coordinated strike against American citizens on American soil? Author and former FBI agent Mike McPheters paints an unsettling picture of US vulnerabilities in his new political thriller *Lit Fuse*. . . . Like a Mormon Tom Clancy, the *Agent Bishop* author weaves an exciting story that gathers a disturbing sense of authenticity from the reams of behind-the-scenes knowledge."

— CODY CLARK, Daily Herald, *Provo, Utah*

MIKE McPHETERS

To Ann Tolman —

Best Wishes to a
faithful reader!

Mike
McPheters

LIT FUSE

Bonneville Books
An imprint of Cedar Fort, Inc.
Springville, Utah

ISBN 13: 978-1-59955-978-0

Published by Bonneville Books, an imprint of Cedar Fort, Inc.
2373 W. 700 S., Springville, UT 84663
Distributed by Cedar Fort, Inc., www.cedarfort.com

LIBRARY OF CONGRESS CATALOGING-IN-PUBLICATION DATA

McPheters, Mike, 1943-, author.
  Lit fuse / Mike McPheters.
    p. cm.
  Includes bibliographical references and index.
  Summary: Delisha and Lufti Ahmed, children of Pakistani immigrants, have
been raised as potential suicide bombers. Then they meet two young Mormon
missionaries who change Delisha's life forever.
  ISBN 978-1-59955-978-0 (alk. paper)
  1. Child suicide bombers--United States--Fiction. 2. Terrorism--United
States--Fiction. 3. Mormon missionaries--Fiction. I. Title.
  PS3613.C58745L58 2011
  813'.6--dc23
                            2011031092

Cover design by Brian Halley
Cover design © 2011 by Lyle Mortimer
Edited and typeset by Melissa J. Caldwell

Printed in the United States of America

10 9 8 7 6 5 4 3 2 1

Printed on acid-free paper

To the brave men of the FBI,
especially Jordan Naylor, Joe Frechette, Frank Duffin,
Gene Flynn, James P. Hufford, Denny Campbell,
Ben Grogan, and Samuel Cowley

ALSO BY MIKE McPHETERS

Agent Bishop: True Stories from an FBI Agent
Moonlighting as a Mormon Bishop

Cartels and Combinations

Contents

Contents

AUTHOR'S NOTE

WHEN I WAS HIRED BY DIRECTOR J. Edgar Hoover—the first director of the FBI—in 1968 as a special agent, I had not yet earned the prestige and honor that goes with the motto of "Fidelity, Bravery, and Integrity." When I launched my career with the FBI, I needed examples—mentors—to eventually earn that prestige by the time I would retire thirty years later.

I found my first mentor in Bishop Jordan Naylor, a veteran agent in San Diego—my initial assignment. He was both my church leader and my example in the FBI. When there was a "Top Ten" fugitive to go after or a tough assignment to be filled, Jordan was one of the first agents to get the nod. Although Jordan's life ended abruptly in an explosion shortly after his retirement, his sterling example has always been there to spur me on.

In my second assignment in the Miami Division of the Bureau, I found men that continued to inspire me, mold my character as an agent, and make me laugh. I will always honor Special Agents Joe Frechette, Frank Duffin, and Gene Flynn, my Irish Catholic friends and buddies, for demonstrating through their actions and personalities how to work hard and smart, get along well with everyone, and have outrageous good fun. Frechette was shot down over Germany flying a B-17 in World War II at the age eighteen and was a POW for eight months until the Russians finally liberated his camp. Duffin fought the Germans on skis as part of the

US Army's Tenth Mountain Division in Italy. Flynn was a crack investigator whose intuitions and uncanny "sixth sense," bordering on the supernatural, led him to unbelievable accomplishments in solving major cases.

To this day, I honor these three men.

It was also in the Miami Division that I met my first partner, James P. Hufford, who I worked with ten hours a day and loved as a brother. We became known as The White Knight (Hufford) and The Holy Crusader (Me). I have never met anyone who enjoyed working so hard and so meticulously and who took more pride and satisfaction in being an agent. We would drive to the office each morning with our plan of attack for that day in hand, execute it, and then spend the ride home figuring out what dragon we would slay the next day.

Then there was special agent Denny Campbell, a black belt in martial arts and fellow SWAT team member, who by suffering through an unbelievably tragic accident that would take most men out of their game, demonstrated the willpower and the strength to rehabilitate his body and remain totally productive after retirement.

Denny's example is priceless.

They say the best die young and soonest. That would be the case with special agent Ben Grogan, who died in the worst gunfight in the history of the FBI—the same friend who fronted me several thousand dollars when I had to transfer across the country and my advance of fund was late in arriving from the government. Ben was just like that. If a vote were taken among the Miami Division agents for who was closest to being the perfect agent of all time, Grogan would come out way ahead. He could—and did—do it all, including laying down his life.

The last hat I have to take off is to an agent that I never met: Inspector Samuel Cowley, a young Mormon attorney from Utah, who joined the FBI in 1929 and became one of J. Edgar Hoover's right-hand men. He was assigned to bring in the infamous gangsters of the 1930s, like John Dillinger, Charles Arthur "Pretty Boy" Floyd, Lester Gillis (also known as "Baby Face" Nelson), and a host of others. He was also killed in the line of duty. When I was transferred to the San Diego Office for my first assignment, I read a letter from Director Hoover that stated, "Sam Cowley was one of the greatest examples of physical and moral courage that I have ever known."

I have been truly blessed to be surrounded throughout my career by the kind of men I just introduced you to. This book is dedicated to them.

ACKNOWLEDGMENTS

In every book, there are always people in the background that contribute to its development. I would be remiss if I didn't acknowledge the many US Border Patrol officers and Immigration and Customs Enforcement (ICE) agents that I have met this past year at book signings in Arizona and Utah. All of them have indicated to me their great concern for not only drug cartels wrecking havoc in America, but also another threat that has much more serious consequences: the immigration of radical jihadists from the Middle East who are now embedded in our society—due to the porous and unprotected nature of much of our two-thousand mile southern border—and are waiting for the right moment to strike. I appreciate their hard work and the frustration they feel when so often they are not provided the resources and manpower they need to do their job.

My sympathy and support especially goes out to the residents, law enforcement communities, and leaders of Arizona, California, New Mexico, and Texas who are experiencing the greatest challenges to America in fortifying and protecting our southern borders . . . and particularly to Arizona's great sheriff, Joe Arpaio of Maricopa County, who has personally met with me and made me aware of those challenges.

Again, I wish to recognize the efforts of my wonderful daughter, Marni Wilks, who helped with the editing of this book, along with the editors at Cedar Fort, Inc., my publisher.

PREFACE

I'M SURE MANY OF YOU HAVE ASKED yourselves this question: "Why has America escaped the horrible suicide bombings that have occurred in so many other countries throughout the world?" Perhaps you, like me, have come up with only one answer that makes sense, given the extremely porous nature of our borders with Mexico and Canada: "We are in the palm of God's hand."

On the evening of May 1, 2011, the president of the United States officially announced that Osama bin Laden, the leader of al-Qaeda, had been killed by American forces in a mansion just outside of Islamabad, Pakistan. With that announcement came the warning of possible retaliatory attacks on America by al-Qaeda cells throughout the world that have been developed since 9/11.

On May 6, 2011, an article was published by msnbc.com, quoting "the general leadership" of al-Qaeda, stating that America's "happiness will turn to sadness," referring to forthcoming retaliation for bin Laden's death. Apparently, the terrorists feel that another attack on America is more important now than ever to show they are still relevant.

This is the story of how that attack could happen.

Just what and who are the suicide bombers? It has been stated that suicide bombers are clearly the weapons of choice for international terrorists. In the Middle East, most suicide bombers are chosen as teenagers. Some are educated before being sent to accomplish their missions in their late teens or early to mid-twenties.

When recruited, they are encouraged by the terrorist groups to sever all relations with their peer culture. They are steeped in radical interpretations of the Koran and instructed to memorize much of its content. From an early age, they are raised in a culture honoring those who sacrifice their lives in the cause of Islam.

One strange anomaly is that parents are more than willing to sacrifice their children for the "honor" of martyrdom, all in the interest of radical Islam.

In order to protect American lives, it is imperative that the US government tighten our borders and increase our intelligence gathering capabilities, the first and foremost actions needed to defend our country against suicide missions.

The FBI is aware that al-Qaeda is actively recruiting female suicide bombers, along with their male counterparts. You will read about several of them in this book. More and more frequently, suicide missions are being attempted in the United States. On Christmas Day 2009, Umar Farouk Abdulmutallab, a Nigerian, attempted to blow up a Northwest Air Lines plane flying from Amsterdam to Detroit. On May 1, 2010, Faisal Shahzad, a budget analyst from Connecticut, attempted to detonate his car—loaded with bombs—in Times Square in New York City. Afterwards, he commented, "If I'm given a thousand lives, I will sacrifice them all for the life of Allah." In late November 2010, the FBI was successful in thwarting an attack by a Somali-born US citizen, Mohammed Osman, who attempted bombing the annual holiday Christmas tree lighting at the Pioneer Courthouse Square in Portland, Oregon. Today, FBI vigilance remains a major key in preventing terrorist assaults.

Suicide bombings have evolved from being a common tactic of terrorist groups in the Mideast to an aggressive experiment in the United States, because we have provided a fertile field through our negligence of the border.

In certain locations in the Mideast, parents send their children to street *madrasahs* or Islamic fundamentalist organizations to be educated. Often they are turned into extremists. I believe the same kind of diabolical metamorphosis is occurring here in America, but under the radar.

My account of Delisha and Lufti Ahmed typifies the genesis of homegrown terrorists raised up as suicide bombers in the
United States. It exposes the emotion and turmoil within both
the parents called upon to sacrifice their own flesh and blood
and the children who are being sacrificed to the radical cause
of Islam. It will highlight the confusion that must ebb from the
would-be martyrs, who must surely at some point find themselves questioning their commitment to a rendezvous with Allah
through self-destruction.

This is the story of the al-Qaeda attack that we pray will never
happen, but most surely will . . . an attack that will not be prevented by our government, as currently constituted. It is an assault
upon our country that could only be prevented through human
compassion, a change of heart, and the love of Jesus Christ.

CHAPTER 1
INFERNO

OMAHA, NEBRASKA
JULY 4

GHANI HUSSAIN RESOLUTELY PUSHED the wheelchair occupied by his sister, Kareema, toward the center of the crowded mall, brimming with shoppers preparing for their Independence Day celebrations. The siblings of Pakistani descent anticipated their impending deaths with frayed nerves as they contemplated their last day on earth.

Kareema wore her long dark hair curled meticulously and was attired in a bright yellow caftan with black embroidery on the sleeves and neckline. Ghani, stocky with handsome bronze facial features, wore a loose-fitting, light blue *guayabera* to cover the harness of lethal explosives suspended from his shoulders. A similar quantity of instant death was secreted in the arm supports and under the seat of Kareema's wheelchair and on her person. The Hussains cautiously scoured the crowd for any sign that the FBI or Homeland Security may have taken them under surveillance.

Never before had their aspirations been so close to fulfillment. Armed with the conviction that they were born for that moment in time, they had prepared themselves for what they knew would last for but a second, then Allah would embrace them in his loving arms and make them his affectionately—forever. Their rewards would be both infinite and eternal. The blessings reserved for

1

martyrs of the highest order guaranteed the prestige of Paradise with every heavenly consideration—freed from mortal prison.

Their anticipation heightened as they proceeded past the Orange Julius stand and several designer clothing stores en route to the food court. Their thumbs rested lightly on the detonator buttons rigged to trigger the forthcoming explosions. They became even more exhilarated as they checked their watches.

It was 12:17 p.m., thirteen minutes before the assigned moment.

The lunch crowd on July 4 had invaded the limited seating areas adjacent to the mouth-watering array of culinary choices . . . soul-satisfying foods that Ghani and Kareema would never again taste. The tables were filled to capacity with hundreds of men, women, and children—all misled American infidels, just standing there in line, wearing American flags embroidered on their apparel. Most eagerly anticipated that first scrumptious bite into one of the juicy hamburger holiday specials, covered in red, white, and blue wrappers for the special occasion.

Ghani glanced at his wrist watch.

12:20 p.m.

Ten minutes more!

The would-be assassins, although trembling inwardly with fear, were encouraged, knowing that the damage they would incur upon the enemies of Islam would be significant.

As they approached the food court, Ghani and Kareema proceeded slowly and cautiously, careful not to reveal the weighted containers strapped to their bodies. Years of preparation and dedication for their final mission were not to be deterred by a foolish mistake that might inadvertently reveal their purpose. Not now!

Kareema looked up at her brother. Her normally aggressive and gung-ho sibling was pale and sweating profusely. *Is he having a change of heart?* she thought. *Now isn't the time!*

"Don't worry," she said calmly with a forced smile. "Soon we will be with Allah."

Ghani glanced down at his sister and nodded. Wiping the sweat from his brow with the sleeve of his guayabera, he began mouthing words from the Koran that he had memorized from his youth. Anything to keep calm and focused on his mission.

"I love you, sister," Ghani said, bending down to embrace her for the last time in their mortal life.

"I'll see you in the arms of Allah," she whispered into his ear.

12:29 p.m.

Silently, without any form of communication except hand signals, they pointed to the two locations in the food court most densely populated: the Ben and Jerry's ice cream stand and the Caribbean Food Café. They fingered the thin cord attached to the explosives. Seconds away from their chosen targets, they moved closer to the exaltation reserved only for a dedicated martyr. It was now well within their reach.

Never had the American infidels experienced such an attack within their borders by God's "real" people. The difference between Kareema and Ghani and their infidel targets was the siblings' conviction that once engulfed in flames, they would ascend upward toward their heaven—a place of great peace and bliss— while the Americans would descend into a fiery abyss reserved for the unbelievers.

Kareema and Ghani smiled at each other triumphantly, then Ghani left Kareema in her wheelchair at the ice cream concession and with a quickened pace, proceeded to his destination approximately fifty feet away.

Kareema wiped the tears from her eyes and adjusted the detonator in her left hand, her thumb already on the button.

Ten seconds later, the siblings glanced at each other furtively. Both gave a thumbs-up.

That was the signal.

They glanced at each other one last time and closed their eyes.

"God is great!" Kareema heard her brother yell.

Suddenly the world came apart inside the mall. It was as if the entire food court was engulfed in the jaws of flaming hell. Glass shards, needles, nuts, screws, and other metallic objects shot out like missiles in every direction, bringing down scores of dazed shoppers as far out as the main corridor of shops leading into the food court.

3

Dismembered body parts were strewn throughout the remains of the food court area. Burned blood spatters covered tables and walls. Although the suicide bombers had disintegrated with the multitudes of victims surrounding them, their handiwork was manifested by a blast radius of seventy-five to one hundred feet around them, and a large crater had been created into the marble floor under them.

* * * * *

The economic fallout from the Omaha mall bombing was yet another disaster. Once news of the assault broke out, it caused ripples of panic throughout the country. The intimidated Americans were afraid to shop in malls and other public retail outlets. Sales were at historic lows as retail sales figures throughout the nation plummeted. With the reliance on mall security diminished, Americans could no longer trust their previously secure venues for retail purchases.

Unlike 9/11 where the attacks were focused on specific buildings that represented national icons of historic significance, the Omaha attack brought threat levels to every shopping mall in every state throughout the country, making it a national assault not only in the real sense, but also psychologically. Over three thousand souls had perished in the unbelievably devastating 9/11, but the Omaha incident mentally impacted countless millions of US citizens. Shoppers were held hostage by their doubts and fears.

Even though the White House responded to the Omaha disaster by implementing every security measure at their disposal, they were at a loss on how to deal with the economic disaster. Never before in America had anyone walked into a mall on such a significant holiday and succeeded in attacking with suicide bombers. People chose to just stay home.

American perception drastically changed in Omaha, Nebraska, the heartland of America, on its Independence Day.

Waves of panic and trepidation emanated from the center of America. History was again rewritten. Every American had been put on notice that no city in the United States was immune from terrorist attack.

How many more were there? When would they come next? And where would they hit? Those three questions had to be answered. And they were now in the minds of every American.

CHAPTER 2
CAUGHT SHORT

THE WHITE HOUSE
JULY 5

GIFFORD PIPPS, WHITE HOUSE chief of staff, called a priority meeting with White House press secretary Jim Murray. There was ground to cover and plays to call. The president was attending to other matters.

Murray almost fell over himself, scurrying down the halls of the White House to meet with Pipps. He'd been up all night upon hearing of the Omaha bombing. The dark circles under his eyes did nothing to add to his normal emaciated, tired demeanor. With his mind working full-speed and a body pumping adrenaline, he looked like a poor excuse for someone who had spent almost a full decade working for Fortune 100 companies prior to becoming the president's spokesman—a task he had excelled at for over two years.

However, Murray felt oddly intimidated by the Omaha incident. He had deftly handled all the press inquiries regarding the bombing but was finding it increasingly difficult to cover for his boss, who seemed casual and unresponsive to the turmoil at hand. The president had issued a vow to track down and punish those responsible for the assault, but other than that, he was missing-in-action. With the nation reeling back from this attack, the president needed to be front and center for the public—fast. The Commander-in-Chief had refused to meet with Murray face-to-face, and Murray felt Pipps had done nothing to help arrange that meeting, even though it was vital to the public relations guy to be responsive to press inquiries. Each time Murray had contacted Pipps for a meeting with the president, he came away rebuffed. Now, a day after the bombing, Pipps was *finally* working him in.

Instead of just barging into Pipps's office, he stopped short, took a few breaths, and then proceeded. He had conditioned himself from his career in public relations to try to refrain from going into something with a chip on his shoulder, knowing it could only make things worse. If he kept cool, maybe Pipps would still set up a personal meeting for him with the president where Murray could learn why the country's leader was hesitant to make a statement following such a national catastrophe.

When Murray entered, Pipps had the phone pressed to one ear and was typing as he spoke. He motioned for Murray to take a chair in front of him. Pipps's face was red, exposing his high stress level. He was balding, short, and about one hundred pounds overweight—a heart attack waiting to happen.

Pipps ended the call and started speaking before Murray could say one word.

"Glad you're here, Jim. This Omaha thing is blowing up in our faces. Did you hear—?"

"Poor choice of words, Gifford, considering the number of people that died yesterday." Murray's staccato voice resembled the blasts of a machine gun.

"Well, all right, Murray. That's why you're the guy that's always in front of the cameras. Now where was I? Oh, poll numbers. They're plummeting. This Omaha thing has to be handled with kid gloves. You know what I mean? The Tea Party people have been on our backs for years about securing the border, and guess what? Now they've got even more fodder for their cannon! This thing has got to be couched right, Murray. We're talking serious damage control here. Got it?" Pipps was adamant.

Jim Murray was more prepared than anyone to be the PR point man for the president. He was a Harvard graduate with years of experience in public relations . . . and a glib tongue at that. But the foul balls being hit by the administration on the

Mexican border issues were getting progressively more difficult to field.

"You know, Pipps, the conservatives are going to kill us on this one! They've been on to us for a long time, figuring out the vote-gathering thing. Sure, there are fourteen million illegal immigrant votes at stake here. Once the President gives them amnesty—sure, they'll vote our ticket. But I don't know if I really buy the administration's view that there will be enough votes to perpetuate a one-party system *ad infinitum* and that doing so will be the remedy we're seeking for our tanking poll numbers."

Pipps hit a couple more keys on his laptop, turning it so Murray could see the spreadsheet of all major polling data extracted since the bombing. "Well, Jim," responded Pipps, "you gotta buy it! Look, the president's numbers are plummeting. He's already down ten points since yesterday. We've got to stop this trend . . . and fast! He needs amnesty for these folks, and he needs those votes—big time! You're the point man here for our entire PR. It doesn't matter how you feel personally. You know that. You're the president's man. That's the line!"

Murray sighed. Poll numbers. Five hundred people dead and Pipps was only thinking about his boss's re-election.

"Look, Pipps, I know all that. But we're going to be up to our behinds in alligators here, and no one's draining the swamp! Unless the president gets out in front of the American people on this bombing, there's no end to the free fall. He needs to reassure them and promise them with his own word that the perpetrators of that mess in Omaha will be brought to justice. This Tea Party crowd is ready to convince the whole country that those two suicide bombers in Omaha came across the Mexican border, whether they find evidence to the contrary or not."

"Yeah, Murray, and that's exactly why you have to find a way to head this thing off at the pass!" Pipps snapped.

"And don't forget about Congresswoman Smith's allegations that there's an alliance in place between al-Qaeda and the Culebra drug cartel and all the collusion being suspected between those groups," added Murray. "There was the allegation a couple of days ago about an al-Qaeda plot to blow up the Falcon Dam on the Rio Grande that almost came to pass, and would have, had it not been for a quick border patrol investigation that nipped the thing in the bud. That would have adversely impacted over four million US citizens' commercial and agricultural activities. This news is just getting out, making the general public—our future voting electorate—wonder when and what we're finally going to do about protecting the border."

"Our Homeland Security Director is looking into that," responded Pipps. "She still maintains that the border is more secure than it has ever been."

"Yeah, right!" snorted Murray. "The obvious indifference to the concern of so many citizens, especially those living along the border in places like Pinal County in Southern Arizona, where so many Mexican illegals—and who knows who else—are crossing the border with impunity, is driving those people crazy. They feel like the current administration has betrayed them and couldn't care less about what happens there. They keep alleging that it's all about vote-gathering. Adding another fourteen million voters to our support. They know exactly what we're doing, and they don't like it. Bottom line is they have our number, Pipps!"

"That's politics, Murray! We won the election . . . remember?"

"It's worse than just that, Pipps. And people are wanting to learn a lot more. Problem is, I don't have enough answers to give them."

"Think of some answers, Murray," Pipps said, getting angry. "That's your job! And one other thing. The president's going on the air in two hours."

Murray nearly jumped out of his seat. "What did you say? Why wasn't I notified?"

"Easy, Jim! I just got confirmation when you walked in. That's why I was on the phone. You may not believe this, but the president and his speechwriter have been working on this all night. When you leave here, you can immediately advise the press."

It's only a day late, Jim thought. "So what's he going to tell America?"

"Basically, the standard stuff: America will come out on top on this. A full investigation has been launched by the FBI. The same stuff you've been wanting him to say. But all this is not your concern. Your marching orders are to diffuse Congresswoman Smith's accusations that the bombers came across our southern border. Her allegation of cooperation between al-Qaeda and the Culebra drug cartel is gaining traction and making the president look weak and ineffective."

"Then I suggest the president address the border issue in his speech," Murray advised. "We need to squash the rumor about the bombers coming over the border from Mexico. I'll write it for him."

Pipps put his hands together, leaned forward, and spoke very softly. "This country has problems, Jim. Big ones. This morning, the president received some intel from the FBI. Two Bureau sources—who apparently don't even know each other—in San Diego and Los Angeles are saying the same thing . . . something about a hundred more terrorists in the Tijuana area preparing to hit several major American cities all over the country. Two different, unrelated sources, Jim . . . both saying the same thing! Another attack like the one yesterday and you can kiss good-bye to another four years in the White House."

Murray was momentarily speechless. "So the Congresswoman's allegations are well-founded?"

Pipps shrugged. "We don't know enough about yesterday's bombings yet to be sure where the perpetrators came from. FBI headquarters has a new team of super sleuths that think they can find the answers."

"So we need to assure the press, correct?" asked Murray. "More border fencing, increased border surveillance, additional manpower—"

Pipps jumped out of his seat, gesticulating wildly. "Look, Murray. The president has six words for this problem—six words only. 'Get this monkey off my back!' And I'll tell you right now, if you think this Omaha bombing incident is going to precipitate some big swing toward sealing the border, you're just living on another planet . . . 'cause it's not. With the poll numbers tanking out, he's going to need the Mexican vote to get re-elected. No way does border security get anything more than window dressing right now!"

"And you're saying that in spite of the information from the FBI that we just talked about? Is that right?" asked Murray.

"You said it."

"I still need a half hour with the president," Murray said somewhat stubbornly, "so I can synchronize my message to the press with his. How about it? I could have handled it at breakfast, but I couldn't get in touch with you or anyone else."

"Come on, Murray! You knew the president was playing golf today. I was with him. I'd left my cell phone at home, and they didn't want to contact the president until he'd finished the nine holes. He needed a break, Murray. As I said, he spent the night up and needed a couple hours nap this morning and a little diversion."

"It's not about the president playing golf, Pipps. It's about his lack of sensitivity regarding the threat at our back door with Mexico. Here's the thing, we're not looking at the whole picture here. Have you ever seen a 'suitcase nuke'?"

"Not really," said Pipps.

"If you think the president's numbers are bad now, wait until a weapon of mass destruction is brought over the border," Murray said. "Let me tell you about a suitcase nuke. They'll fit a bomb into a regular-sized briefcase with no sweat. If the Mexicans can get thousands of pounds of cocaine into this country in briefcases, just think how easy it would be to bring in a nuke or several pounds of poisonous bio toxins in one. Then, with the help of the Culebra cartel's contacts with the American street gangs to distribute those bio toxins, and the suitcase nuke going to the right party at the right price . . . BINGO!—a big part of American population just disappeared. Americans were beginning to get psyched out about this *before* the Omaha bombing. Think what's going through the average public mind now.

"Combine that with what happened in Omaha and the president's got to come up with something really spectacular to defend his lack of action along the border."

"Listen, Murray," said Pipps. "This really doesn't change the argument. There are fourteen million Hispanic votes here, and we're going to need every one of them to win this next election." Pipps started pacing. "The president has been on the verge of proposing a bill to give illegals citizenship. I'm talking amnesty. Fourteen million more votes we could count on, Murray. That bill won't have a chance if word gets out that terrorists are being trained south of the border to come over and kill us. Think about the big picture."

That was one of the sickest comments Murray had heard coming from this administration. Not caring about weapons of mass destruction or terrorists being trained in Mexico to come over and kill Americans? Keeping it all concealed to secure votes? Murray's mind was buzzing.

"You know, Pipps, if this rumor is true about the training camps and the terrorists coming over and we have 'poo-pooed' border security and have tried to cover it up, the president will lose the election even if every Hispanic in the country votes for him . . . and maybe we'll all go to jail."

Now Murray really had Pipps's attention.

"You're right, Murray," Pipps conceded. "As much as I hate to admit it, you're right. This new threat from the south, if corroborated sufficiently, could be a game changer. I'll set up a meeting with the president for you and me later this afternoon, after his speech . . . around four-thirty. In the meantime, I'll call the FBI director for more clarification. Then we can all come up with a game plan on handling this in the most discreet, favorable manner possible. But I reiterate, Murray, that your job right now is to let me worry about the plans and you deflect the allegations from Congresswoman Smith and do all you can to make the president look good. In the meantime, get in front of the camera and make sure everyone knows the president goes live in two hours."

Murray stood to leave.

"One more thing before you go, Jim. Nothing—I mean, *nothing*—goes out to the press on these training camps in Mexico and the possibility of terrorists coming from down south. Your job is to run interference on this issue. Understood?

"I get it," said Murray. "Four-thirty. Where?"

"The Oval Office."

Murray nodded and turned without a word. He felt torn. As the PR guy for the president, he often felt that he was only telling half the truth. It made him feel like a creep. He had so much more bottled up that America should hear, news that belonged to the whole country, not just a select few in the administration. The conversation with Pipps had once again left him with the same conclusion. He was just buying time for the president; once again he was running interference.

It's the same old game. Politics first! Murray told himself. He knew the party line was beginning to weave a little too much to one side. He was being pushed out of his comfort zone . . . way out. *Almost five hundred people in Omaha either dead or dying. What if a sealed border could have made the difference?* he asked himself. *And what about these other killers . . . maybe a hundred of them, being prepared in Tijuana to hit us again? And I'm to say nothing? To do nothing?*

Jim Murray was beginning to like his job less and less.

CHAPTER 3

JAWBONE MATCH

OMAHA, NEBRASKA
JULY 5

FBI FORENSICS EXPERTS WERE slowly and methodically sifting through the residuals of the Omaha bombing, working in tandem with the Bureau's disaster response unit. The day after the attack, the stench of death still lingered over the whole area. Coupled with the acrid scent of burnt and charred walls and furnishings, the odor was overwhelming. Sifting through the wake of the July 4 tragedy to obtain post-blast evidence was daunting, but not an unfamiliar task for the men and women of the FBI assigned to respond to such calamities.

From the scores of victims hewn down lengthy distances where the bombs were deployed, it was obvious that the most potent killing had not been caused by the explosions alone, but by the huge quantity of shrapnel emanating from the explosions. The bomb had been filled with steel mini-balls, screws, nuts, bolts, needles, and pieces of thick wire, which were launched in every direction from the blasts. Each fragment had an impact similar to that of a bullet. Victims in every direction from the two explosions were laid low by a battery of artillery, creating an impact similar to that of a machine gun mounted on a rotating swivel.

FBI technicians were bagging and labeling hundreds of fragments and dating them to be preserved as evidence in a gargantuan effort designed to piece together the type of bombs used by the subjects. The steel balls were described as ball bearings three to seven millimeters in diameter, the type most widely used by terrorists and the most dangerous form of shrapnel.

Based upon the kind of metal fragments used, the harnesses worn by the bombers were presumed to be "fragmentation jackets," a label given to the explosive harnesses Palestinian suicide bombers and other terrorists in the Middle East used in similar attacks. It was a cheap and effective way of massacring maximum numbers of victims with every self-detonation.

The technicians discovered additional evidence that pointed to the use of either acetone peroxide or TATP (triacetone triperoxide) as the initiating explosive and ammonal as the main explosive. The FBI concluded that the ammonal was "homemade," and that it had been mixed with ammonia nitrate, coal, and aluminum powder . . . again, the category of bomb frequently used by Palestinian terrorists. The difference, however, was that unlike with Palestinian assailants, the detonator in this incident was probably a hand-held device rather than breaking a light bulb and lighting the wire coated with flammable material, which was the simplest kind of detonator.

The technicians ruled out both TNT and C4. They felt both of these explosives would have been much more difficult to obtain, when acetone peroxide could be purchased in household stores without making anyone suspicious. Hydrogen peroxide was used for bleaching hair, and acetone was used for nail polish. Another reason acetone peroxide was suspected was that the "sniffing dogs" had not detected it, since this substance prevents dogs from being able to smell it.

The crime scene investigators concluded that the "body bombs" were somewhat sophisticated. The metal cylinders were filled with explosives and shrapnel, then connected to a wire that ran down the sleeve of the bombers' clothing leading to the trigger, where it could be manually accessed. The cylinders had most likely hung in the inner lining of the sleeves.

A perimeter was formed within the mall, encompassing the entire food court area, which only the police, forensic examiners, and emergency personnel could enter. The mall had been thoroughly evacuated and searched for any secondary bomb devices or bombers. The area was also searched thoroughly for any abandoned vehicles that could possibly contain additional explosive devices. Uniform and plainclothes officers from the Omaha Police Department had been tasked to search for suspicious persons.

As the FBI forensics people combed through the charred remains of the Omaha mall, one of the agents observed an odd piece of burnt bone mass hanging from the limb of an artificial tree about fifty feet away from one of the craters. A hydraulic jack was brought over and hoisted up with an FBI agent on top, enabling him to grab the object for analysis. Upon close observation, it was apparent that the object was the jawbone of someone involved in the bombing, either a victim or subject.

The jawbone contained four teeth on one side and three on the other that had not disintegrated. The piece was carefully preserved and passed on to the forensics people. A minimal amount of dental work had been done on a couple of the teeth, which could be used to identify the deceased.

Since all the reports had been submitted to the Omaha Police Department regarding any suspicious happenings in the city, as well as the arrest records going back to a month before the bombings had occurred, comparisons of the dental records of the suspects involved could be made against the recovered jawbone.

One of Ghani and Kareema Hussain's neighbors had reported that both of them, along with their parents, had left mysteriously and had not returned. Their sprinklers had been left on, flooding not only their front sidewalks, but also those of their neighbors. A neighbor had knocked at their door but had gotten no response. This neighbor had invited the parents over to play cards with them the night before on July 3. Since the police and the FBI had done several joint news conferences claiming the Omaha attack had the trappings of a suicide bombing, the neighbor had suddenly become curious about the Hussains and had filed a suspicious person report.

Dental records were secured for the Hussains and all others

reported as suspicious persons and were compared with the dental fragments on the newly-discovered jaw bone.

A "hit" came back on Ghani Hussain's dental records. He had indeed been there at the scene of the bombing.

When it was announced over the television that Ghani Hussain was a "person of interest" in the bombing of the mall, a close high school friend called in another report to the police.

The complainant related that on July 2, Ghani had told him he was flying out with his parents to Afghanistan to visit relatives on July 4. He was very curious why Ghani would still be in Omaha at the mall on that day.

A subsequent review of airport flight manifests determined that Ghani and Kareema Hussain were not on the flight manifest sheet as having boarded the aircraft, although airplane tickets had been obtained for them along with their parents.

The obvious began melding together. Those facts were bolstered by the reality that the Hussains had flown in a hurry to Islamabad without their children, leaving their home and all their belongings.

It became clear that Ghani and Kareema Hussain were indeed the suicide bombers.

Pictures of the two assailants were obtained from the Nebraska state drivers' license bureau and were exhibited to employees of the various stores and shops in the mall who had survived the bombing. Both Kareema and Ghani were identified entering the mall just before the bombing. Ghani had been pushing Kareema in a wheelchair. Both were wearing loosely-fitting, long flowing clothing that could easily have hidden explosives. Although there were no living witnesses who had observed Kareema and Ghani set off the explosives, it was clear that the brother and sister team was responsible for the attack.

The police findings revealed a new face to the *modus operandi* of potential suicide bombers in the United States. Authorities would now consider the possibility of brother and sister attack teams. Siblings made sense to the authorities. Familial loyalty and easier accessibility to one another for planning and mutual motivation were perfect prerequisites for carrying out the attacks.

The concept of deploying females on suicide missions was an established trend in the Middle East. In fact, the FBI's International Terrorism Unit was aware of this method of attack by Palestinian terrorists. Seventeen of the established terrorist organizations were turning to women to carry out their attacks.

One suicide bomber trainee, Hiba, last name unknown, a twenty-eight-year-old mother of five, had made the statement, "I have to tell the world that if they do not defend us, then we have to defend ourselves with the only thing we have: our bodies. Our bodies are the only fighting means at our disposal."

The FBI was aware that suicide attacks, including the use of women, had evolved into a very efficient method of terrorism, probably the most efficient. They discovered that from the years 1980 to 2001, although suicide missions accounted for only three percent of terrorist incidents, those same attacks were responsible for half of the deaths related to terrorism.

The FBI also discovered that the use of women as suicide bombers contributed to the added advantages of surprise and accessibility to targets, because women drew little suspicion.

Prior to 9/11, the FBI had not considered suicide bombers a great source of concern. However, in December 2003, New York City was on high alert over warnings of an attack by a female suicide bomber. And the Department of Homeland Security had been warned of the potential repercussions of ignoring the possibility of a female suicide bomber.

After 9/11, the official profile the Department of Homeland Security used to describe the typical terrorist for checking out resident aliens and visa applicants had applied only to men, specifically "males aged between sixteen and forty-five." When they implemented the sibling team attack concept, al-Qaeda operatives like Bashir Sayed and Rashid Siddiqui were quietly encouraged by this lack of scrutiny for women as a potential threat.

Law enforcement authorities now needed to be on the alert for this new type of suspect: siblings raised in the United States by parents who had been conditioned to sacrifice their children for "holy" missions. These young men and women of minority descent resembled so many others that constitute America, the mixing pot. They would be youth who were scholars, athletes, and friendly neighbors raised by immigrant parents who had fraudulently professed a desire to become citizens of the United States.

This new breed of terrorist was home-grown in the real sense—someone who could easily be a confidante of other Americans and an excellent example in the classroom, one who combed his hair like any other American and liked to eat fast food. It could be one who saluted the flag, attended Christian churches, and kept out of trouble with the law. Indeed, it could be one who was clean-cut and wholesome—a youth raised by model immigrant citizens.

No longer was there a standard profile.

CHAPTER 4
CELEBRATION AND INDOCTRINATION

ISLAMABAD, PAKISTAN
NIGHT OF JULY 5

IN THE OPULENT RESIDENCE of Abeer Hussain, paternal uncle to Ghani and Kareema Hussain, glasses were being raised by uncles, aunts, and cousins to the family's recent martyrs in the holy cause of Islam. Wine was poured freely as more and more relatives swarmed in to celebrate. Ghani and Kareema's parents, Ghafir and Raaida Hussain, had purchased their flights out of Omaha the day before, ensuring they would be already heading back "home" a couple hours before the attack. They were the honored guests.

Ghafir and Raaida Hussain had not shed tears over their son and daughter but had gloried in their children's new position and prestige in the Afterlife. Their children had done Allah's bidding and had gone to their reward. They were born and raised for that purpose.

Having given up their home, cars, and personal property in Omaha, taking only what they could carry with them, the Hussains would now live comfortably in the home of Abeer, Ghafir's brother, for the rest of their lives . . . subsidized by al-Qaeda funding. Ghafir and Raaida would also be regarded as heroic, having given up their flesh and blood in such a noble cause.

Ghani and Kareema's parents had not dared to put their home in Omaha up for sale. Neither had they tried to sell their cars or any other property that might hint at their departure. They were careful to do nothing out of the ordinary that could possibly draw suspicion to their children's forthcoming attack, orchestrated by al-Qaeda. The militant Islamic group had been formed a few years earlier by Osama bin Laden. They called for global jihad against non-believers. The Hussains knew appearances needed to be maintained. They would never seek remuneration or compensation in America for their earthly goods, nor did they need it. They would live handsomely for the rest of their lives, supported by al-Qaeda money, with relatives who would cover for them.

Prior to their departure from the United States, Ghani and Kareema's parents had been awaiting their flight to Islamabad in a restaurant at the Kennedy International airport in New York when the welcomed reports of the Omaha tragedy came over the television. Their hearts had leaped for joy while watching the news report of the wreckage and carnage in the mall in Omaha. They rejoiced inwardly while observing the devastating results of their children's mission. As they toasted one another, smiling broadly, people seated nearby stared suspiciously at them with expressions of curiosity and disgust. Aware they were being watched, the Hussains ceased their revelry instantly. They knew once they were on the plane headed to Islamabad they could more appropriately vocalize their exultation.

To understand how parents could celebrate sacrificing children for such a cause, one must go back in time.

In the year 1991, when Ghani and Kareema were infant children in Islamabad, one of al-Qaeda's most influential clerics, Rashid Siddiqui, an *imam* or "holy man" who presided over their local mosque, selected six families from his congregation with two children each: a brother and sister. These families met his criteria as fervent and dedicated believers in the cause of radical Islam. Siddiqui approached the Hussains with his plan to "raise martyrs up unto Allah" from the children's tender age in the infidel nation of America, their enemy. Eventually, when the time was right, these young people would make some of the most noble and far-reaching sacrifices ever in the cause of Islam.

Siddiqui had explained that through an alliance with and financial support from al-Qaeda, the families would be blessed to live well while raising their martyrs-to-be in America. The families would be furnished papers created by a drug cartel in Mexico that would facilitate their "immigration" into the United States. There they would establish roots in the cities of Omaha, San Francisco, Los Angeles, Chicago, New York, and Miami.

The families were also advised that a Pakistani al-Qaeda operative in the United States, Abu Khan, would meet them, handle their financial arrangements, and help integrate them into American society. The fathers would have the kind of employment they were accustomed to . . . just for appearances and not far from where they lived. The mothers were to be "stay at home" types that would raise their children, see they were well-educated, and constantly inspire them as to the great and final achievement of their life's mission.

The plan had gone into effect. The families were successfully transplanted with fabricated documents throughout the United States. The children were raised normally, like other American children, but always in the shadow of Siddiqui and other Muslim clerics in the United States who sympathized with the radical jihadist movement.

Knowing their lives would be short, there would be many tender moments for these parents in nourishing their "martyrs-in-embryo," but those feelings could in no way eclipse the parents' mission to instill in their children the noble cause of martyrdom.

Prior to the Omaha bombing, Ghani, Kareema, and their parents, along with the other five families, had met faithfully at a Los Angeles mosque once every three months to listen to either Siddiqui or another *imam,* or cleric presiding over the mosque. The young martyrs-to-be, who would become known as "The Twelve," were being "incubated" under the watchful eye of the al-Qaeda. Quarterly joint meetings of The Twelve were held with Siddiqui, but the identities and residences of the other youth and their parents were not disclosed from one family to another, nor would their lives associate, except in the quarterly gathering. That way, the al-Qaeda were convinced, there would be less chance of the young aspirants inadvertently disclosing information about al-Qaeda's plans to attack America to authorities who resided in the various venues where the "offerings" were to be made.

Additional anti-American propaganda would be spewed forth at other meetings where the families resided. If that were not enough, the parents were encouraged to follow the same line of hate-mongering at home, picking apart the Americans, and portraying them always as evil and decadent.

The al-Qaeda sponsors continually assured that "blessings" kept flowing in to the sacrificial families with seemingly unlimited funds for nice homes, cars, clothing, food, and the best education money could buy. The refrain was always: "Spare no expense in the cause of Allah!" Al-Qaeda funding was made abundant through their monopoly on the heroin trade, bolstered by lush, ubiquitous fields of poppies, harvested with impunity in the fields of Pakistan and neighboring Afghanistan.

* * * * *

Los Angeles, California

Upon being apprised of the devastating consequences of the Omaha assault, there was a mosque gathering of the remaining martyrs—now to be referred to as "The Ten"—and their parents. Rashid Siddiqui addressed those present.

"Dear parents . . . Dear children, praise Allah! You are the great ones. Not only will your sacrifice raise your names in Holiness forever, as that by Ghani and Kareema has done, but each day, each week, each month and year that you prepare for your union with Allah, you will cause His blessing to flow into your families.

"In the Koran, we read of the outrage and disorder caused by the western world . . . especially the Americans. We watch with trepidation and disdain as the infidels persist in tearing out the roots of humanity. But we are taught from the Koran how to cope with this. I read from Sura 8, page 120:

"I will cast a dread into the hearts of the infidels. Strike off their heads then, and strike off from them every finger-tip. This, because they have opposed God and his Apostle: and whoso shall

oppose God and his Apostle . . . Verily, God will be severe in punishment. This for you! Taste it then! And for the infidels is the torture of the Fire!"

Siddiqui distributed at these "religious" gatherings anti-"Western World" rhetoric, making sure the poison flowed fully into his young audience.

Rashid Siddiqui, accompanied by Bashir Sayed, the principal coordinator of the al-Qaeda cells in America, looked out upon all the pairs of brothers and sisters, all in their early twenties, seated in the mosque with their parents.

The success of Ghani and Kareema Hussain the day before in Omaha signaled to the other Ten that their missions were possible and well within reach. The al-Qaeda leaders counted heavily on the other volunteers becoming empowered and emboldened, now that the city of Omaha, the heart of the infidel dog, had been brought to its knees.

Rashid had declared the meeting a day of rejoicing. He stated with great emphasis, "This is an occasion of celebration! On July 4, the infidel day of celebrating their independence, two of us, Ghani and Kareema Hussain, successfully struck at the heart of this blasphemous country at a mall in Omaha. Hundreds of enemy souls were turned to ashes. Praise Allah!"

"Praise Allah! Praise Allah!" came the refrain from all in attendance. The fervor and enthusiasm from those who would soon follow in the Hussains' footsteps was obvious.

Siddiqui forged ahead. "From a very young age, Ghani and Kareema, along with their parents, prepared faithfully to launch their sacrifice of blood and body, as you will soon do."

Heads were nodding in affirmation. The imam was lulling the attendees into enthusiastic agreement.

"I have something here for each of you that I will ask Delisha and Lufti Ahmed to distribute. The gifts are necklaces venerating Ghani and Kareema as the first martyrs to take a giant stride forward in America through their courageous and historical attack on Omaha."

Siddiqui had carefully chosen the Ahmed siblings, Lufti and

Delisha, to be his assistants. They were not only the most educated of the group, but seemingly the most aggressive in courting
Siddiqui's philosophy in his crusade against the Americans. The
Ahmed siblings had been particularly good at disguising their real
motives while in their host country.

Twenty-one-year-old Lufti, athletic and intelligent, had
excelled in sports in high school and in college baseball. He
was soft-spoken, yet always animated when discussing his
forthcoming destiny as a martyr for Allah. He was undeviating in
his commitment to self-sacrifice . . . and always a favorite of the
Muslim holy men for that commitment.

Delisha was slender, fit, and pretty, with long black hair setting off an attractive dark complexion. She was twenty years old.
Her dark brown, oval eyes were alluring, seeming to contain
thoughts, the meaning of which one could only guess at. She had
been an honor student, a leading thespian in high school stage
productions, and had even obtained a scholarship to attend Bro-
ward County Community College near Plantation, Florida, the
community where the Ahmeds resided while preparing for the
long-awaited Christmas Eve "event" at a mall near Miami.

The Ahmed siblings were deeply devoted to their Islam foun-
dation. Whatever Siddiqui asked, Delisha and Lufti had tried to
deliver. They were looked upon as leaders among the youth of the
local Muslim community in South Florida, none of which were
aware of their mission for Allah. Only those other martyrs-to-be
that met in these periodical gatherings with Siddiqui knew of one
another's real destiny.

Each participant received a necklace engraved with the words
"Praise to the heroes of Islam!" Bashir Sayed, the al-Qaeda coordinator, encouraged the young people to wear them with honor
as an assurance that what the Hussains had accomplished, the rest
could also bring to pass.

As Delisha and Lufti passed out the necklaces, they stepped
around posters that Siddiqui and Sayed had placed in front of
the group, extolling the virtues of past suicide bombers. Missing
this day were the music videos often played at these meetings to
inspire even more confidence in the glory of past suicide bombers

in the Mideast. All present sensed that something different was going to be presented.

Bashir Sayed had a presentation. He stood to address the gathering. "You will now be given the opportunity to hear and see Ghani and Kareema one last time."

Heads jerked up in disbelief. Sayed introduced a video, accompanied by a rousing al-Qaeda battle hymn with the words "A Last and Final Testament" flashing across the screen. Ghani Hussain, representing both him and his sister, had prepared it, just prior to their attack on the Omaha mall. As those in the gathering watched, Ghani's words came out slowly and deliberately.

"Kareema and I are honored to sacrifice ourselves in the cause of Islam. We are proud to spread Mohammed's sacred teachings to all the world through this sacred act of jihad. The unholy character of the western world must be vanquished, that the true religion of Islam might fill the world.

"We plead with you who yet remain with your glorious missions still unfulfilled to do your part faithfully and effectively, so that you also may join us in the sacred embrace of Allah. Praise Allah!"

After seeing the video, the ten young adults seemed mesmerized by Ghani's words. It was obvious to all present that the remaining martyrs-to-be had become even more galvanized in their determination. The cult of martyrdom had spread its roots deep into the hearts of Siddiqui and Sayed's following.

Referring to the forthcoming Christmas Eve attacks on the remaining targets, Siddiqui stated, "Even though the American dogs think themselves indomitable, they will be humbled when you, the ten champions of Islam, make your marks on the heart, breasts, belly, and hips of the infidel nation."

"What are these words?" asked one of the parents.

The head cleric smiled broadly. "The dog's heart was the American city of Omaha. That has now been ripped out. Next will be the breasts: San Francisco and New York. Also the belly: Chicago. And the hips: Los Angeles and Miami. You see?" Siddiqui produced a map of the United States. "The heart," he said, pointing at Omaha, then to other locations, "the breasts, hips, and belly, which correspond to the various parts of the body." Siddiqui was openly proud of his metaphors.

The imam continued, "The unique aspect of your demographics is that you are all brothers and sisters. You will be faithful to one another and to your mission and will be less conspicuous, pretending to be a couple, entering a mall, or other public place, holding hands . . . until that last exalting moment." Siddiqui, the major architect of what he often referred to as "The Dream Attack," smiled inwardly at his cleverness.

The cleric had also provided for any mitigating circumstances, by emphasizing the need for two people to carry out their holy mission, in case one became ill or unable to fulfill his or her commitment. The idea then would be for the surviving sibling to strap on even more explosives.

Siddiqui continued. "The attack on September 11, 2001, preceded by other attacks on American embassies, military establishments, and naval vessels, was isolated, planned more at random and somewhat unrelated in nature. They will not hold a candle to what you will accomplish on what the Americans call 'Christmas Eve.' We are much more organized. The Omaha incident not only struck terror into America's gut, but also has prepared them for even more suffering. Within just five months, you'll repeat the Omaha success in America's five largest cities on Christmas Eve—a fitting date to strike down the misled adoration the Americans profess for this Jesus they call a Savior . . . one they have the gall to compare with Mohammed!

"I assure you that these attacks by The Ten will inflict overwhelming anxiety on America. It will be an overpowering psychological crisis for the infidels, apart from the many deaths of all those who will perish. All the world will read of it in their newspapers and on their televisions and Internet. All mankind will become aware of the consequences of betraying the true followers of Allah. Praise Allah!"

"Praise Allah!" came the responses.

The imam Siddiqui, bought and paid for by al-Qaeda, was indeed pleased with the control he had over the mind, and hearts of his congregation. He concluded his remarks, heaping praise upon those gathered before him.

None of the attendees were more captivated by the electricity in the meeting than Lufti and Delisha Ahmed—Lufti because of his compassion for martyrdom and Delisha because of a need to reinforce her personal conviction of her forthcoming mission.

Delisha recalled in detail the years of preparation for her "Meeting with Allah," including the several trips she and Lufti had made back to their native Pakistan starting at age sixteen. There, they had attended clandestine training centers where al-Qaeda operatives taught them certain warfare techniques. They were taught how to wear explosive harnesses so as not to be detected and how to most effectively detonate them. She and Lufti had been trained by four al-Qaeda instructors in four two-hour sessions each day for the ten days they were in Islamabad at the training compound, only a few miles outside of the city.

Delisha and Lufti learned how to handle explosives, operate Kalisknikov sub-machine guns, and assemble and take apart AK-47 assault rifles. They listened to instructors who taught them about the weaknesses in American law enforcement and police tactics. The priority emphasis was always on the explosives training. They practiced moving around with the explosives distributed on their legs, arms, backs, and bellies. Each participant was shown the best way to strap on his explosive harness, based upon his individual build.

Delisha was impressed by the thorough, all-inclusive nature of the al-Qaeda training and was convinced it was only a matter of time until the questions that were gnawing at her would be answered and her doubts would abate.

CHAPTER 5
THE SURVIVALISTS

HAYDEN LAKE, IDAHO
JULY 5

BUCK BOWEN WAS SIPPING coffee when the details of the Omaha incident flashed over Fox News. Bowen's six-foot-five-inch frame, anchored by a ~~ pot belly bulging out against the k~~ igure. He made quick work on a huge plate of ham and eggs, mountains of hot cakes, and several mugs of coffee. The more he ate, the more food seeped onto his ample handlebar mustache. His salt-and-pepper hair and wrinkled brow portrayed a man making absolutely no effort to mask the approaching seventies.

The log house in Northern Idaho near Hayden Lake had been built by Bowen and many of his "survivalist" associates. It was located on land that bordered an area previously occupied by the Aryan Nations, an extremist group formed by the Reverend Richard Butler, who focused on white superiority, hate toward blacks and Jews, and a disgust for the American government. They were a neo-Nazi group inspired by Adolph Hitler followers. From the 1970s until 2001, the headquarters of the Aryan Nations was a twenty-acre compound located 1.8 miles north of Hayden Lake.

Bown and his associates had reportedly tried to form an alliance between their white supremacists and al-Qaeda, hoping to exploit the shared hatred of the American government and the Jews. They had been successful.

Bowen's group hated America as it was and had allied themselves with al-Qaeda's clandestine cells embedded throughout
America via the Mexican border. Bowen's men were a mixture of
survivalist fanatics, Jew haters, Ku Klux Clan sympathizers, and
followers of the Freemen of Jordan, Montana. All these groups
believed that the federal government had failed in its responsibili-
ties and should be disregarded and replaced . . . that it had no right
to inflict laws upon the people.

Bowen's group called themselves the "Mountain Patriots,"
although they were anything but that. They believed the end was
coming soon and when it did, they would persevere with their
survivalist culture and establish a new and more effective form
of government. However, they recognized they could not do this
alone. Entering into a compact with al-Qaeda's Pakistani representative, Abu Khan, was proving very advantageous, both politically and financially.

Bowen had signed a very lucrative contract with Khan, who
had carefully researched Bowen's organization and was delighted
when he became aware of Bowen's hate for the American government. Khan subsequently offered him five million dollars a
year to covertly manufacture and deliver portable harnesses filled
with explosives to al-Qaeda operatives in the United States and
to assist in transporting those operatives to US destinations they
had targeted. The understanding was that if word got out at any
time about the al-Qaeda connection, the payments would be discontinued immediately. Bowen had sworn his men to absolute
secrecy.

Each Mountain Patriot fully understood that the difference
between becoming a millionaire or living in log cabins surviving
on elk and deer meat the rest of his life depended on how well he
could keep his mouth shut. On the Middle Fork of the Salmon
River in Idaho, they had a clandestine lab used for manufacturing
the explosive harnesses. It was well-hidden in a large cave with an
entrance only big enough for one man to crawl through at a time.

When Bowen saw the residuals of the Omaha attack on Fox
News, he was captivated but really not surprised. He had known
for months that something big was going to happen. He'd

traveled to George Town, Grand Cayman, periodically where he would meet with Abu Khan in his plush room at the Marriott Hotel to discuss the quantity and quality of the required explosives, as well as the eventual delivery sites. Bowen was awed at the amount of money Khan was paying him and his men and couldn't care less what the explosives would be used for. He had already received the first two million with the promise that the remaining three million dollars would be delivered the week prior to Christmas Eve.

Neither Bowen nor his followers suffered any remorse for their fellow countrymen in Omaha who were so gullible, misguided, and ignorant enough to support American leaders. *To the Devil with them!* he thought.

Bowen picked up his cell phone and dialed Ike Grimsley's number. Grimsley was in charge of the plant in Idaho's Parrot Creek drainage off the Middle Fork. Now in his early seventies, Grimsley had been a bomb technician in the US military before deserting to avoid ever having to fight for a country he no longer believed in. He had stated his objections to the war due to "significant disagreement" with American leaders regarding their support of Israel. He had been extremely embittered since his release from incarceration, subsequent to his arrest by the FBI for desertion.

"Yeah, it's Ike," Grimsley answered. "What's up?"

"It's started Ike," Bowen said. "The first of your goodies went off last night in Omaha. Fox News reported three hundred and seventy-one are dead. Another hundred and twenty-three are hospitalized."

"That's good! The more the better!" Even Bowen was somewhat startled by Grimsley's response. He decided it would do no good to tell Grimsley how many of the victims were children. *Grimsley's a hard one!* he thought.

Grimsley's hatred for his own country was insatiable. He had lost two sons in the war in Iraq, which he considered a sham. He was convinced that Saddam Hussain was a victim of American imperialism and that no weapons of mass destruction existed that the former administration said were there. Although his sons had volunteered for duty and had gone to war willingly, he always thought they had been naïve. They had been raised mostly by their mother, who had always tried to keep them away from Grimsley's influence. She had succeeded for the most part after their divorce. He had limited contact with the two boys, but had just enough to grow close to them. Their deaths in Iraq had only exacerbated his hatred for the government. He loved the idea of helping who he called the "ragheads" attack the country.

Grimsley had pushed another concept of his own. He had tried to convince Bowen to dispatch several Mountain Patriots to various major interstate overpasses throughout the country as snipers. His idea was to take out fifteen or twenty truck drivers hauling groceries to the major food outlets of the country . . . all in the same week. He figured all the drivers would go on strike until the truck manufacturers reinforced the truck cabs with several inches of steel and installed bullet-proof windows. He insisted that would quickly empty the shelves of retail food outlets throughout America so people couldn't eat. He delighted in imagining what degree of chaos that would cause . . . a major step in bringing America to her knees prior to bringing in a new form of government.

Unbeknownst to Grimsley, Bowen had already turned that concept over to Abu Khan for a big chunk of pocket change and it was already being implemented in the training camp in Mexico.

Bowen liked most of Grimsley's concepts of revolution and destruction but wanted to wait until Abu Khan's plan for the suicide bombings materialized. Bowen's philosophy was always to "Let the ragheads take the heat!" Once the suicide bombers were through, then Bowen and his men could perpetrate their own assaults, and the government would blame al-Qaeda.

Bowen reveled in the hope that the resultant hate crimes toward all Mideasterners throughout the country after the suicide bombings would cause such chaos and mistrust, it would create the perfect environment for him and his men to carry out their havoc with impunity.

"Maybe those stupid jaybirds at the seat of government will start getting the message," Grimsley stated bluntly.

"Well, that's neither here nor there," answered Bowen. "We're going to need everything ready for this next event coming up in December. How are you doing for ingredients?"

"It's tricklin' in. Getting the stuff flown in from Stanley to Indian Creek landing is the first problem. Those freaking bush pilots can't seem to get over the fact that we've got all this stuff in wooden boxes weighing a ton that they know nothing about and we can't tell them. I've got to slip them a couple hundred here and there to keep their mouths shut. I keep telling them time and time again that if anything leaks out, the dough disappears. The slush fund here is hit hard."

"That's not a problem," Bowen said. "There's plenty of money to cover that."

"Can't we get our own plane and pilot?" Grimsley asked.

"We had two, remember?" Bowen reminded. "But they both got cold feet when they found out what we were flying in. I haven't been able to find anyone else since."

"Well, just keep that in mind," growled Grimsley. "Any one of these flyboys could blow our thing here, unless we keep 'em happy."

"We will. Don't worry about it. That's my job. What else?" Bowen asked.

"If we're putting on a full-court press to get this stuff down the river, we need to change out a few rafts. Some of these old military fourteen footers are no good when you have to keep everything dry. Even though we're putting everything in river bags, there's always a little seepage. Remember, if we can't keep the acetone peroxide dry, we're going to be hurtin' big time."

"You mean the TATP, right?" asked Bowen.

"Yeah, that's what the sophisticated folks call it. But if it gets mixed with river water, forget it!"

"What about just going with the TNT?" Bowen asked.

"It's harder to come by. Got to get it out of old mines or shells or on the black market. You think we got the time to run the risk of developing contacts to store that stuff?"

"Probably not," Bowen said.

"Besides, with TNT, dogs can sniff it out." Grimsley wondered if he was impressing his boss with his knowledge.

"Okay, Grimsley. So what are you asking for?"

"Let's get more money out here into the slush fund for payin' off these bush pilots, and let's change out these old military rafts for new Avon self-bailers. But we need to do it fast if you want all that product done before December. And, remember, since we can't fly in any noise here as in helicopters and so on, without giving away our position, everything has to come down the river. It's three hard days rafting from Indian Creek to get here at Parrot Landing and another two days to convey the finished product down to Cache Bar on the Main Salmon, where it can be off-loaded onto pickups."

"Done," Bowen answered.

"And another thing. Who knows what the weather will be like here in December? Snow for sure and some ice on the river. We'll need to ask again for half again the requested quantity of materials just in case we lose a raft or two. Only two harnesses can be placed on each raft, since they have to be triple-wrapped for insulation and protection from seepage. They'll take up a lot of room. Three men hafta go with each raft: one to oar and two armed lookouts, just in case somebody down the river wants to try some funny stuff. I'm talkin' seven rafts for the four extra harnesses and twenty-one men. I only have eight people here now."

"Good grief, Grimsley. That's almost our entire contingent!" Bowen said, becoming impatient.

"That's what it'll take, boss. Take it or leave it."

Bowen could tell Grimsley couldn't care less. It would have to be his way or nothing.

"All right, you hardhead!" Bowen said. "We'll get you the rafts and the extra money. We'll have to dig hard for the manpower, but if we're lucky, we'll get you all the bodies you need. We'll do it within the next few days, so you'll have plenty of time to make this stuff and wrap it right. Just keep working and don't disappoint me!"

"One more thing, Bowen," Grimsley said. "Goin' into this here cave through that small opening one man at a time is takin' its toll on my rheumatism. But there's no place else to hide this operation. Can't store this stuff in the cabin. Plan on fixing me up with a little extra cash incentive, will ya?"

Now Bowen was really upset. "What's that supposed to mean, Grimsley?"

"I mean a measly ten thousand bonus—ya know, Christmas money in December? Half now and half then. Okay?"

Money was no object for Bowen, but this underling had him over the barrel. No harnesses in December meant forget the other two million.

"Okay, Grimsley. It's added to your other cut you have coming, all right?"

"Right, boss. Just a little something ta keep body and soul together, you know!"

Bowen knew Grimsley was just like him and the others: greedy. He had no recourse but to say, "Yes."

CHAPTER 6
THE CARTEL CONNECTION

TIJUANA, MEXICO
JULY 5

THE RESIDENCE OF CARLOS Quesada, leader of the "Culebra (Snake) Cartel," lacked nothing of opulence. Each year, Mexico did forty billion dollars of drug trade with the United States to satisfy the insatiable American cravings. Quesada had carved a huge piece of that figure out for himself and his henchmen. Their lives of luxury carried an overwhelming appeal to scores of policemen and military personnel who had deserted their prior stations in life to join Quesada's organization. The "If you can't beat them, join them" attitude eclipsed any principled behavior or concept of loyalty to these individuals.

Quesada had entered into an agreement ten years prior, just after 9/11, with Abu Khan, who lived in Los Angeles *officially,* but spent most of his time in George Town, Grand Cayman. Quesada was impressed with the power and nerve of this blend of militant Mideasterner who would so blatantly attack the United States. Quesada should have been grateful for the prosperity America's drug dependency brought him, but instead he looked at America and her leaders with disdain. He saw how prone America was to allow her borders to remain unprotected in order for liberal-leaning politicians to gather the Hispanic vote by trying to grant illegal immigrants amnesty. Even Quesada could see clearly that with allowing the illegals amnesty and with the Hispanics having the highest birth rate in "Gringo Land," America's liberal element would eventually succeed at perpetuating a one-party system in the United States.

Quesada ruled the Tijuana cartel with an iron fist. For him, human life held no real premium. He battled viciously to maintain his territory as he killed scores of competitors in turf battles, mainly along the United States border. The fact that stray bullets from Quesada's border wars were also killing Americans meant nothing to him.

From the time Mexican President Felipe Calderon went to war against the drug cartels in 2006, over thirty-five thousand people had died along the American border, including many US citizens. The wars—resulting from drug traffickers jockeying to fill vacant positions created when Calderon's forces killed, arrested, or jailed a cartel leader—left an unclaimed legacy of valuable drug distribution territory open. Flexing their muscles in order to make statements to competitive cartels, Quesada's minions would decapitate his opposition's people, roll their heads onto the lawns of their families, then hang the bodies upside down from bridges spanning across nearby highways. These inhumane demonstrations of power enticed young drug runner wannabes to join the organization, galvanizing their lusts for wealth and power.

Mexico was out of control. It was feared that it would become a "failed state," causing a domino effect on the world economy and in the societal structure of other countries, especially America. The United States did over 130 billion dollars a year in trade with Mexico, their third biggest trading partner.

Men like Quesada and his minions capitalized on this kind of societal chaos and human frailty. They used it to their advantage, sending willing young Mexican men in alligator boots, silk shirts, and cowboy hats in new pick-ups to Gringo Land with hidden loads of marijuana, cocaine, methamphetamine, and opium derivatives to capitalize on the insatiable demand for drugs.

Quesada himself typified the blended nature of the Mexican people and their mestizo culture. Five feet six inches tall, with an ample protrusion of belly, the forty-two-year-old drug warrior had a face void of hair, reflecting his Amerindian lineage. He had lighter black skin with a hint of Negroid features. His rough face was punctuated with a knife slash from the bottom of his lower lip, right side, up to his right ear, which he had earned in a knife fight. His adversary had stood in the way of Quesada taking over leadership of the Culebra Cartel, which was still in its formative stages. The same knife ended buried in the other man's throat.

Quesada was descended from Arawak Indian inhabitants of Dominica in the Lesser Antilles Islands of the eastern Caribbean who eventually married African slaves that had escaped from two Spanish slave galleons.

Quesada's Amerindian ancestors had been expelled from Dominica late in the seventeenth century by the British and moved to Coxen Hole on the island of Roatan, Honduras, where life was hard. They became known as the Garifuna. With a 72 percent illiteracy rate, few of the Garifuna were prepared for meaningful employment. At any given time in Roatan, half of the men were absent, working jobs in the United States, Central America, or Mexico. Quesada's father left his wife and son in Roatan and found work in Culiacan, Sinaloa, Mexico, where he quickly learned Spanish and began working in the fields. There he met another woman, Quesada's mother, who bore Carlos and one other son. Later, she traveled with him to Tijuana. Quesada's father became an alcoholic, lost his job as a hotel attendant, and left the task of raising Quesada and his brother to their mother.

Carlos Quesada had little supervision from home and had only attended school a few years. In a short time, he took notice of the quick wealth available in drug running and instantly devoted himself to it. He married Safia, the daughter of a wealthy Tijuana merchant, when he was nineteen. She was sixteen. From there, those standing in the way of Quesada's ascendancy to become leader of the Culebra Cartel mysteriously disappeared or were found dead.

Now Quesada had a new line of business, complementing his involvement in running drugs—an agreement with Abu Khan to provide training for al-Qaeda militants bound for the United States, as well as providing passage and protection for them when they crossed over the Mexican border into the United States.

For years, Muslim terrorist organizations had been known to operate drug trafficking rings in South America, especially on the borders of Argentina, Paraguay, and Brazil. Eventually, some of these groups had spread into Mexico where they had initiated discussions with Quesada and other drug lords about transporting al-Qaeda operatives into America . . . for a price. Abu Khan had personally contacted Quesada, who amazingly had eliminated the other competition for the al-Qaeda contract.

Quesada and his wife were also compensated for seeing that the al-Qaeda operatives were taught English and an elementary form of Spanish. After teaching the hundred Muslim terrorists both languages, Quesada was to transport them over the border to the United States and provide them temporary work permits. From there they would be transported by Buck Bowen's Mountain Patriots to the target cities, including all the US state capitals.

As a child, Pakistani-born Safia had accompanied her parents to Culiacan, Sinaloa, where her father's passion for growing poppies to cultivate heroin was given full exposure. They then moved to Tijuana where he could more efficiently market his product. After marrying Quesada, Safia proved of great worth in translating and interpreting for him in dealings with Abu Khan. Khan was pleased to know a patriot of his homeland, also sympathetic with al-Qaeda's cause, was married to his Mexican contact.

Quesada's reward for this work: 150 thousand dollars per person smuggled over the border, each having been taught military tactics, some Spanish, and English, for a total of fifteen million dollars—"chump change" for a terrorist organization backed by huge oil interests and ever abundant poppy fields.

Quesada sympathized with Khan, particularly in his attitude of demeaning disrespect for the Gringos up north. Khan knew that Quesada had connections with American street gangs, specifically the Mara Salvatruchas, who were particularly good at transporting illegals and serving as "enforcers" and "collectors" for Quesada.

Even though Quesada was eager to take Khan's money, he inwardly loathed the Muslim descendants of the fanatical hordes, which the Spanish legend, "El Cid," had driven back into Africa.

Still, while dangling such enormous sums of money in front of Quesada's face, Khan had successfully enlisted him for another al-Qaeda attack on America's capital cities, a devastating attack that would be carried out by The Hundred on yet another Christian holiday: Easter.

CHAPTER 7
SEEDS OF CONFUSION

PLANTATION, FLORIDA
JULY 6

WHEN DELISHA AND LUFTI Ahmed first heard that Ghani and Kareema Hussain had successfully ascended into the Islamic heaven, both siblings suddenly felt their stomachs tightening. *It can be done*, they thought, *and we will be next, along with the others of The Ten . . . in less than six short months!*

"It went so smoothly for them," Lutfi stated matter-of-factly to Delisha. "Just think, sister. They are now in heaven, reaping their eternal rewards. We'll soon be there with them, Delisha. Our day is near!"

Delisha looked at her brother halfheartedly. *How I wish I could feel as enthused about the way I will meet Allah as you do, brother,* she thought.

Delisha had always admired her brother's commitment and dedication for their cause, which admittedly was somewhat stronger than her own. Although she had reflected a strong outward dedication to the Muslim clerics and to The Ten, inwardly she felt herself wavering as the day of self-sacrifice drew nearer. Each family of The Twelve had been encouraged by the holy man, Rashid Siddiqui, to fully assimilate into the infidel culture in every way possible in order to disguise their real motive for being in America. They were even encouraged to associate with American religions . . . anything to deflect suspicion. They had done just that throughout the last twenty years since arriving in America,

41

integrating themselves into the Christian carpet of religions, even attending services with Catholics, Protestants, and Mormons.

Delisha reflected back on that day when she was sixteen and the two young men wearing name tags drove up and parked in front of their house in Plantation, Florida.

When the missionaries drove up in their Camry and parked it about sixty feet from the front door of their residence, Delisha, Lufti, and their parents peered out from the living room window. They observed something that riveted their attention. The driver—over six feet tall and muscular—got out, walked around to the passenger side, and opened the door for the other male passenger.

Then something occurred that imprinted a picture in the Ahmed family's memory forever. The husky driver reached in and with a quick gesture, almost effortlessly placed the frail passenger into his arms, gently and carefully, and began walking with him cradled securely up the path to their home. The apparent invalid was about the same age as his benefactor and had two wooden canes straddled over his lap. As they approached the front entrance to the Ahmed home, moving determinedly and matter-of-factly, it was obvious that the twosome had been through this drill many times before. The one being carried, although tall, appeared to weigh no more than 150 pounds. He wore thick, horn-rimmed glasses, was balding, bore a pallid complexion, and had droopy eyelids that were very obvious.

As the two men approached their home, Delisha's eyes were fixed on the one carrying his companion with apparent ease. She took note of his dark complexion, well-chiseled face, and muscular build. He had a pleasant appearance, graced by a handsome smile and a full head of hair.

Once the young men entered the front porch area, they momentarily disappeared from sight. Then came a rap on the door. Delisha rose to open it. She was surprised to see the disabled man who had been carried by the driver standing upright and facing her, supported with a cane in each hand. The other one stood a little off to the side. She found it interesting that the visitor who had been carried seemed to be in charge. He spoke first.

"Hello! I'm Elder Sterling, and this is Elder Brown. We're missionaries from The Church of Jesus Christ of Latter-day Saints, and we have a message for you about the Savior. May we come in?"

Delisha looked at her father for approval, hoping he would allow the two in, especially the tall muscular one. At first her father hesitated and would make no commitment, but when his wife glanced toward him with a positive look of approval, he nodded affirmatively. Delisha's parents needed to continue their charade—anything to mask their commitment to radical Islam. Her parents allowed them to come in since they knew there were several other Christian families living in their neighborhood. Denying them entry might offend some of those neighbors and perhaps raise a flag of suspicion.

Delisha opened the door widely, gesturing toward the large dining room table for them to sit down, while casting a wide smile at Elder Brown. "Please come in!" she said politely.

Lufti looked on with curiosity toward Elder Sterling, wondering why he would be working in his feeble condition.

Elder Sterling walked in like a wooden soldier, very slowly and painfully. With each step, he placed his weight on one cane and then the other. He grimaced occasionally, dragging one foot after another, refusing help from Elder Brown. Once he reached the dining room table where everyone was sitting down, he turned backward toward a chair and allowed himself to collapse into it. He tried not to express the pain in his countenance that he felt, in order to avoid being conspicuous.

Lufti wanted to toy with the two young men, like he had the Jehovah's Witnesses and some born-again Christians that had come before to "bear witness." "Where are you guys from?" he asked.

Elder Sterling responded. "I'm from Payson, Utah. Elder Brown here, the little fellow who packed me in, is from Atlanta, Georgia." Anticipating Lufti's next question, Elder Sterling continued. "I've been a missionary out here in Florida for almost twenty-one months."

Elder Brown weighed in, addressing himself more to Delisha

than the rest. "I've been out sixteen months. We serve two-year missions at our own expense to tell people about the modern-day prophets and our Savior, Jesus Christ."

Delisha noticed her father rolling his eyes with that condescending "Here we go again!" look.

She thought that Elder Brown was extremely handsome and sweet-spirited. She was willing to listen to anything he had to say . . . regardless of what he might talk about.

Lufti asked, "I've seen lots of you guys biking it and going door-to-door like this. Doesn't that get old? Lots of people your age are either working or going to college. Do you make good money?"

"None," Elder Brown said. "It's all strictly volunteer work at our own expense, as I mentioned before. We've both had some college . . . me one year and Elder Sterling two. We hope to finish after our two years out here."

Mr. Ahmed had had enough. He began thinking of an excuse to leave the room.

Elder Sterling added, "No good money, but great pay!"

Lufti was puzzled.

Elder Sterling continued explaining. "We share our testimonies of Jesus Christ with those we meet, like you, and try to explain His mission on Earth. The only pay we receive is the satisfaction of serving others this way and relaying to people the message Christ has brought to mankind, so all people everywhere can live after the manner of happiness."

That was it for Lufti and Delisha's father. He couldn't stand to hear another word praising the Christian god. He stood up and asked to be excused, indicating that he had some stomach problems. As he slowly left the room, he glanced at his wife, who stared back with disdain.

The two missionaries visited with Delisha, Lufti, and Mrs. Ahmed for another half hour before Lufti's curiosity became insurmountable and he asked Elder Sterling, "What did you say your name was?"

"Just Elder Sterling" came the response.

"No. I mean your first name," said Lufti.

"Well, we don't use first names while on our missions. We just go by 'Elder.' That's an office in our priesthood."

Priesthood? thought Lufti. *These guys are weird. Oh, well . . . they're no different than some of the other 'do-gooders' that come around here.* Yet, deep down, Lufti didn't really believe that, especially as he stared at Elder Sterling again and contemplated the elder's good nature, in spite of his struggles in life. There was just something about Elder Sterling that Lufti couldn't write off. Delisha saw it too. It was something that went far beyond just being weird. There was a determination, a commitment, almost as if this missionary was in a kind of transition, going from one place to another, needing to get his message out before he ran out of time.

Delisha and her mother didn't say much as they observed the interaction between Lufti and Elder Sterling.

Lufti was intent on discovering what was wrong with Elder Sterling and why he would be canvassing neighborhoods when he could barely walk. He noticed that the missionary's breathing seemed labored. Although barely audible, there were underlying gasps for breath as he spoke. Lufti wanted to ask Elder Sterling what was wrong with him, without giving offense and sounding ignorant. Seconds passed without a word being uttered.

Finally, Elder Sterling broke the silence, looking at Lufti. "I'll bet you're wondering what's wrong with me and why I'm out here doing this. Am I right?"

Lufti nodded and looked down, just a little embarrassed that Elder Sterling could read him so easily.

"No problem," Elder Sterling reassured. "Who wouldn't be curious? I have a rare form of muscular dystrophy. I'm not expected to live much longer. Maybe another year, or a few more months. I had a choice between extending my life a couple more years by undergoing certain treatments and procedures that would require staying at home, convalescing, and refraining from much activity, or to come out here on a mission and use up the rest of the time I have left in the service of the Lord. So I chose this one. I'd surely rather do this than just lay around for a couple more years and miss this opportunity. I fall a lot and have some problems getting around, as you can see, but I'm still better off being out here. It was an easy choice."

Heads slowly came up following that remark. Even Lufti's. Lufti had thought he was going to denigrate the motives of these two men his age, just like he did the other Christian church representatives that had come around. It was obvious it would not be easy with these two.

"So," asked Lufti, "what do you really get out of this? Looks to me like you or someone in your family ought to get some serious cash or other compensation for shortening your life, just to tell people about your church."

Elder Sterling just smiled at Lufti. "Exactly right, Lufti," he said. "Exactly right. I am hugely compensated, but not with cash. I'm paid handsomely with the joy it gives me to share the gospel of Jesus Christ . . . the gospel of love."

Lufti was unable to respond with the normal little jab or comeback he had in his repertoire for people like these Christian missionaries. He looked at Delisha and his mother. They seemed captivated . . . intrigued.

Upon hearing Elder Sterling's response to Lufti, Delisha was struck, even a little ashamed, as she contrasted his purpose in the short life he had left with the major goal in life that she and Lufti had been prepared for.

With tears in their eyes as they testified to Christ's divinity, the two young men talked to the Ahmed family about the gift of salvation given by Jesus Christ. While Lufti held back both laughter and disdain, Delisha felt something confusing. It was something warm and enlightening . . . something she had never before experienced in her Islamic upbringing. *Why was this so?* she wondered. *Why am I feeling this so strongly in an infidel religion when I'm giving up my life to comply with my own?* Delisha had to assure herself that the warm feelings she was experiencing were not precipitated by Elder Brown, his handsome countenance, and his special way of communicating. *No,* she thought, *there is more than that here. It isn't just about him. It's something else . . . something I've never before experienced!*

The missionaries remained another fifteen minutes, asking the Ahmeds about life in Pakistan and the contrasts they had experienced living in the United States. Then once the family consented to having them return to share their message, Elder Brown helped Elder Sterling to his feet, then asked if they could leave a word of prayer in the Ahmed home. The mother gave permission. Elder Brown offered the prayer, asking blessings of peace, comfort, and protection upon the Ahmeds.

As Elder Sterling shuffled slowly out the door, leaning on his two canes, the Ahmeds knew they had experienced and felt something during that visit that was unlike any other visit they had ever had in their home. Lufti, his mother, and even his father, who was still in the kitchen next to the living room listening, were perplexed by the visit, not really knowing what to think about it.

Delisha was certain that she needed to learn more about what motivated the two young men. What she had felt from the visit still tugged at her heart and created within her a craving for more of the spirit that the missionaries had brought into her home.

Once the Ahmeds closed the door behind Elders Sterling and Brown, they again looked out the front window. Soft sheets of rain were falling, forming beads of moisture on Elder Brown's back and shoulders as he carefully carried his companion back to their car.

As she watched the two young men, Delisha's thoughts reflected upon something she had memorized from her Koran: Sura X, "Jonah, Peace be on Him!":

> *Goodness itself and an increase of it for those who do good! Neither blackness nor shame shall cover their faces! These shall be the inmates of Paradise, therein shall they abide forever.*

It was much different with Lufti. When Delisha talked to her brother about what she had felt, he just scoffed and said no more about it. She wouldn't even mention the subject to her parents, knowing how it would upset them. She recalled how both of them spoke derisively of the missionaries after their visit, laughing about how naïve they were using the title of "Elder."

Lufti was confused about the way he felt but succeeded in convincing himself that he had felt nothing. He had rejoiced in that his pretending to show attention to the young men evidenced the fact he was successfully deceiving them.

CHAPTER 8
THE FOLLOW-UP

PLANTATION, FLORIDA
JULY 12

DELISHA RECALLED HOW DAUNTING a task it was obtaining permission to have the missionaries back. Lufti and her parents were absolutely opposed, yet still curious. Not so much about the Christian concepts the young men were "peddling," as her father referred to it, but about what made Elder Sterling tick.

Delisha finally won out, and at 7:00 p.m., exactly a week later, Elder Rhett Brown appeared at the door again with Elder Chris Sterling in front of him. Obviously still in charge, he stood with a cane in each hand and a broad smile beaming out to the Ahmeds.

Once the young men were seated on a sofa facing the Ahmeds, including the father whose curiosity was also piqued, Elder Sterling asked if they could all pray together. Elder Brown offered a word of prayer.

"We respect the fact that you are a Muslim family," Elder Sterling said, "perhaps faithful followers of Islam and your prophet, Mohammed. We want you to be assured that we honor that. I, personally, have read the Koran in some detail."

Mr. Ahmed suddenly looked up, obviously surprised and now even more curious. He thought, *This young American Christian has read the entire Koran? Even I haven't read all of it.* Then Mr. Ahmed asked, "What did you think of the teachings in our holy book?"

"Very impressive," answered Elder Sterling, removing his glasses and wiping clean the lenses as he looked at Mr. Ahmed directly.

"I'm pleased with the similarities I found between the Koran and the Old Testament. Many of the same figures are in both books. After all, the Arabs and other Muslims are descended from Abraham through Ishmael, same as the Jews are descended through Isaac, Abraham's other son. I've always thought that the Muslims considered Allah to be the same god as the God of the New Testament."

The Ahmeds were clearly impressed.

Elder Sterling continued. "I also know that your Koran encourages contact and conversation with Christians. There is one Sura in it that says:

> *If you are in doubt about what we have*
> *sent down to you, ask those who were*
> *reading scripture before you.*

"I also recall that in the Koran it states something to the effect that Christians are 'the closest in affection to the believers.'"

Lufti had grown to like Elder Sterling and admired the sheer will he displayed in carrying out his mission under such challenging circumstances, but Lufti still wanted to toy with him. He was ready to stop what he recognized as an attempt by the Mormon missionaries to proselyte his family. He weighed in. "The Koran also states in a Sura that neither Jews nor Christians will be pleased with us unless we follow their religion. Are you thinking we should join your church?"

"We would be delighted if that were the case, Lufti," Elder Brown responded. "We'd love to share the joys of our church with you and with your family." He looked specifically at Delisha and smiled. "However, we recognize that at this point, we're still a long ways from that. We would have a good deal of ground to cover first."

Delisha just gazed at Elder Brown pensively, asking herself what it was that really motivated him to serve two years as a missionary. He assisted Elder Sterling, spent each day carrying his companion from one house to another, and probably had doors slammed in his face. She felt an intense admiration for both young men.

Lufti's father decided to side with his son. "You know, young men, we really don't practice our religion seriously. There is so much work we must do here in this country that consumes our time. However, there are certain customs from our country of Pakistan that we still hold dear. We do keep copies of the Koran in our home, but we also have a Bible that Delisha sometimes reads . . . just out of curiosity, of course. Now, you . . . uhh . . . Elder Sterling, is it? You seem to know a good deal about the Koran. What do you think of the prophet Mohammed?"

Elder Sterling was pleased with the question. "Muhammed bin Abdullah, most often referred to just as Mohammed, spelled a little differently, was an Arabian prophet, the last of a line of prophets running from Father Abraham through Jesus Christ, according to Muslim belief. He is the founder of the Islam religion and is looked up to by Muslims as a messenger and prophet of their god, Allah. I know that as a Muslim, you believe he restored the original faith of Adam, Noah, Abraham, Moses, and Jesus to the earth. I know he accomplished many amazing things in his life during the sixth and seventh centuries AD. He was a diplomat, a general, a reformer, and is regarded by Muslims as one who could do God's will."

The Ahmeds were stunned, absolutely amazed at this physically challenged young person that seemed to know more about their prophet than they did.

"Muhammed was orphaned and raised by an uncle," Elder Sterling continued. "He worked as a merchant and married when he was twenty-five. He later lived in a cave where he started receiving revelations when he was forty."

Elder Brown was just as shocked with Elder Sterling's knowledge of Islam. He knew his companion had been a student of world history at Brigham Young University before coming out on his mission, but had no idea Elder Sterling had such awesome recall. Elder Brown perceived that out of all the Ahmeds, Delisha was the one most moved by Elder Sterling's knowledge.

"Much like Jesus Christ and his disciples, Muhammed and his followers were persecuted by the tribes around Mecca, Arabia, where he was born," Elder Sterling said. "They were not pleased with the fact that he claimed that he was receiving revelation. Also, like with Jesus, the people resented Muhammed. He had to fight the tribes around Mecca for eight years and finally conquered Mecca with about ten thousand disciples. He died at the age of sixty-two, but by that time, almost the entire Arabian Peninsula had accepted Islam and united into a huge Arab organization."

"Have you read all of the Koran?" asked Delisha.

"Yes," responded Elder Sterling. "Much like I have studied many of the world's religions. I know that the Koran was constantly updated through decades of oral recitation. That's why it's considered by Muslims to be the current word of God for his people."

"You know a great deal about Islam . . . more than all of us I think, except maybe Delisha," commented Mr. Ahmed. "We just don't follow religion that closely. It matters little to us at this point in our lives."

Delisha knew her father was lying to allay any suspicion regarding the family's real convictions. Nevertheless, she hated hearing her father do it. She found that his deception made her really uncomfortable.

Elder Sterling had more to add. "Even though I know a good deal about Muhammed and the content of the Koran, I know much more about the Lord, Jesus Christ. I do believe He is the Son of God and the Savior of mankind. I know that although Muslims accept Him as a great prophet and teacher, they do not accept Him as the Savior. Hopefully, in future meetings with your family, Elder Brown and I will have the opportunity to share with you regarding modern-day prophets and other ancient scriptures that you may have never heard of before, but going into that may be pointless until you know more about Jesus."

"Actually," Delisha added, "I clearly see some similarities between Islam and your Christian faith. The Koran teaches that we are forbidden to kill, steal, gamble, and to be unfaithful to our spouses. We are told not to work one day during the week . . . which for us is Friday. We are also taught the concepts of heaven and hell, like the Christians are taught."

"Yes, sister, of course. We all know that," added Lufti. "But the similarities stop right there. We are not so much like them," he said, nodding toward the missionaries. "The Bible does not contain the strong prohibitions that the Koran does regarding drinking, for example. The Koran forbids drinking any amount of alcohol and teaches that one can go straight to hell for doing that. It also forbids eating certain kinds of meat. The Christians are allowed to do all that."

The Ahmeds were becoming uncomfortable with Lufti's argumentative attitude. They were concerned he was becoming too aggressive, maybe even a little combative, which could hint at his hostile attitude toward the Judeo-Christian standard in America. They worried that he might unveil his real motives and attitude toward America and Christianity.

"We're with you on the alcohol question and the idea of abstaining from eating much meat," Elder Brown said. "We have a commandment in our church called the 'Word of Wisdom,' which we'll explain later in some detail. This commandment cautions us to eat meat sparingly and to abstain completely from alcohol and other harmful substances."

Again, upon hearing this, the Ahmeds took notice, thinking only Muslims had these dietary restrictions.

"There are still many other major differences in our religions," Lufti argued. We have a lot more strict rules than you do. We're a more disciplined people. Muslims are supposed to pray five times a day, although we don't."

Mr. Ahmed was nodding in agreement with his son.

He and Father are doing it again! thought Delisha. *Same thing they've been doing ever since we have been in America. Lying and deceiving.* Delisha was well aware of the number of prayer mats that both Lufti and her father had worn out in the Ahmed home.

"And another thing," added Lufti, "look at the young women

around here, dressed in their mini-skirts, bikinis, and tight clothes. You'll never see Muslim women dressed like that!"

Lufti's hypocrisy was annoying Delisha, as she recalled with disgust, some of the pictures over the years that Lufti hung on the inside door of his closet that their father made him remove.

Both Elder Sterling and Elder Brown had to smile as they reflected on the strict dress code required to get into BYU.

Lufti figured he was on a roll in routing the two visitors. "You talk of your Jesus as a savior and the son of God. The Koran denies that. We've been taught that he was only a messenger of God, an enlightened teacher, like Muhammed. It also teaches that Jesus failed in his mission, because his disciples began to worship him, instead of God."

Elder Sterling spoke up. "Actually, Lufti, the Koran speaks well of Jesus. One verse from it really impresses me. It's from Sura 3, verses 40 and 41. I've written it down for your family. I'll read it.

> *His name shall be Messiah Jesus, the son*
> *of Mary, illustrious in this world, and in the*
> *next, and one of those who have near access*
> *to God; And he shall speak to men alike when*
> *in the cradle and when grown up; And he shall*
> *be one of the just.*

"Hopefully, that's what we'll have the opportunity of explaining to your family: Jesus's mission. Then you can draw your own conclusions about Him. But here's what I want you to know. I know personally and with all my heart that Jesus Christ is the Son of God—He's my Redeemer and Savior. Within less than a year, wherever He is, I want to be with Him. I know He was crucified, died, and after three days, rose again, leaving an empty tomb behind. Because of that act of resurrection, I will rise from the dead also, minus my canes, and will have my life restored without my physical impairments. I'm talking not being carried around, not limping, and having all my hair back."

Elder Sterling was smiling again. His enthusiasm was palpable. "And when I do come back to life, I will be standing next to this big guy here," he said, motioning to Elder Brown, "shaking his hand and thanking him for all those 'piggybacks.' And I'll even be able to beat him in a foot race!"

No one in the room could resist laughing at that remark. Then there was a silence, with no response from the Ahmeds . . . only a quiet sentiment of reverence filling the room, a sentiment that both puzzled and intrigued the Pakistani family.

Permission was granted for another concluding word of prayer, which Elder Sterling offered. Then the elders left again, with permission to return the following week.

As the missionaries closed the door behind them, the Ahmeds once again moved to the front living room window to watch Elder Brown carry his friend and companion to their vehicle.

As the ensuing weeks went by, the Ahmeds were taught all the elders knew about Jesus Christ. Delisha became increasingly interested in experiencing more, much more of what she felt when Elder Sterling was talking about Jesus and when Elder Brown was praying. She retired to her room after their final visit. She brought out the Bible and turned to the Beatitudes from the book of Matthew. She then placed the Koran next to the Bible, staring at both books intently, where they lay side by side.

Over the next few days, Delisha spent time each evening comparing the basic tenets of the Koran that Rashid Siddiqui had used to emphasize the reasons for her suicide mission, with the teachings of Jesus Christ.

Delisha was aghast as the comparisons struck home, noting the extreme differences between what Jesus and Muhammed taught. She wrote them down in columns across from one another, so she could carefully compare them. The comparisons were chilling.

THE KORAN	THE BIBLE (THE BEATITUDES)
SURA 9:29 *Fight those who do not believe in Allah.*	
	MATTHEW 5:9 *Blessed are the peacemakers: for they will be called the children of God.*
SURA 48:29 *Be ruthless to the infidel.*	
SURA 9:123 *Make war on the infidels who dwell around you.*	
	MATTHEW 5:7 *Blessed are the merciful: for they shall obtain mercy.*
SURA 4:56 *They that deny our revelations we will burn in fire. No sooner will their skins be consumed than we shall give them other skins, so that they may truly taste the scourge*	
	MATTHEW 5:3 *Blessed are the poor in spirit: for theirs is the kingdom of heaven.*
	MATTHEW 5:10 *Blessed are they who are persecuted for righteousness' sake: for theirs is the kingdom of heaven.*
SURA 2:191 *And slay them wherever you find them, and drive them out of the places where they drove you out of . . .*	
	MATTHEW 5:39 *Resist not evil.*

THE KORAN	THE BIBLE (THE BEATITUDES)
SURA 3:49 *And as to those who believe not, I will chastise them with a terrible chastisement in this world and in the next; and none shall they have to help them*	**MATTHEW 5:4** *Blessed are they that mourn: for they will be comforted.* **MATTHEW 5:5** *Blessed are the meek: for they will inherit the earth*
SURA 9:124 *Believers! Wage war against such of the infidels as are your neighbors, and let them find you rigorous: and know that God is with those who fear him.* **SURA 47: VERSE 4** *Strike off the heads of infidels in battle* **SURA 28: 86** *Never be a helper to the disbelievers.*	**MATTHEW 5:11–12** *Blessed are ye when men shall revile you, and persecute you, and shall say all manner of evil falsely for my sake. Rejoice, and be exceeding glad: for great is your reward in heaven: for so persecuted they the prophets which were before you* **MATTHEW 5:44** *Love your enemies, bless them that curse you, do good to them that hate you, pray for them which despitefully use you.* **MATTHEW 5:40** *If someone takes your coat, give them your shirt also.*

In the five years since the first visit of the missionaries, Delisha had never considered joining their church, but she had attended several of their meetings, much to the chagrin of her brother and parents, who also had attended a few church activities. This was only to "keep up appearances" and to deflect second thoughts anyone may have had that they were traditional followers of Islam and affiliated with radical al-Qaeda extremists.

Delisha eventually befriended Madi Southerland, a young girl whose father was an FBI agent who eventually became a Mormon bishop in the local ward in Plantation, Florida. They became close friends. Madi invited Delisha to many church activities, including a dance the Mormons called the "Gold and Green Ball." It was a family "punch and cookie" dance celebrating the New Year. Both girls had just turned sixteen. This was their first dance upon arriving at the Mormon timeline for group dating. Delisha's mother had consented for her to go with Madi, but when her father returned from work and heard she was "dancing with the infidel rabble," he was infuriated and stormed down to the chapel. While Delisha was dancing with a young man at arm's length, her father crossed the dance floor, grabbed her by an arm, and forced her to leave with him. Delisha had never been so humiliated.

The following Monday, Delisha called Madi, asking her to meet for a few minutes at a nearby McDonalds. Madi was shocked to see her friend's swollen face.

"Delisha, how could your own father do this?" Madi asked.

"He felt I had betrayed him," Delisha responded. "Where he was raised, women have no rights . . . no freedoms. Daughters especially. That's the way he still wants it. I have no special rights."

Madi was speechless as she embraced her friend and viewed the facial abrasions up close. For five minutes the two cried together. Then Delisha asked, "Madi, some of the girls at the dance were talking about their hope chests. Do you have one?"

"I do. It is a beautiful rectangular wooden box on wooden legs made of cedar."

"What is it used for?" Delisha asked.

"It's for collecting items I will need when I'm married and start my own home, like sheets, pillow cases that are embroidered, and tablecloths. Maybe even a starter set of china and silverware. My grandmother actually contributed much of it. She knew how to do 'tatting,' It's like crocheting, but different. It's beautiful!"

Delisha's face saddened and reflected noticeable remorse.

"Delisha, what is it?"

"Nothing, Madi . . . really nothing."

"Delisha, tell me the truth. You're lying! What's wrong? You look like you've lost your last friend."

At first there was no response. Then Delisha turned toward Madi with the most forlorn expression Madi had ever seen in anyone. It was a look that was now turning to acceptance and resignation. "I'll never need a hope chest!" Delisha said.

"Delisha, what are you telling me?" asked Madi.

"Madi, it's okay. I was just talking. I really need to go. I'll be able to attend the youth activities again in three months, after I complete my father's punishment. But in the meantime, please stay in touch. I've got to go, or I'll be in more trouble."

"For sure, Delisha . . . absolutely!" Madi stared at Delisha as she pondered the meaning of her comment about never needing a hope chest. It was a chilling thought. *Why not?* she asked herself.

The girls squeezed each other by the hand and departed.

After being banned from any contact with Madi or the church for three months, Delisha was again permitted to attend a few church meetings and activities.

* * * * *

After July 4, Lufti began approaching Delisha in earnest regarding her interest in the American Christian faith of the Mormons. He was alarmed by his sister's growing support for the concept of Jesus Christ being anything more than a popular Jewish prophet/teacher.

"Delisha, are you seriously considering this? Do you know what these Christian heretics can do to us? Both you and I? If one word gets back to Siddiqui or any of the holy men in Islamabad that you are in touch with those Christian dogs for any motive other than for our real mission, we will both die, but not as martyrs." Lufti was referring to the penalty for any one who might "stray from the path." The al-Qaeda would send operatives to kill not only them but would also execute their parents for failing in their mission to successfully launch their children into their course of martyrdom.

"Of course I would never go against the desire of the holy men or compromise our mission, Lufti. It's just that it's all become so confusing. The Christians from The Church of Jesus Christ of Latter-day Saints teach that their God loves all mankind of every race, color, and religion. Sometimes it's just difficult for me to feel good about killing all those around me because they don't believe as we do. As good as Allah has been to us throughout our lives, why would he desire that we would do as Ghani and Kareema Hussain did to so many people in Omaha? Why is it really necessary to exterminate so many people . . . people we don't even know or have a personal argument with, just because they don't believe as we do, in order to satisfy Allah? I struggle sometimes to think that it is really what Allah wants to happen . . . that that is really the message of the Koran."

"Delisha, you must divest yourself of this kind of thinking! You know it's blasphemy. You know it, and so do I. You must promise me, Delisha, as your brother, that you're going to follow through with me on our mission. Tell me. Are you with me?"

"Of course I am, Lufti. What do you think? That I would be a traitor to the cause I was created for and raised to achieve?" Delisha's face reddened.

Lufti grunted, not entirely satisfied; nevertheless at least he could report to their parents, who had been very concerned about Delisha's potential deviation from her destiny with Allah, that everything was okay and on course.

With Delisha it was different. Her words to her brother had rung hollow as she had responded to him. There had been occasions in the Mormon meetings when she had again felt the same stirrings she had experienced when the missionaries had come over. Delisha had observed how this fast-growing American-born religion, centered in faith in a living resurrected Christ, had such a positive effect on its followers, much more than just an emotional appeal to its adherents to suddenly die for their reward, killing scores of other human beings in their wake. She admired the Christian concept of wanting to *live* for their beliefs and wanting to bless the lives of all people, not just those of their own faith. It seemed so much more fair and logical to her than a call to martyrdom—a call to ravage scores of human beings in a cruel and unimaginable death in a selfish act to receive a personal reward.

Delisha was caught in the biggest struggle of her life . . . and she knew it.

CHAPTER 9
THE A TEAMS

FBI HEADQUARTERS
WASHINGTON, DC
JULY 12

OP PRIORITY COMMUNICATIONS HAD been sizzling back and forth between the Omaha field office of the FBI and FBI Headquarters regarding the Omaha bombing incident from the hour it had occurred. Dave Cowan, Special Agent in Charge (SAC) of the Omaha office, had requested all the help he could get within minutes of being notified of the attack in Omaha. The International Terrorism Unit at headquarters had dispatched investigative teams to assess the situation and provide assistance. They were working in tandem with local police authorities in Omaha while determining what agency would have primary investigative jurisdiction. Once the attack was believed to have been the result of international terrorism, it was agreed the FBI would have primary jurisdiction.

At first glance for the Bureau, all indications pointed to the modus operandi of trained terrorists. Al-Qaeda had their prints all over it. Although what happened in Omaha, Nebraska, was the first successful suicide bombing attempt of its kind ever occurring in the United States, it was very similar to roughly two hundred others that had already occurred in other parts of the world. The local authorities in Omaha were more than ready to give the FBI the lead in investigating this case. They began supporting them in every way possible by affording them access to local informants, any logistical resources they had, and all their available manpower.

As FBI agents streamed into Omaha from neighboring divisions to assist, along with disaster squads from Bureau headquarters dispatched to identify victims and preserve evidence, something new and unusual was evolving at FBI Headquarters. For several months, a new concept for immediate response to terrorist assaults had been incubating at Bureau headquarters under the supervision of the International Terrorism Unit. It was Supervisory Special Agent Denny Campo's brainchild.

The concept embodied the formation of ten five-man teams geared to respond to terrorist attacks. They were a hybrid mix of proven expert investigators with at least ten years investigative field experience who had also specialized in special weapons and tactics (SWAT) maneuvers for a minimum of five years. Each of these fifty agents had to have been graded "superior" in their performance ratings, both as investigators and as SWAT operatives for both the five- and ten-year periods. They had to commit to at least five additional years service to the FBI upon receiving their appointment. They had to be willing to undergo highly intense and stressful physical training, along with prolonged periods of sleep deprivation. And they were required to travel anywhere in the world where the Bureau was authorized to conduct investigations. Their spouses would be furnished information regarding their companion's missions on only a "need-to-know" basis."

The men and women involved in these teams would be recommended by their field authorities—the Special Agents in Charge—once they had formally volunteered for the assignment. They would be called the "A Team."

Supervisory Special Agent (SSA) Campo had been pushing this concept for years within the FBI since the 9/11 attack, when he was first assigned to the International Terrorism Unit. Prior to the Omaha bombing, the current administration had fought the A Team concept, insisting it would breed a form of profiling against people of Mideastern descent that would be unacceptable. They argued that the idea of a more aggressive approach to deterrence might have negative social ramifications for American society.

The July 4 incident changed all that and finally gave Campo's dream its birth.

Special Agents in Charge (SACs) throughout the United States and several FBI legal attaché officers abroad had already submitted their lists of volunteers. A Team One (A1) and A Team Two (A2) were the first teams chosen, evaluated, and oriented to their tasks. A1 had been dispatched two months before on a pilot project to investigate the bombing of a federal reserve bank in San Francisco that had occurred on May 2,. The group taking credit called themselves the Mountain Patriots. This group had issued a public statement advising they were opposed to the government's methods of "controlling the free enterprise system through the use of bogus currency." They were regarded as a nut group but were of great concern because of the nature of the explosives they had developed. Their bomb precursors had proved extremely potent, more so than any other explosives identified as of that date that had been used by "homegrown" terrorists.

To date, A1 had established those responsible were from somewhere in the Northwest, probably the Hayden Lakes, Idaho, area. A recent resurgence had occurred there of leftover discontents.

Since A1 was absorbed in the San Francisco matter, investigative jurisdiction for the Omaha incident was assigned to A2. Those five agents were instructed to work closely with the new strike force formed in Omaha from local, county, and state officials. Code word for the new investigative thrust was "Operation OMAMALL."

On August 5 at 2:30 p.m., SSA Campo met with A2 in his office at FBI headquarters at 935 Pennsylvania Avenue in Washington, DC. A2 team leader, Joe Fredette, was accompanied by Hank Duffin, Ken Grogan, Jim Flynn, and Ridge Southerland.

Fredette spoke first. "You sure you got the right guys, Denny? We're fresh off the boat on this A Team thing. We want to do it, and we've volunteered for it, but nothing exactly like this has ever happened before in the good old USA, and after going over this most of last night with my buddies here, we first need to know that you're comfortable with us—I mean, *real* comfortable."

The other four agents nodded affirmatively, looking directly at Campo.

Forty-eight-year-old Supervisory Special Agent Denny Campo was into karate. The only thing he loved more than his martial arts was a good case. Each time he made a trip to the *dojo*, he would burn off stress while sparring with a good opponent. He knew that releasing pent-up energy, often caused by frustration at work, was best done in a gym. He had learned the valuable lesson so many other administrators missed: that grown men with years of experience don't like to be micro-managed. That made him "one of the boys." He had been a crack field office investigator in New York City and Miami before choosing the administrative route. He first went through FBI "Charm School," where he was evaluated for his capacity for administrative advancement. Campo had pressed all the right buttons and, with a stout athletic build, it was obvious he had taken advantage of the three forty-five minute work-out sessions each week, rather than going shopping after lunch. He was low key, fun to be around, and unlike other supervisors in their "ivory towers," was indeed the street agents' guy.

"Well, I'll tell you the truth, Joe. You guys ain't much, but you're all I got!" Campo broke out in a smile, while continuing to pop his chewing gum.

"You know, when I envisioned this unit, I felt deep down that it would never be activated until some major event like 9/11 came along," Campo continued, still making those funny crackling noises with his gum. "And bingo! Suddenly we get the nod. Well, that's how it is, guys. Are you totally ready for any contingency that comes up? Probably not. Are you going to make mistakes here and there while covering new ground . . . some challenges you've never seen before? Probably. But guess what? I'm in this with you. You mess up. I've messed up. You miss something. I've missed something. I'm letting it all hang out on this A Team concept, and my butt's on the line. But I believe in it. And more important, I believe in you guys. What else can I say about that?"

"That's good," responded Special Agent Fredette. "Because what you see is what you get."

"Question," Hank Duffin said. "So we can be called anytime and could be sent all over Kingdom Come and back, right?"

"Affirmative," answered Campo.

"Okay, one more question. So, being gone all the time, the Bureau will pick up the tab for our marriage counselors, right? I mean, we can put that through with vouchers?" Duffin said, never cracking a smile. His faint, raspy remarks usually put the other guy off guard a little.

"Doesn't it amaze you, Duffin, that I actually approved you for this assignment, even though you're always trying to get to me . . . I mean, ever since we served together in New York City?" Campo looked at Fredette, pointing at Duffin, and said jokingly, "Will you give this guy a banana so we can get on with this?"

"No, thanks," replied Duffin. "I just had a bar of soap." Duffin, the Irish Catholic Bostonian, never missed a good one-liner. Forty-six, slender, just over six feet tall, and well-framed, Duffin had excelled as a field agent. He was the "go-to guy" on more priority bureau operations than he could remember. By the time he was selected for A2, Duffin calculated that he had spent more time on federal toilets than some of the rising star supervisors at Bureau headquarters had in their careers. Duffin was regarded as "cozy" and the dark, wavy hair, Bostonian accent, and his flair for speaking Spanish and French sporadically drew a lot of attention.

"You other guys got anything to say?" asked Campo, as he focused his attention on Ken Grogan, Jim Flynn, and Ridge Southerland.

Grogan, forty-five years old and a twenty-one year veteran of the FBI, affectionately known as "The Grinch," was the only member of A2 who had no military background. He had actually studied for the Catholic ministry to become a priest before being appointed a special agent in what he jokingly referred to as the "XYZ." He had decided, however, that his propensity for living more on the edge and wanting to experience the real world would one day drive him nuts if his own reality became ecclesiastical and nothing more. He had lived a Spartan lifestyle as a single man well into his late forties before becoming enamored with and married to a pretty FBI secretary. His self-effacing lifestyle was reflected in his apartment's furnishings, including only a single kitchen table with a couple of chairs, a bed, and a few other items of furniture. Marriage, of course, changed all that . . . somewhat.

Grogan stood a slender five feet ten inches with dark hair, graying at the temple, black rimmed glasses, and piercing brown eyes. If he liked you, he'd call you "doctor" or "friend" with a strong southern accent. If he didn't, he was charitable enough not to let you know it. His personal creed was spelled out on a laminated piece of paper on his desk. It contained this quote from a speech President Teddy Roosevelt had made in 1910:

> It is not the critic who counts; not the man who points out how the strong man stumbles, or where the doer of deeds could have done them better. The credit belongs to the man who is actually in the arena, whose face is marred by dust and sweat and blood; who strives valiantly; who errs, who comes short again and again, because there is no effort without error and shortcoming; but who does actually strive to do the deeds; who knows great enthusiasms, the great devotions; who spends himself in a worthy cause; who at the best knows in the end the triumph of high achievement, and who at the worst, if he fails, at least fails while daring greatly, so that his place shall never be with those cold and timid souls who neither know victory nor defeat.

Grogan defined the term "loyal." He would follow his team leader, Joe Fredette, into the depths of hell with the clip in his M-16 rifle empty, if that's what he was called on to do.

"Not really, boss," replied Grogan to Campo's question. "The *jefe*,"—Spanish for *chief,* a term of affection the A2 Team had for their leader, Fredette—"he's got it all figured out. I can play along."

A few people—not everyone, but a few—knew just how well The Grinch could play along. He had not only been a field supervisor in Miami and a SWAT Team leader but was also a trained "sound man," meaning he was expert at inserting covert tracking

devices into suspect vehicles, figuring out how to pick locks, setting up wiretaps, and conducting a list of other covert operations.
The Grinch could doctor up just about anything.

Flynn had one statement to make. "I'm ready to roll, Campo.
No questions."

Jim Flynn was a combination of a "whirling dervish" and a
Sherlock Holmes. The man was perpetually in motion. The idea
of grass growing under Flynn's feet was comparable to hair growing on steel. There was no case anywhere under the stars that
he didn't want to be a part of if it meant "putting one of those
bottom-feeders in jail," as he put it. Flynn dressed funny. Green
tennis shoes in the office, complementing his open sport shirt and
slacks, were the order of the day. After all, he needed to identify
with his "sources," meaning the top echelon criminal informants
that he specialized in developing.

Flynn was the master interviewer and the epitome of the guy
with the sixth sense. On one prior occasion while assigned to
the Miami FBI Division, during a complicated organized crime
trial, one of Flynn's subjects had somehow escaped from a temporary holding facility. His subject's whereabouts were unknown.
Shortly thereafter, Flynn visited the facility and began staring at
the graffiti riddled walls. A common practice, prisoners often left
addresses and phone numbers for wives and girlfriends to find
them after they were released. Women would also leave phone
numbers there for their men to contact them.

On this particular occasion, Flynn had stood in front of one
section of the graffiti and honed in on one particular address in
New York City. That sixth sense kicked in. Flynn quickly scribbled
down the address as his partner just looked at him, wondering
what was up.

Later that night Flynn sent a message to the New York FBI
office to check out that address where he felt the escapee would
be. The next morning a message came into the Miami office that
the fugitive had been apprehended at that same address, his girlfriend's apartment, and was being transported en route to Miami
by US Marshals.

Next SSA Campo looked at Agent Southerland. "Come on,

Ridge, don't hold back. Go ahead and weigh in on this!" Campo insisted.

Southerland, age forty-eight, was from Idaho. As a devout Mormon, he practiced his faith but did not push it down anyone's throat. He had served as a bishop to a congregation in Plantation, Florida, while assigned to the Plantation Resident Agency of the Miami Division of the FBI, prior to volunteering for A2. At six feet two inches tall and two hundred and fifteen pounds, he was an imposing figure but had a gentle disposition. He loved to tease and be teased and had an ever-present grin you would only observe in the kid who had successfully swiped not only the cookies, but also the whole jar. When the other team members wanted someone to go with them through a door of the residence of an armed and dangerous subject, the call usually went to Southerland to back them up.

One of the great mysteries on A2 was how Ridge Southerland could smile about anything. His father, a church leader who had served a congregation in a small Idaho town for almost ten years, had taught Ridge to substitute a powerful positive thought at each juncture in his life when he was challenged. For Southerland, it worked. He had faced some big challenges,such as overcoming stuttering and playing football as a running back for Brigham Young University's Cougars in Provo, Utah. That was where he had met and married Stella, a Utah girl.

"Mr. Campo, when I raised my arm and swore an oath to defend the Constitution of the United States and the people of this country as a special agent with the FBI," Southerland said, "that was a sacred oath for me. I believe that document, the Constitution, is an inspired instrument of God. I wasn't thinking then and I don't think now that I should take a smorgasbord approach to what I'm going to do in this organization. I've always worked where I've been assigned and I've been glad to do just that. It was different with this assignment. I wanted it. I wanted it bad and, yes, I asked for it. That's why I'm here. That's about all I've got to say."

Supervisory Special Agent Campo knew he had the right guys.

"All right, gentlemen," Campo stated resolutely. "As you approach your first assignment on A2, just remember this: hundreds of American men, women, and children were slaughtered indiscriminately at that mall in Omaha by those bottom-feeders. The only mistake those poor folks made was being at the wrong place at the wrong time. The terrorists, on the other hand, were the end product of a diabolic scheme al-Qaeda wants to perpetuate on all of us, because of their hatred for the stars and stripes. They want to kill all of us, because we prefer not to believe what they believe. That's who you are up against. They are the perpetrators . . . the ones who are calling the shots. It's either them or us and on a personal note, 'us' includes our wives and children." That statement raised the eyebrows of everyone in the room.

"The problem with the Omaha crime scene is in coming up with clues," Campo continued. "There are no 'snitches' who can report on anything that happened. There are no remaining victims that were within proximity of the explosion. All those that had any kind of a view are dead. Unlike criminals we have dealt with traditionally, who have murdered people and left tracks, these subjects disintegrated, along with those who witnessed their actions."

"What makes these suicide bombers tick?" asked Ken Grogan.

Campo answered. "Some say it's religious zeal from their upbringing with promises of paradise as a reward for doing themselves in. Many are selected from Islam mosques where their parents have actually encouraged them to commit acts of martyrdom to bring prestige and financial remuneration to their families."

"That's sick!" Fredette said. "What parent would give up a kid for money and glory? You gotta' be kiddin'!"

There was a low, guttural mumbling with a New York accent in the background. It was Flynn, talking to himself. "Mental cases!"

"No. Not at all," answered Campo. "I actually viewed a news flash where the father of a bomber told the Associated Press he was very happy and proud of what his son had done by killing twenty people in a suicide bombing in a public gathering. So there you go . . . support for these atrocities from parents who are willing to sacrifice their own flesh and blood!"

"They're sickos no doubt," Hank Duffin chimed in, "but they're sickos who have thought out the end results of their actions. We need to realize that the bombing in Omaha has caused people in all fifty states to think twice about ever entering another mall to shop or hit a movie. Has anyone even began to calculate the economic impact this bombing will have on the overall economy of this country?"

"Yes," responded Campo. "The President has already assigned experts to assess the devastation to the economy nationwide this assault has caused. The initial assessment is that the repercussions will be disastrous . . . and if it happens again, even one more time within the next year, the results could be catastrophic. The fear and anxiety caused by another bombing like the one in Omaha would produce an irreversible mental anxiety throughout the entire nation, not just the Omaha victims and their families."

Ken Grogan asked, "The use of the Hussain girl is a new twist, isn't it? What's that all about?"

"The female terrorist idea is still pretty new. The Palestinians have used women successfully a few times in the past. Women have been great for media shock value," Campo answered. "The Palestinians use them to embarrass the Israelis. Sometimes they are younger women who have lost a loved one to their enemy and are depressed and grieving. They are often under personal stress of one kind or another. Other young women are drugged or threatened with rape if they don't participate. Women who kill or threaten to kill are great stories for the news media."

Campo continued. "It's really difficult to profile the female terrorist . . . mainly because there are not enough reports available to build case studies on.

"The first attack using a girl was in 1985 when Khyadali Sana, age sixteen, drove a truck into an Israeli Defense Force convoy. She killed two soldiers. Since that incident, women have been used to drive vehicles full of bombs into targets, detonating themselves. This has occurred numerous times in Turkey, Chechnya, Israel, Lebanon, and other places. Lots of terrorist organizations have claimed that using females has made it easier to accomplish their purposes. This has been especially true with the Palestinian

Islamic Jihad, the Syrian Socialist National Party, Hamas, and now we suspect al-Qaeda is following suit. The Liberation Tigers of Tamil Elam have used the most suicide bombers . . . more than two hundred attacks. They used women in thirty to forty percent of them."

"What's been the age breakdown on the female bombers?" Fredette asked.

"The youngest was this Khyadali Sana girl that I mentioned. She was sixteen." Campo had his facts down. "The oldest was a woman by the name of Shagir Karima Mohumed, age thirty-seven."

"How much damage did these ladies inflict?" asked Grogan, who appeared shocked that so many women were involved. The whole idea of capitalizing on the use of the opposite sex to inflict this kind of misery was nauseating to Grogan. It went against his instincts as a southern gentleman.

Campo responded, "In June 1996, one of them, who was pregnant, killed six Turkish soldiers. Another one, the Russian woman, Hawa Barayev, killed twenty-seven Russian Special Forces in June 2000 for the Chechen rebels. In January 2002, the first female martyr in Israel, Wafa Idris, representing the Al Aqsa Martyr's Brigade, detonated a twenty-two pound body bomb filled with nails and killed an eighty-year-old man and injured more than a hundred people. In October 2003, another woman killed twenty-one Israeli and Arab people in a restaurant. Then in January 2004 another woman, Reem al-Reyaashi, the first female Hamas bomber, killed four Israeli soldiers. Incidentally, she had a husband, a three-year-old son, and a one-year-old daughter."

"So that means Kareema Hussain, in the Omaha incident, was probably the first al-Qaeda female bomber?" asked Fredette.

"Looks like that's what it means," said Campo. "The bottom line is this trend of using women will probably continue, particularly as a powerful combination in sibling relationships, because females provide a stealthier attack as an element of surprise, they provide a nonviolent stereotype, and they get more publicity and have more of a psychological effect. Basically, it's a minimal-risk and minimal-cost approach to terrorism."

"What's the general profile on female bombers? Is there one?" asked Southerland.

"Other than the ages I mentioned, the other profile characteristics all vary too much for accurate comparison," responded Campo.

"I heard of one instance where the bomber trainee was shown a film of a dead boy beckoning her to join him in a state of Paradise only accessible through self-martyrdom," Ridge Southerland added. "I think it boils down to brainwashing and constant reinforcement from a depraved society."

"It was different with the two Hussain kids," stated Campo. "They were raised in the American culture with doting parents and given every social advantage that al-Qaeda money could buy. They were college-educated with absolutely no prior contacts with law enforcement, not even a traffic ticket. They had no personal beefs with America that they had articulated in public or to other Americans. They were just religious fanatics."

"Just religious fanatics," repeated Flynn. "Right! *Just* religious fanatics who prayed and fasted, then killed and wounded hundreds of people. That's all!" Flynn was muttering again. "Scumbags!"

"I've come up with the typical profile for Palestinian bombers overall," Campo continued. "I'm not sure if this would apply 100 percent to our Pakistani subjects. Forty-seven percent of them have some education. Only twenty-nine percent have a high school education. This description obviously doesn't fit the Hussains who are college-educated.

Campo paused. "Eighty-three percent were single."

"The single part fits, but the sibling thing's a new twist," said Fredette. "The Omaha subjects were single and siblings."

Campo continued. "Sixty-four percent were between the ages of eighteen and twenty-three. The remainder are under thirty. That profile fits the Hussains.

"Sixty-eight percent of the Palestinian bombers come from the Gaza Strip. Our Omaha subjects are homegrown. Huge difference!" pointed out Campo, who was becoming more and more enthralled in his own findings.

"Even though al-Qaeda has refrained in the past from using women as bombers except in supporting roles, that was all changed in Omaha. Where there is an advantage to using women, al-Qaeda will do it if it's convenient."

"Sounds like there's a lot of flexibility in implementing the teachings of the Koran for these pukes," said Fredette. "Whatever is convenient for them becomes their scripture, right?"

Campo proceeded ahead as if he never heard Fredette. "The kids that hit the mall in Omaha had not been socially isolated like the Palestinian bombers. They had actually been encouraged to blend into their environment while in America and to be a part of everything in order to avoid suspicion as to their eventual goal."

"I attended an in-service training on terrorism just last year where we were told that even in war time, harming innocent people was forbidden by the Prophet Mohammed," Ridge Southerland added. "In fact, a supreme religious leader had just issued a *fatwa* or religious edict indicating that suicide bombing was the same as suicide and was forbidden in Islam."

"Right," affirmed Campo. "However, other doctrinal authorities in Islam claim that if a person blows himself up in a holy cause to spread Islam, he's a martyr. However, if he kills himself to kill babies, women, and old people who aren't fighting a war, then he is not a martyr. The problem is that Muslim clerics aren't in full agreement over what constitutes martyrdom and what doesn't, so in the meantime al-Qaeda construes it just to fit their purposes.

"The sad part," continued Campo, "is that these young people are courted by fanatics who use anti-American rhetoric to stir up feelings of national patriotism and hatred of the enemy so that these suicide bombers view their mission as driven by a higher order. They really believe they will be rewarded richly in the afterlife.

"Oh, there's one more twist, guys," Campo said. "We're receiving intel from the Los Angeles Division indicating that al-Qaeda has created an alliance with the Culebra drug cartel down in Tijuana, run by Carlos Quesada. If this is true, that could be bad—as in BAD bad!"

"Lay it on us," said Fredette.

"We're hearing that al-Qaeda has formed what has been referred to as an 'unholy trinity' with not only Quesada's organization, but also with several American street gangs on our side of the border, including the Mexican Mafia, Mara Salvatruchas, and a few others that the Culebra cartel is using as 'collectors' and 'enforcers.' If that is truly the case, the Mexican border will become the major freeway for terrorist ingress into the United States. This alliance between the Culebra people and the American gangs with al-Qaeda constitutes the worst crossover threat to the country we've ever known."

"So what we got here" added Duffin, "is a trio of money-grabbing drug dealers and fanatical jihadists scratching each others' backs in some kind of a mutual agreement involving drugs, terrorism, and high-level crime in general, right?"

"Something like that," responded Campo.

Duffin continued to weigh in. "The cartels throwing in with these fanatical camel jockeys doesn't resonate. Something's wrong here. The American street gang informants we've contacted from the Mexican Mafia say they don't like associating with the camel jockeys. The gangs have killed guys in prison that they discover are Muslim fanatics. It has to do with the Mexican Mafia code of conduct."

"So they actually have one," said Campo. "Well, that code of conduct is being bought out, apparently, because the power and impact of Osama bin Laden's memory has overshadowed that of Montezuma, the Aztec chief, whose image these Hispanic gangs have always liked to celebrate. The bad guys are teaming up, gents. I'm talking the cartels, the street gangs here in the states, the terrorists, and you can also throw in the American extremists . . . particularly the ones in the Northwest. We've got our hands full, boys.

"Okay, gents," Campo instructed. "You've been furnished the tactical gear and equipment you need. Take your wives out to dinner tonight, then pack up and head out to Omaha first thing tomorrow. Our phones are global and secure. Oh—unlimited minutes, by the way, and I want you to use them to call home . . .

a lot! Report to Omaha Special Agent in Charge Dave Cowan. He'll orient you on everything going on and will give you *carte blanche* to whatever information those guys have available. Work as fast and as effectively as you can."

"And another thing, guys," added Campo. "The whole game has changed now. The new Attorney General has seen the light. Waterboarding is no longer synonymous with the boogeyman. Get the picture?"

There were affirmative nods.

As Ridge Southerland drove back to his apartment that afternoon, contemplating his new assignment, he asked himself, *Just what is it, really, that motivates these young people like the Hussains, in their early twenties with a whole life ahead of them, to strap on a bomb and set out to kill themselves along with hundreds of innocent victims?* He recalled the answer that President George W. Bush gave in response to the 9/11 attacks on the World Trade Center buildings and the Pentagon. President Bush had called it "evil." *But it has to be more than that,* Southerland concluded. *The term "evil" alone can't adequately describe it.*

As Ridge continued down the highway, reaching the outskirts of Washington, DC, he considered the terrorists' claim that upon sacrificing themselves, they would be rewarded with a new home in paradise, surrounded by adoring virgins and eternal joy. Having previously served as a Mormon bishop in Florida, he compared the requirement of martyrdom as a prerequisite to entering paradise with the tenants of his own faith in The Church of Jesus Christ of Latter-day Saints that were necessary to enter into the presence of the Lord Jesus Christ in the hereafter. *For us, even taking one innocent life would preclude that,* he thought, *let alone killing hundreds of people.*

He continued weighing the requirements for exaltation with God as he had been taught—devotion, serving others, and respect for all other faiths. He compared those prerequisites with the diabolical goals of suicide bombers weaned on hate and prejudices.

He recalled being advised that 50 percent of the suicide bombers were typically single young men between eighteen and twenty-three years old, bent on inflicting a violent death on as many as possible not of their faith. In contrast, in his church, young men in the same age group would be traveling throughout the world, serving missions voluntarily—missions of compassion and service to anyone that would receive them.

He was perplexed at how concepts emanating from religion could become so twisted.

CHAPTER 10
THE CONSPIRATORS

ISLAMABAD, PAKISTAN
JULY 13

AL-QAEDA LEADER BASHIR SAYED and Rashid Siddiqui sipped coffee at a deli in downtown Islamabad. A few days ago, they had held their meeting with the recruited families in Los Angeles.

"Aahh, Rashid, this plan of ours has truly been inspired by Allah," Sayed said with satisfaction. "The egos of these young innocents and their parents are inflated so easily as we teach them the ideologies of martyrdom. They really believe all we tell them. They follow like sheep." Sayed grinned lavishly.

"Yes, they are quite naïve . . . but still have Allah's blessing," responded Siddiqui. "They believe they are what Islam is all about, when it is really we in the clergy that keep the candles burning. We're the ones that are next to Allah while these young dilettantes are only doing the easy part. After all, how much heart does it take just to walk into the infidel's presence and pull a cord? Dying to enter into paradise is the easy step. We in the clergy are the ones who must endure day by day, year after year, and throughout the decades. We are they who choose the young people, take them by the hand, and teach them to hate the infidels."

"And how clever you of the clergy have been in orchestrating these attacks, insisting that brothers and sisters attack together," Sayed said. "Two mid-eastern men would create much more suspicion entering a public place since the event the Americans call

9/11, and if it were a man and woman unrelated, without family loyalty toward one another, they may foolishly fall in love, get to know each other intimately, and then develop emotion which, when they are jilted or betrayed, may result in compromising one another and our mission with them."

Siddiqui nodded in agreement. "You're right, my friend. Here in Pakistan we control our women, but only heaven knows what could develop with married couples outside of familial relationships who have had years to be seeped in American idealism. At least a brother and sister with a common purpose will not be as easily distracted."

"Someday, when *Sharia* law is imposed upon the Western World and women are put in their proper place, the infidels will bless us, eh?" Sayed smiled broadly.

"Bashir, do you think the repercussions of the incident in Omaha will in any way compromise or endanger the assignments of the other Ten?" Siddiqui asked.

"No, they have been in their target cities now for almost twenty years," Sayed answered. "Even though the American intelligence agencies will be contacting their informants everywhere to identify individuals of mid-eastern descent previously involved in suspicious activity, The Ten and their parents have no criminal records, have all been furnished adequate documentation, and have no known contacts with individuals suspected of terrorist activity. They are beyond reproach and undiscoverable.

"Also to our advantage is the fact that when the slaughter of the infidels occurred in Omaha, both Ghani and Kareema disintegrated," Siddiqui said gleefully. "Nothing remains to identify them. The American intelligence will surely attribute what they call a suicide bomber attack to us, but no evidence remains. The only thing that could possibly draw suspicion would be the sudden disappearance of all the Hussains, but Ghani and Kareema had already advised their associates that their father's brother in Islamabad had passed away and that they would be gone for several months while their father took care of the affairs of his brother's estate. The family had even purchased plane tickets to Islamabad in advance for all four family members. It will take literally months for the FBI to investigate that family . . . if they do it at all." Another smile crossed Siddiqui's face.

"Right, my dear friend. Absolutely correct," said Sayed. "Yes . . . all contingencies are well covered. Praise Allah!"

"Praise Allah," responded Siddiqui. "It may take the Americans months to sift through all this and to determine who was behind the Omaha incident."

"All our operatives have been instructed that no one is to send any form of communication to American news media taking credit for the Omaha bombing, as we did in the attacks on the World Trade Centers, the US Pentagon, and other prior attacks. We will not have to claim credit in that manner any longer in order to rally the Islamic World."

"Yes, we will remain quiet on the issue," assured Siddiqui. "The American dogs will have to scramble to rule out another Oklahoma City bombing by a soured American like Timothy McVeigh. They'll spend months thinking it may have been one of their own."

"By that time The Ten will be ready to attack the 'breasts, belly, and hips' of the infidel dog on their holy Christmas Eve," said Sayed. "They love presents at that time. We'll give them one they'll never forget!" Both men laughed loudly.

Siddiqui asked, "Do you think we have planned well, attacking on their Independence Day, then delaying almost six months until their Christian holiday? Will they have too much time to recuperate?"

"No, it's perfect!" said Sayed. "The security measures around their malls and public places will triple . . . even quadruple after this attack in Omaha. The Americans are great ones to react, but not to act. That's their problem. Just look at their unprotected borders with Mexico and Canada. Look at how easy it was for our people to take over their planes and fly them into their most significant buildings on September 11, 2001. They weren't ready then. They're never ready, and they won't be ready on December 24. By then, nothing else significant will have happened. They'll drop their guard again and The Ten will walk in unabashedly and unleash fiery hell on them: North, south, central, east, and west. This attack will be without precedent and will bring them to their knees. Their economy will collapse."

The two men were practically overwhelmed with exhilaration as they discussed the forthcoming slaughter. They could barely draw the coffee to their lips without spilling it.

Finally gaining his composure, Siddiqui asked Sayed, "Have you been in contact with Abu this week?"

"Yes, I called him in the Cayman Islands three days ago. He's still in George Town. We just wired two million dollars into our account there for him to take care of additional expenses for The Ten and their families. He also needed more funding for Mr. Buck Bowen, the American in Idaho in charge of manufacturing our explosive harnesses."

"Ahh, yes. Mr. Bowen did fantastic work with the explosives Ghani and Kareema wore under their clothing," Siddiqui said. "Never before have our explosives made such an impact as they did in Omaha."

"Yes," responded Sayed, "Mr. Bowen and his people in Idaho are to be commended. We will deliver them the money they need through Abu. Between now and December 24, Bowen's people will have ample time to produce explosives even superior to what we used in Omaha."

"One other thing, Bashir," said Siddiqui. "Has Abu determined from the people in Mexico how much they'll need for the next stage of our operation?"

"From his last contact with Carlos Quesada, Abu calculates it will cost one hundred thousand dollars per person to bring The Hundred over the border prior to next Easter. That's ten million dollars for getting them across the border from Tijuana and providing identification." Then Sayed added, "A small price to pay to hit each state capital."

The Hundred would not be raised in America, trained in their ways, and educated in their schools like The Twelve. Once they were escorted into the United States over the Mexican border, they would simply walk into a store or other public building in a state capital and pull their cords simultaneously. They would be ushered through Tijuana by Carlos Quesada's "gate keeper," who would have access to a tunnel eighty feet deep, paved with concrete, and big enough to drive a truck through. The tunnel would lead north under the border and come up in an American warehouse one-quarter of a mile over on the United States side.

"Our plan is all so clever, Bashir!"

Bashir nodded. "The Hundred will be given phony papers provided by the Mexicans, then transported to all fifty state capital cities by Buck Bowen's people. Our other brothers and sisters—Pakistanis, Afghans, and Iraqis who will have crossed the borders by then—will shelter them temporarily until their meeting with Allah. As they disintegrate into Paradise, so also will a large portion of America dissolve into the hell prepared for them."

"I think, Bashir, that our plan is most pleasing to Allah. Once the heart, shoulders, breasts, belly, and hips of the infidel dog are blown apart and their major state capital cities are struck down, it will be easy for future martyrs to pour into America at a rate the infidels would never have believed possible. Our people will be so emboldened through these attacks on America that this will signal to all other Western infidel nations in Europe and other places of inequity that they also will eventually feel America's pain."

"There could not be a better plan," agreed Sayed. "It's simple and forthright. Since the martyrs will disintegrate, no escape route is necessary, and there will be no need to rescue anyone. It ensures killing not just a few, but scores of people."

"It's wonderful, my friend. Absolutely wonderful!" Siddiqui answered.

"Oh, there's more," Bashir added. "Much more. The other advantage is not having to worry that if the bomber is caught that he will give up information under interrogation. After all, his death is assured."

The two men raised their coffee cups in a toast.

CHAPTER 11
ABU KHAN

LOS ANGELES, CALIFORNIA
JULY 14

ABU KHAN, A PAKISTANI-BORN immigrant, came with his parents to Los Angeles in 1991 at age twelve, but adjusted poorly to the American culture, partially because his father had only negative comments regarding the "American Dream." His parents had expected much more than what they found in America. They had no idea they would have to work so hard at menial jobs in their adopted country to get ahead.

Although Abu was brought to America with his parents' dream that he would one day rise to the challenge of sacrificing his life as a suicide bomber, he had other ideas as to how he could accomplish his mission in the cause of Islam. He was a great disappointment to his father, who had looked forward to the wealth, prestige, and blessings his son's martyrdom would have brought to his family.

Abu's father spent his days and nights driving a cab, always discouraged, believing his talents for management would place him in a supervisory capacity once he had a minimal grasp of English. That never materialized. His attitude became sour and rebellious.

Abu's mother remained silent for the most part, fearing her husband's attitude would precipitate a return to Pakistan and a life of depravation. She relished life in the United States where she finally enjoyed human rights and some degree of respect.

She enjoyed living in an environment where women all around her were being treated as equals to their husbands. She secretly enjoyed the squeamishness Abu's father displayed when he had to come face-to-face with the fact that his neighbors would not appreciate witnessing him force his wife into a submissive role as he was accustomed to do in Pakistan.

Abu's father didn't like it, to say the least.

As a child, Abu listened day after day to his father's rants regarding the "imperialistic, money-grabbing American dogs" that cheated him on fare tips and "talked down" to him. Abu's mother, taking note of Abu's growing resentment for his adopted country, tried unsuccessfully to temper her husband's criticism, but it was to no avail. To his mother's dismay, Abu learned to hate Americans with a passion from an early age.

From the age of twelve to eighteen, like the other children being prepared to attack America as suicide bombers, Abu had been brainwashed by radical jihadists, military operatives influenced by both the Taliban and al-Qaeda. He had been taught that in heaven, he would find rivers of milk and honey, virgins, and many other heavenly rewards for offering himself up.

Like other Pakistani children, Khan's mentality changed from that of an innocent child into that of a cold-blooded assassin, bent on murdering as many people as he could in his religious fervor.

Abu first went to a training center near Islamabad when he was twelve years old. The compound consisted of a building with four rooms, each wall painted in bright colors with wondrous scenes designed to help each child draw a strong contrast with the drab, harsh surroundings in Pakistan.

"Abu, my child," advised Abu's father, "this is what heaven will look like." His father anxiously awaited Abu's response.

Abu just stared at the bright and beautiful depictions on the walls, saying nothing, seemingly transfixed. Then the "teachers" came in and greeted both Abu and the older Khan. One of them began explaining the paintings.

"Look, Abu, these are rivers of milk and honey. The beautiful women standing next to the rivers are virgins. That means they are special people waiting to make you happy. If you will give yourself completely to Allah, many of them will be yours in heaven. You could live there with the Holy Prophet Mohammed and eat great feasts whenever you want them. What do you think of that, Abu?"

Abu had remained silent, appearing embarrassed, not fully understanding the concept of virgins. He limped over to the wall, staring again at the paintings, saying nothing.

Before being brought by his parents to the United States, where the plan was to raise him as a human sacrifice, Abu had been used to living in abject poverty in Islamabad in a dusty, hopeless neighborhood in a home with a dirt floor and farm animals running in and out of it. The bright, elaborate paintings with heavenly images had imprinted heavily onto his mind.

The teacher approached Abu where he stood staring at the wall, placed a hand on his shoulder, and whispered softly into his ear, "You know, Abu, life has little value for you here in Islamabad. You are so poor. But if you do a good thing by giving your body to Allah in the United States against the infidels there, you will immediately go to heaven."

Abu was convinced. He had little hope to ever better himself where he was. His family had no wealth, other than a few pigs and chickens. He had no rich relatives. His family had no social connections. Through giving his life to Allah, he could assume a much better life in the hereafter.

Abu recalled that many of the children at the center were sent there by their parents just to get free food. Most parents knew nothing about the nature of education their children were receiving. He reflected on how the training at the center evolved as he got older, thanks to transportation from the states to Pakistan, paid for by al-Qaeda. He was trained in the use of weaponry, in the preparation of explosive harnesses, and in various military tactics. He recalled some of the youth his age being killed while conducting dangerous training procedures. The deaths were passed off by the teachers as "small prices to pay for inhabiting heaven."

In spite of all the descriptions of glorious accomplishment and heavenly reward, Abu was not impressed by hearing that the majority of the suicide bombers that were killed "in the cause of Allah" were only twelve to eighteen years old.

Once Abu became an American teenager, he voluntarily jumped off the track leading to martyrdom but remained thoroughly committed to the holy war. He demonstrated the ability to carry out other important assignments the terrorists gave him.

Abu's father made sure his son accompanied him regularly to a mosque in Los Angeles that preached hate and disdain for the ways of western culture. Abu became an avid student of the Koran. He became increasingly intolerant of heathens who wouldn't recognize Islam nor deify Mohammed. He eventually came to regard Americans as sub-human . . . individuals who needed to be eliminated rather than take up space on earth.

The Khan family had remained in contact with family members in Islamabad and routinely associated with al-Qaeda operatives and militant holy men who promoted al-Qaeda activities. Abu's relatives were proud that he was being groomed to become a major player in the militant Islamic movement in the United States.

The die was cast.

Abu never adjusted well in the American schools. He became the subject of ridicule by his peers as he struggled to learn English and to adapt to his new environment. The ridicule served only to deepen the hate he had for Americans. Although he walked with a limp due to a congenital defect, he became a devotee of weight-lifting and began competing successfully in many events at a local gym. The holy men at the mosque had previously put him in touch with al-Qaeda leaders in Afghanistan and Pakistan and they began communicating with him. Eventually, they successfully recruited him to the cause of militant Islam *jihad*.

At five foot ten inches tall, with a muscular build, Abu made an impressive figure in spite of his limp. His ego expanded as he hung pictures of his bodybuilding poses throughout his home. As an excellent student with a cultivated hate for America, Abu had become the perfect candidate to carry out al-Qaeda's bidding in the United States.

Abu continued to visit Islamabad numerous times to train

with al-Qaeda militants. He became proficient in military tactics, including firearms, building entry, rappelling techniques, helicopter extraction, and fast roping out of helicopters. When he returned home and reported his activity to his parents, his father rejoiced while his mother became increasingly alarmed.

By the time Abu was thirty-three, he was a major resource for al-Qaeda in America and became a wealthy man for his work on the militant group's behalf. His parents also benefited enormously. His father retired from working "beneath his station in life" when Abu began funneling money to him. With this newfound wealth, Abu's mother was content enough to hold her tongue and not protest Abu's continuing genesis as a militant who hated his host country.

Although Abu resided in Los Angeles, he spent considerable time in the Cayman Islands, 480 miles south of Miami in the Caribbean. In this George Town tax haven, he oversaw millions of al-Qaeda dollars tucked away in several of over six hundred banks. It was Abu who controlled the money for terrorist activities throughout America.

While traveling extensively throughout the Caribbean, Abu managed his employer's money effectively. Many of those funds— banked in the Cayman Islands, San Juan, Puerto Rico, and in St. Thomas, Virgin Islands—were raised by al-Qaeda sympathizers in the United States as well as in Pakistan and Afghanistan. The money had been laundered by individuals who, under Abu's direction, made deposits into various accounts throughout the United States in amounts under ten thousand dollars to avoid suspicion by banking authorities. Next the funds were "layered" by switching the money around through different US banks, then running the money through accounts in Panama and the Caribbean. Abu would even ensure the currency was changed into foreign denominations, making it even more difficult to trace, prior to the terrorists pulling it out for their activities.

Original sources of funding were never detected and always protected. Abu Khan was the man to contact in the major infidel nation where the fuse would be lit.

CHAPTER 12
THE OMAHA RENDEZVOUS

OMAHA, NEBRASKA
JULY 14

WHEN A2 TEAM ARRIVED at the Omaha office, SAC Dave Cowan was waiting with Omaha police chief Jack O'Malley. SSA Denny Campo had called ahead and made the appointment for his team's orientation.

SAC Cowan spoke first, eyeballing each of the five agents individually while sporting a taciturn expression. "So you guys have come to bail us out on this one, have you?"

"Don't bust our chops, Cowan," team leader Fredette responded. "We're just the new kids on the block, here to do our job, not to hinder."

"So you're not the Mongol hordes from the East? The Genghis Khans? The Attila the Huns? Here to wreak havoc with our investigations and steal our evidence?" Chief O'Malley said, looking serious.

Upon observing that team leader Fredette was taking their attitudes seriously, both Cowan and O'Malley broke into wide grins and began guffawing. "We're just pulling your chains, Fredette," chuckled O'Malley. "We're laughing to keep from crying. You bet we need you and your men here. We need all the help we can get, and with the mobility and funding you guys have with this new A Team program you got, you could be a real boon to us. Sit down here, and we'll line up some sodas and sandwiches."

"Make that ice water, boss," Duffin chimed in.

SAC Cowan stared at Duffin, then at his team leader. "Who is this guy, Fredette? Is he an Irish Catholic and is this the season of Lent? Ice water!"

Cowan seemed to be a fun-loving, happy guy. The A2 team breathed easier. It appeared that he and O'Malley, the chief, were a lot alike. They would be good to work with.

"Actually, Ridge Southerland over there, our Mormon tee-totaler, is the only real abstainer, besides me," Fredette said. "We really gotta watch him. He's always trying to steal the milk and cookies." Fredette loved poking Southerland a little here and there.

"Right!" responded Southerland. "That's the way it is. Any-time someone retires back at headquarters, they call upon me and the jefe here to tend the bar . . . only because they know we won't be helping ourselves to anything except sodas. It's like Fredette is always observing Lent '24-7,' and they all know I'm an abstainer."

O'Malley spoke up with his Irish brogue slightly exaggerated. "That's awful, Ridge, me boy! My dear old mother told me once I never should trust a man who won't drink with me!"

"You'd be pleased to know, chief," responded Ridge, "that I could get just as happy as you and your dear mother with a cold glass of 7-Up topped off with vanilla ice cream! We call them 'Mormon Martinis' back in Idaho."

Laughter broke out in the room—much needed laughter. Laughter that could perhaps ease the pain of what was ahead. These seven men faced huge challenges in solving one of the most serious crimes in the history of America. Now the A2 team knew Cowan and O'Malley would work with them and share their information and evidence in an environment of mutual trust and cooperation.

"I'll ask Chief O'Malley here to summarize our findings so far." Cowan sat back as the chief took over.

"Gentlemen, we know only two things: the identity of the two bombers and the type of bomb used. Beyond that, we're in the dark and have no idea where we go from here. The suicide bombers were Ghani and Kareema Hussain—young Pakistanis in their early twenties raised by previously thought to be legal migrant parents. Now we know they are radical Islamists from Islamabad, who brought up their children solely for doing what they did in our mall. We identified Ghani from some residual dental remains. The parents left their kids to do the dirty work, then high-tailed it back to Pakistan.

"The bombs were accelerated by acetone peroxide, known as TARP and were loaded with miscellaneous pieces of shrapnel. Two hundred and seventeen people were killed just with the shrapnel. Several hundred more were wounded. Only about fifty of those were killed by the actual impact of the bomb.

"We've already interviewed a couple dozen people, mainly bystanders at the mall, who survived. Some of them saw the brother push his sister in a wheelchair. We have interviewed known acquaintances of the bombers, who characterized them as good neighbors, presumably loyal citizens, void of contempt or hatred toward Americans, and faithful attendees of a local mosque That's all we got for now."

"Questions, gentlemen?" Cowan asked.

"Yeah," said Jim Flynn. "Any leads at all to work with?"

"Absolutely none," answered Cowan. "Ten days since the bombing and no good leads, but you have all our resources at your disposal and access to all the evidence, both here and at O'Malley's department."

The A2 guys just looked at one another with that "Are we going to be plowing in the sea?" look.

CHAPTER 13
THE PANIC BUTTON

WASHINGTON, DC
JULY 15

PIPPS LOVED THE OVAL Office. Deep in his heart, he yearned one day to be there and to occupy that chair behind the historic desk. Any time the president was out of town, he scheduled his meetings there . . . with the president's blessing. It gave Pipps clout, the kind of power and prestige that he thrived on. He loved it.

With the president on a South American tour, where he was to attend special meetings with the presidents of Chile and Brazil, Pipps was assigned to call the FBI director on the carpet and determine why more progress hadn't been made on solving the Omaha case. After all, eleven days had passed with no arrests. Pipps, who had no background in law enforcement and no knowledge of its challenges, couldn't understand why subjects hadn't been apprehended. Obviously neither could the president. *Eleven days since the incident*, he thought, *and no perpetrators identified? What's the FBI doing? Sitting on their haunches?*

Pipps was working himself up for this one. When the director arrived, he would lean on him big time.

There was a knock on the door. Pipps opened it and with a curt "Hello," signaled for Director Paul Hagen to sit down in front of him . . . with only a coffee table between them. Pipps enjoyed proximity between him and his victim when he was about to chew someone out.

Looking straight into Director Hagen's eyes condescendingly, Pipps asked a question that he already knew the answer to. "I'm sure you know what this is all about. Right, Hagen?"

The director answered matter-of-factly, staring right back at Pipps. "I have an idea . . . yes."

Director Hagen wasn't the least bit surprised when he had been summoned in by Pipps. He was well aware that the man sitting across from him was a "climber," and that he had stepped up in his career by stepping down on many of his past work associates. Director Hagen had a multitude of pressing matters on his desk, all related to coordinating the Omaha bombing investigation. He was receiving reports from SSA Denny Campo and others on almost an hourly basis. This was not his day to be badgered by a politician obsessed only with his own future in politics.

"Hagen, the Bureau has had five days to develop some concrete evidence regarding who was behind the Hussain subjects in the Omaha incident and the recent allegations of the possibility of another major attack in December, according to the two informants in Southern California."

As Hagen looked Pipps in the eye, he thought *What kind of an idiot am I dealing with? Surely he must realize I'm the one that passed this information on to the president. Here he is . . . reprimanding me for not already having solved possibly one of the most significant criminal cases in US history in just five days!*

Pipps sensed he may have put the director a little off balance. He wanted to close in for the kill. With his head tilted down and pointed in Director Hagen's direction, and he furrowed up his eyebrows and asked pointedly, "Is this matter really being pursued as vigorously as it should be, Hagen?"

Director Hagen's friendly countenance became sober, very sober, then extremely guarded. His eyes took on that steely look, accompanied by that affidavit half-smile appearance that many men in his organization were known for.

"That's Director Hagen to you, Mr. Pipps," came the response, direct and ominous. "I'm the director of the Federal Bureau of Investigation, the premier law enforcement agency in the world. You and I have had very little contact with one another, so you don't know me well, do you?" The director still had that chilling expression on his face. It was a no-nonsense look that unnerved Pipps.

"Well, now . . . that's . . . uhhh . . . ," Pipps was completely unprepared for this kind of insubordination toward his *authority*. Yes, authority that had been delegated to him directly from the President of the United States. This wasn't supposed to happen! He was not used to having his bluff called.

The director had more to say. "Furthermore, Mr. Pipps, I have now been in charge of the FBI for well over six years. I have less than two left. I have weathered many gigantic storms both from this administration and from the challenges of my appointment. What you are trying to create for me today doesn't even qualify as a light sprinkle. I'm not worried about losing my position. I have numerous options. So don't try to badger me, Mr. Pipps. I don't fear repercussions."

The director had scored a knockout punch. Pipps was momentarily tongue-tied.

Director Hagen had more to say. "However, Mr. Pipps, this isn't about you or me. This is about our country . . . a country threatened with a disaster that could well surpass the devastation of 9/11."

Pipps could barely wait for the director to finish what he was saying, so he could continue with his own rhetoric.

"Okay . . . Director Hagen. How's that?" Pipps asked. "This is the story. The president contacted me from Chile yesterday, where he's currently involved with straightening out our image down there. He's beside himself over the fact that no degree of measurable success has been obtained in prosecuting the Omaha incident and determining where and when these alleged attacks reported by your sources are to take place. He's still being hammered by all those Tea Party activists clamoring for his head, alleging that the Omaha incident was a result of his border policies. You know, yourself, that no evidence has been documented proving the Hussain family came across the border illegally, and even if they did, that was over twenty years ago."

"The Hussains came two decades ago with their infant

children. That's correct. Their documentation and point of entry
are still in question," responded Director Hagen. "So it's true that
we don't know for sure how they got here. However, their documentation closely resembles that currently being produced by the
Carlos Quesada drug cartel in Tijuana, Mexico. Quesada's people
have been pumping out false documentation for the purpose of
supporting illegal entry for over three decades. We cannot deny,
with certainty now—like you in the administration have been
denying—that the Hussain siblings' involvement in the Omaha
bombing isn't related to an illegal crossing from Mexico."

Suddenly Pipps looked pale. He thought he had just put an
end to that rumor with his absolute, yet undocumented, denials
to the press that the Omaha bombing could in any way be tied to
illegal border entry from Mexico.

"Director . . . please! For the sake of this administration, let's
keep this under wraps for now, okay? Especially since there is no
positive proof to indicate with any degree of certainty that Ghani
and Kareema Hussain came over the Mexican border."

"No worries, Mr. Pipps," replied the director, with the air of
one assured of having the upper hand. "We'll treat this with the
utmost confidence . . . like always."

"Thank you, Director Hagen. Thanks very, very much,"
replied Pipps as he took the director's hand and shook it vigorously.

Director Hagen paused until he was sure he had Pipps's full
attention.

"Mr. Pipps, I want you to understand that this possible illegal
border crossing by the Hussains doesn't hold a candle to the concern I now have for this possibility of another attack—an attack
on an unknown date in unknown places in December. This
intelligence comes from two informants in Southern California whose past information has proved reliable. After all, they're
talking about possibly one hundred al-Qaeda assailants preparing
for armed attacks at some undisclosed location in Mexico, where
they'll coordinate a hit on numerous American cities, after crossing the border."

Pipps couldn't pretend he was surprised. The director had

filtered that information down to the Oval Office several days before. Director Hagen knew Pipps knew that. Few issues had been more ticklish for the president than the potential of a terrorist attack coming from south of the border at the same time he was pushing for amnesty for fourteen million illegal aliens—aliens who had crossed that border and now resided in the United States and whose votes he was counting on for his re-election.

Pipps stuck with the party line. "Director Hagen, with all due respect for your intelligence gathering, we in the administration also have information coming from our Homeland Security chief that contradicts some of your intelligence. We appreciate your concern for the possibility of a pending attack, but countering that concern are the comments of the Director of Homeland Security, who has advised us repeatedly and continues to do so, that there is really no threat of consequence coming from the border. The Homeland Security director was also furnished the information you received but feels additional corroboration is necessary before lending it much credence, or at least enough to where the administration should take that threat seriously."

Director Hagen knew from past experience what the administration's real motives were for not addressing the border issues. He was well aware that vote-gathering was at the top of the list. He also knew his role was to protect the country and uphold the Constitution, not to meddle in politics.

"My own opinion, Mr. Pipps," Hagen said, "is that it would be extremely irresponsible to disregard or even minimize that information. I know it's not what the administration wants to hear, but that doesn't preclude such information from being a very dangerous allegation, and it should not be taken lightly."

Director Hagen could see that he wasn't getting through to Pipps. He knew that nothing he could say would convince the president's chief of staff—Pipps's rise to prominence was tied to the president's signature.

"Let me just ask you this, Mr. Pipps." Director Hagen's countenance again became very serious.

Pipps looked intently at the director, listening carefully.

"What's preventing al-Qaeda, Hezbollah, or any other

terrorist organization today from just marching over that border with the scores of Mexican illegals that cross it unabashedly every day? And once they cross over, what do you think their purpose would be here? Maybe just to soak in the rays of Christian freedom?

"Another thing, Mr. Pipps." The director looked directly into Pipps's eyes. "At the press conference with Jim Murray regarding the Omaha tragedy, you referred to the terrorists as having ties to the Taliban. Nothing could be further from the truth. Your remarks were embarrassing and disclosed an extreme lack of understanding—totally unbefitting for a top representative of the president's office. It was the al-Qaeda terrorist organization. That's a-l-Q-a-e-d-a," Hagen said slowly. "There are also other ways to spell it, but they are nothing like the Taliban. It's defined as a radical Islam organization operating through an international network of secret cells. It claims to be engaged in a jihad, or holy war, and has been responsible, as you know, for many acts of terrorism. It was the al-Qaeda organization that our informants indicated were behind the attack, not the Taliban."

"Well, big deal! Do you really believe the garden variety American really cares whether they're called one or the other?" Pipps asked.

"Yes, Mr. Pipps," answered Hagen. "I believe they do. You don't give the 'garden variety American' much credit for intellect, do you? Just for your information, the Taliban is a fundamentalist Islamic religious group that has no agenda outside of seeking control of Afghanistan. They resented us for taking it over. It's true that both the al-Qaeda and the Taliban are terrorist organizations that originated from Islamic roots and seem to be the same in many ways, but they definitely are not the same organization.

"Mullah Mohammed Omar founded the Taliban. Osama bin Laden founded al-Qaeda.

"The Taliban is Pakistani-based. Al-Qaeda is Saudi-based.

"These are just a few of the differences. Does that clear it up for you, Mr. Pipps?"

Pipps knew the director was being condescending, but he saw very little he could do to retaliate. He had been trapped in a void of ignorance. He was red in the face and so angry, he couldn't respond. Tongue-tied, he knew he had met his match . . . and then some. He remained silent, seeking desperately for the appropriate response, but came up empty.

Director Hagen stood up. "Mr. Pipps, you can advise the president we're working hard to develop the intelligence we need to prevent another attack on our country. Supervisory Special Agent Denny Campo has implemented the A Team, which has taken a while because of the obstacles your administration has set before us. You finally gave us the green light to deploy this group to pursue the perpetrators of the Omaha mall case because you had no other option . . . nowhere to turn. Campo's men are working ten to twelve hour days, six days a week, contacting key informants and following up with every lead available in order to gain the intel we need to obtain arrest and search warrants. Nothing of substantial value has been developed yet, other than the identity of the Hussain bombers and the informant data we have discussed. Tell the president we'll keep working until we find what we need. That's my report, Mr. Pipps."

By the look on the director's face, Pipps knew that their conversation was finished.

"I have other matters pending, Mr. Pipps. Please give my regards to the president. Good-bye!" Director Hagen shook Pipps's hand briskly and walked away without looking back.

Pipps remained in a daze. *The Hussains may have crossed the Mexican border! How do we spin that one when it leaks out? You gotta be kidding!*

CHAPTER 14
A NEW POLITICAL CLIMATE

WASHINGTON, DC
JULY 16

JIM MURRAY CALLED A SPECIAL press conference with the White House reporters. Gifford Pipps was behind him. Murray began reading from a prepared statement.

"The tenor of the White House has changed considerably since the Omaha incident. Since the president took office, there have been a few isolated attempts by al-Qaeda operatives that have failed. Very close to success, yes . . . but still failed, like the shoe bomber airplane incident, the 2009 Christmas Day bomber, and the attempted Times Square bombing. No other major attempt to attack the United States has been successful since 9/11 with the exception of the attack by a United States officer, Major Nidal Malik Hasan, who shot thirteen of his fellow soldiers at Fort Hood, Texas.

"The Omaha incident has placed the president on a new learning curve and has precipitated a much more aggressive stance toward security issues. The Mexican border will now be secured with tens of thousands of additional United States troops, returning from Afghanistan and other foreign assignment. A massive steel wall will be constructed, manned by United States troops who will have eye-to-eye contact with one another, tower-to-tower, the entire two thousand miles along the Mexican border with California, Arizona, New Mexico, and Texas. Those steel walls will be sensitized in such a way that signals will be given off if breeching attempts are made. Sensory devices, like those used by the military, will probe underneath the ground for tunnels intended to breach the borders.

"The area adjacent to the walls and guard stations will contain a highway accommodating ground units with drills, explosives, and whatever else is needed to neutralize intrusions.

"Illegal immigration issues will be prioritized with the path to citizenship being carried out only after an obligatory return to the country of origin. The illegal immigrant will become a citizen only by standing in line, going through the hoops, and paying a hefty fine for illegal entry. Border authorities and law enforcement agencies will be mandated to arrest and deport those without proper identification. The president will ask Congress to issue stiff penalties for US employers who hire illegal immigrants without legal documentation authorizing their presence.

"In addition, law enforcement on all levels—federal, state, and local—will be given continuing authority to use all necessary investigative means, within the boundaries of judicious and humane enforcement, to investigate and pursue those in America who would kill us . . . given the opportunity. Once the images of the carnage of the Omaha victims was flashed over the screens of American viewers, Congress moved quickly to ensure that advanced interrogation techniques, including waterboarding, were no longer considered torture. The president has signed off on these measures."

Murray took a few questions. The reporters appeared eager about returning to their news stations to announce the changes in American policy toward terrorism. Questions flew around in a frenzy.

"What else are we going to do about this? Are we really, finally, following through with protecting the border and all these other measures you have mentioned, or is this all talk?"

These kind of questions had been spawned from a very liberal policy regarding leaving the border alone in the past. Murray answered every question in a positive way, trying to assure the reporters that the president's response to the Omaha attack and any forthcoming assaults would be both immediate and aggressive. Doubt was still present though. All had heard the party line numerous times without witnessing the actual fulfillment of commitment. Finally, the press conference began winding down.

Murray concluded his remarks by saying, with an air of seriousness, "Just one more thing, folks. The 'same old story' has again repeated itself in America: the United States has gone soft until it had to go hard. No happy medium. We can't afford to make this mistake ever again!"

Gifford Pipps wasn't happy with that comment, but Murray was elated.

"It's true that the White House has allowed trying the Gitmo detainees who have been working for al-Qaeda in federal courts in several instances . . . the same terrorists that orchestrated the 9/11 attack and prior terror attacks against the United States. They have gone as far as to extend to them as enemy combatants the same privileges that they would to United States criminals. It isn't working. Too much evidence is being discarded on technical error. Too much lenience for those who delight in killing Americans. Too much turning the cheek and saying, 'Here! Hit me again!' I think you all get the point. Things are changing around here."

Although Gifford Pipps left the gathering red in the face, for the first time in ages, Murray felt good about his job.

* * * * *

New York City, New York
September 15

In the months following the Omaha incident, a newly-appointed United States District Court Judge in New York—assigned to hear cases involving terrorist attacks in the United States—had stepped forward with a "hanging judge" temperament. This judge, Clyde Alan Jeffreys, never agreed with having al-Qaeda terrorists tried in federal courts and was successful in postponing, or at least delaying, that action wherever he could. Nevertheless, he tried them when it was apparent that he had to, but invariably they were found guilty and were dealt harsh sentences.

Judge Jeffreys was particularly offended that certain Muslim imams were pushing to build a mosque near "Ground Zero" in New York City in the shadow of the attack on the Twin Towers. He vigorously expressed his views against that action, influencing many of his friends in Congress to oppose it.

The al-Qaeda rulers became convinced something had to be done about Judge Jeffreys. They called upon Abu Khan.

* * * * *

George Town, Grand Cayman
September 20

The phone rang in Abu Khan's richly furnished apartment in the Marriott Hotel, on Seven Mile Beach in George Town, Cayman Islands.

"Abu, this is Bashir." A sense of urgency was in his voice. "I have something very important, good brother. Something only you can help us with. We have met with the holy man, Rashid Siddiqui, and he also gives this request his blessing."

"Yes, Bashir . . . anything. What would you have me do?" responded Abu to his al-Qaeda superior in Islamabad.

"It's our brethren being tried in the New York federal courts. As you may be aware, the infidel judge there, Clyde Alan Jeffreys, is doing us no favors. He seems to have a personal vendetta against the cause of Islam. Can you help us with him?"

"Of course, Bashir, of course. Tell Rashid and the other holy men it will be taken care of, but give me a few weeks. I will deliver," Abu assured.

"We know, Abu," Bashir said. "We have such faith in you for your devotion to Allah in all you do: handling the funds in the Caymans, coordinating the logistics with the Mountain Patriots and Quesada's Culebra Cartel, and keeping The Ten and their parents happy. Now that you are also working with the Mexicans to bring The Hundred and the others to their destinations, do you want help there? Is it too much?"

"Please, Bashir, send no one! It is hard enough for me to avoid attracting the attention of the FBI and the other infidel authorities who monitor the monetary proceeds here in the Caymans. Curious questions are asked, and I must always pacify.

"Having another here for me to look after and keep track of could only cause more problems," Abu said adamantly. "For what we have to do, I can accomplish either here or home in Los Angeles. I need no one else. They would be in my way." Abu disguised his real motive for refusing help: having to share his al-Qaeda proceeds with someone else.

"Of course, brother, but you should always know that we, with the holy men, offer you our sworn support. Praise Allah! Good-bye for now, brother."

"Good-bye, my friend. Praise Allah!" Abu responded.

CHAPTER 15
THE CAVE

PARROT CREEK LANDING
MIDDLE FORK OF THE SALMON RIVER, IDAHO
SEPTEMBER 21

THE SEVEN NEW SELF-BAILER rafts—fourteen-foot Avon models—pulled up into the Parrot Creek landing, all loaded down with wooden boxes roped securely to the side retainers and carefully placed on cargo platforms on the end of each raft. Each box had been flown in by Cessna aircraft from Stanley, Idaho, to the Indian Creek landing strip, where they were loaded onto the rafts.

The flight into the Indian Creek landing itself had been an adventure. Each aircraft contained one raft and two boxes with precursors for explosives and harness fabric, along with metal objects for shrapnel: needles, nuts, screws, nails, and so on. As the landing at Indian Creek had loomed into sight, the pilots yawned while the passengers held their breath. The Cessnas tentatively approached the narrow, winding, dirt airstrip, tucked into the dense growths of pine adjacent to the river. Once the cargo was unloaded, Bowen's river men had inflated their rafts with foot pumps and lashed the heavily-laden boxes onto the new rafts.

Idaho's Middle Fork of the Salmon River was a legend. The river was so pure and clear that every rock could be seen on the bottom, right up to the time it converged with the Main Salmon. The free-flowing river dropped three thousand feet in a one hundred and five mile stretch. It was called the "River of No Return" by the native Indians. Natural and untamed, it was protected by Congress as one of America's wild and scenic rivers. The landscape was rugged and diverse with no roads. Only a few old rundown log cabins could testify that men ever lived along its banks. The fir and spruce presented a gorgeous yet primitive setting of a western frontier, still partially undiscovered.

The Parrot Creek Placer Mine drainage—five hundred yards from the Middle Fork, up the tributary on the Bighorn Craig side—was nothing but rough, craggy mountain terrain. The east side of the river was probably the most remote place in Idaho's Frank Church Wilderness Area, the largest wilderness area in the United States.

The trip down the Middle Fork during the fall presented a real challenge, even for experienced river guides. The water was low, barely two and a half feet deep, where the Mountain Patriots had launched at Indian Creek. Jagged rocks had to be expertly navigated and accounted for. Big fir trees that had slid into the river during spring runoff were now lurking barely underneath the surface of the river. They could snag a raft, forcing the oarsman to proceed cautiously downstream, following the "V slick," or main area of current flow.

From the Indian Creek landing strip, they had spent three days traversing those one hundred white water rapids, some of them gigantic. The oarsmen picked their way through rapids with names like Velvet Falls, Pistol Creek, Devil's Tooth, and House Rock. As the river deepened and widened, the rafts' occupants could see native rainbow and cutthroat trout, scurrying around for a swipe at a loose angle worm or salmon egg.

The surrounding mountains with granite cliffs that projected two thousand feet up from the river were inhabited not only by bighorn sheep, bear, and elk, but had also become densely populated by gray wolves introduced into the area from Canada twenty years earlier. The wolves fed on diminishing elk herds. By the time Bowen's men were floating in the explosives, the animals were becoming much more emboldened in their hunting patterns and were less and less hesitant to surround hikers and hunters in near approaches.

Luckily, not one raft had flipped. Since the agreement was reached with Abu Khan to manufacture the explosives, Bowen's men had run the Middle Fork numerous times over the previous months with old military surplus rafts for training purposes. Several rafts had flipped in training trips as the men became familiar with the treacherous challenges of the Middle Fork. Bowen felt his people had to do this themselves. He feared hiring some nosey river guide could compromise their operation.

As the raft convoy finally approached the landing and worked slowly down to the shore's edge, several of the Mountain Patriots staying at Parrot Creek, including Ike Grimsley, came out with two pack mules to meet them.

"We've been waiting!" hollered Grimsley. "Thought maybe you boys had gone out on your own to greener pastures. We was expectin' you early this mornin'."

"Well, Grimsley," responded the rower in the lead boat, "maybe you ought to try runnin' this river yourself, then tell us about the timing."

"Don't take offense, fella." Grimsley half smiled. "Just glad ya made it. Got some chow waitin' up at the cabin. Let's load this stuff on these critters and get up there."

The men had to make numerous trips with the pack animals to the site. They placed the cargo at the mouth of an obscure cave covered by heavy brush, just across from the cabin.

The river men had taken note of the gray, fleeting forms of several wolves close to the shore and had been curious at the apparent interest the animals seemed to have in human beings. There had been incidents at Stoddard Creek, upstream from Parrot Creek, a few miles down from the Flying B Lodge on the west side of the river, near an old lookout. The wolves had come dangerously close to some river runners eating lunch, before they were chased away by folks banging on pots and pans.

At that point, no one thought much about it.

CHAPTER 16
THE TRAINING ACADEMY

TIJUANA, MEXICO
SEPTEMBER 23

CARLOS QUESADA'S PAKISTANI-BORN WIFE, Safia, fluent not only in her native tongue, but also in Spanish and English, spent several hours each day coordinating language classes for The Hundred. This was taking place at the abandoned military outpost just a few miles outside of Tijuana.

English classes were taught by four al-Qaeda sympathizers from various cells in the United States . . . US citizens of Afghan, Pakistani, and Iraqi descent, all of whom were dedicated to the cause of one day instituting Sharia law and customs into America.

Most of The Hundred were young men and women, like The Ten, in their twenties and early thirties, willing to wreak havoc on American infidels to comply with their commitment to holy *jihad* . . . young adults intent on eventually meeting up with Allah through one last, final act of self-martyrdom. They were now in their fifth month of training at the compound.

Safia Quesada had divided The Hundred into four equal groups with one teacher apiece. The teachers were fluent in languages common to The Hundred. They had the very best English texts available, as well as instructive CDs they could listen to throughout the day. They were taught with the goal of producing a student that could represent himself as having lived in the United States for several years, but who was still struggling somewhat with the English language. If they could pass them-selves off in that way for two or three days, they could stay in the target cities' hotels and go where they had to go to accomplish their missions without arousing suspicion.

Safia insisted that the teachers spend at least four hours a day with the students. They had remodeled the interior of an old military installation with the finest furniture, technology, and equipment that money could buy for language instruction.

An additional hour each day had to be spent learning Spanish. The Hundred were to grow facial hair similar to their Mexican counterparts and be dressed as other illegal aliens of Mexican descent when they cross the border with Carlos Quesada's men. That way, there would be no question about the visitors being anything other than what they were characterized as . . . Mexican illegals.

Quesada knew that if his contacts among the *coyote* trans-porters and corrupt border officials were aware he was bringing al-Qaeda terrorists across the US border, he would be charged ten times what he normally had to pay them. And, after all, the one hundred thousand dollars per person was a tidy amount that he didn't want diminished, so it was imperative The Hundred appeared as Mexicans.

During the remaining three to four hours a day reserved for training, Quesada supervised a core of his own men who provided training in surreptitious border crossings and other helpful tech-niques: how to interact with the coyote transporters until they were handed over to the Mountain Patriots; what to say if border authorities questioned them; and how to escape or evade authori-ties in the event of attempted apprehension.

In Quesada's view, the crowning achievement of the training he afforded The Hundred was the two-hour instruction given by four Gitmo detainees who had eventually been released by US authorities. They had subsequently returned to Mexico to teach The Hundred how to attack their former captors. Inspired by their resentment to their American captors and their deep-seated hatred for the United States, they had committed to do everything pos-sible to see that America was brought to her knees.

The up side for Quesada in having the Gitmo detainees was that they could pour their venom on the trainees *and* also communicate directly to The Hundred without a translator. They were relentless in teaching tactics of destruction, poisoning, and harassment—methodology that would constitute the daily fare of The Hundred right up to the coordinated, simultaneous attack on Easter.

On the evening of September 23, a man showed up at the academy whose visit had long been anticipated: Bashir Sayed. He was accompanied by Abu Khan. A special dinner was held for Sayed and Khan at the Quesada residence. The four American English teachers were present, along with the four ex-Gitmo detainee trainers.

Safia translated for her husband, as Carlos welcomed the visitors. "What a pleasure to have you both here, Señor Sayed and Señor Khan. You'll have a perfect opportunity to see the progress we have made with The Hundred. Tomorrow morning, we will start early, so we can thoroughly acquaint you with what we're accomplishing here. Thanks to my dear wife, Safia, these fine English teachers, and the gentlemen teaching the assault tactics, we have prepared an awesome contingent of warriors for you."

"The pleasure is ours," Bashir said, speaking slowly and methodically, so that it could be translated. "We have heard much about what you have been doing here and have seen some of the results in the videos you have sent us, but I'm sure I am speaking for both Abu and myself when I tell you that seeing this in person will prove an extraordinary experience."

Dinner was served, consisting of roast pork marinated in a wonderful combination of herbs and salsa. There was also a plate of tortillas by each guest's dish, accompanied by dishes loaded with stuffed potatoes and succulent vegetables. It was followed up with the traditional Mexican dessert of *tres leches* cake and coffee or hot chocolate. Once the meal was over and the conversation stalled, the guests turned in.

The following morning Khan and Sayed spent a few minutes in the Spanish and English training sessions, but what drew their attention the most were the contraptions Quesada had devised for what he referred to as " simulated training scenarios."

The first demonstration was an overpass built over what was obviously meant to be a four-lane highway. Only one lane was paved—the lane directly adjacent to the base of the overpass. It was built next to a dirt lane of the same dimensions.

"Come on up to our overpass," instructed Quesada, accompanied by Safia, who once again translated for him. Khan and Sayed followed Quesada and Safia up the staircase leading to the top of the fake overpass, which extended out just over the paved lane.

"You can imagine," added Quesada, "that the overpass goes all the way across the interstate, but we are only concerned with this position of advantage." He pointed out to the place where the overpass ended just over the first lane.

He spoke directly to Bashir Sayed. "To go along with your plan for interrupting commerce and stalling delivery of foodstuffs and other commodities to the Americans, we have devised this scenario. Here is what will happen."

Khan and Sayed listened intently.

"There will be a three-day attack period, according to your request, starting with Good Friday. On that day the fifty two-man teams will mount an overpass on a major interstate in or near each state capital. They will use the high octane rifles, .308 caliber-scoped sniper weapons. Using bicycles in the early morning, just when there is visibility, they'll keep the weapon in a long bag strapped under the frame. One person will pick the target through high-powered binoculars. It will be an eighteen-wheeler transporting food items like meat, fruit, and vegetables. We're already aware of which companies transport food, when they make their deliveries, and where. Through photos and videos, our students have learned to identify those kinds of trucks. When the truck comes within approximately fifty feet of the overpass, our sniper will fire at the driver through the front window. We've chosen ammunition that can penetrate effectively for your shooters."

"Ahh . . . Carlos, this is all too amazing!" said Bashir Sayed.

"Now watch!" ordered Quesada.

Two of The Hundred mounted the overpass, walking in front of the onlookers. One had a .308-scoped rifle and the other binoculars. Approximately one hundred and seventy-five yards up the paved road, an old dilapidated eighteen-wheeler transport truck came down the road, accelerating. Another individual operated it by remote at the foot of the overpass. When the truck was within forty feet of the overpass, the sniper fired a round directly into the front window where the driver would normally be seated. The glass did not totally erupt, but the shot had left a clear hole through the front leading into the cab. It clearly would have hit the driver.

The truck came to a stop approximately fifty yards down the road, once it had passed underneath the overpass.

As Sayed and Khan examined the damage to the window and noted the hole in the top portion of the driver's seat, Sayed remarked, "No wonder we're paying you the fortune that we are, my good man. You have remarkable insights!"

"I'm sure you understand the ramifications these attacks will have on the Americans in each of their capital cities," Quesada responded, "once fifty of these attacks are reported. The truck drivers will refuse to deliver until the owners refit all their trucks with bullet-proof glass and reinforced steel. This will take time . . . a good deal of time. In the meantime, the shelves in the super markets will empty. People will panic when they see there is no more food. There will be rioting and stealing like never before. People will overreact everywhere."

"You see," remarked Safia, "my husband has given all this great thought."

"Indeed, my dear . . . indeed," said Sayed.

Quesada and Safia then accompanied the two men to another old building, shaped like a half cylinder, with a pitted metal surface.

Quesada spoke again proudly. "Here's where we have our laboratory. The Hundred are instructed on the effects of certain chemical compounds they will place in the water systems of the American cities . . . chemicals that can at a bare minimum make people deathly ill, if not kill them. The second day, the day after Good Friday, they will poison some of the water systems in each city with these chemicals. Again, a simulated water supply system has been set up for that purpose, with the students being shown by the Gitmo instructors how to breech the various pipes and duct inlets in order to disperse the chemicals into the streams of drinking supply."

"Fantastic!" said Khan. "This is truly amazing. What will you have for Easter Sunday?"

"We have what Bashir requested. This is the day that the dams will be attacked. This is where The Hundred will 'rendezvous with Allah,' as you call it. We are not considering the major dams, like the Hoover Dam in Nevada or the Grand Coulee Dam in Washington. They are too well guarded. They'll pick smaller, less significant dams, but ones that will cause instant death to many and will diminish supplies of electricity throughout the country. Dams that are not guarded and are left unprotected . . . for the most part. These locations are where The Hundred will drive their boats, loaded with explosives, right up to the face behind the dam, then pull the cord on their harnesses. That feat of martyrdom will ignite the loads of heavy explosives, breeching the face of the dam and causing chaos below."

"Remarkable, Carlos," said Sayed. "But I do have one question. Does the supply of explosives seem sufficient for what The Hundred will need for the Easter event?"

"So far, each order we have recommended and sent to Mr. Bowen in Idaho through Abu has been cleared, meaning they have it ready and can ship it out when needed," said Quesada.

"Then we are on track," remarked Sayed. "I assume your payments are coming in here on a timely basis?"

"Absolutely," responded Quesada. Stretching his arm out over his training compound. He added, "Of course, I would not be doing all this otherwise."

Fully satisfied with the training for The Hundred in Mexico, Sayed and Khan left the following day for Los Angeles, from whence Sayed departed the same day for Islamabad.

CHAPTER 17
THE MEDALLION

PLANTATION, FLORIDA
SEPTEMBER 25

DELISHA AHMED RETURNED WITH her brother Lufti from another meeting at the mosque near their neighborhood in Plantation, Florida. After the regular services, Tahir Kauser, the local Muslim imam, had met separately with the siblings and their parents. He repeated the same rhetoric as he always did regarding their infidel host country and the glory of martyrdom, showering the four people with anti-American demagoguery for a full hour.

Lufti and his parents ate it up. What the imam critiqued was what they wanted to hear, what they had always heard, and what they knew was appropriate to hear for the forthcoming missions of the two young martyrs.

It was different for Delisha. She retired to her room, pensive and confused. She struggled with the memory of Elder Brown with Elder Sterling in his arms, preaching a gospel of love and compassion. She contrasted that picture with the mission she and Lufti had prepared themselves for. She questioned the purpose for which she had been raised. It was something that was beginning to tear her apart. The thought of killing herself in the cause of Allah did not intimidate her. She understood the concept of self-sacrifice for a higher cause. It was well imbued within her. But there was a tinge of doubt, a questioning as to "Why?" that continued appearing on her horizon. *Why take so many lives, including innocent children and their mothers? Why hate the way we have been taught to hate? Does the Koran really require this kind of bloodletting? Is this really what a just god like Allah would want? Elder Sterling was ready to die also, knowing that he would soon . . . but maybe for a cause that was much higher, much nobler?*

Delisha slipped into a deep state of reflection, as she was becoming more prone to do. Each session of thought and introspection regarding her future destiny with death was tugging frequently at her heart and was introducing more confusion.

As Delisha massaged a gold-colored medallion hanging from her neck, highlighted by a picture of a multi-spired temple in the center, her memory was turned back four years.

✵ ✵ ✵ ✵ ✵

Several months after Delisha turned sixteen, she attended a youth activity night at the Mormon chapel in Plantation. Afterwards, Bishop Southerland, the father of her closest friend, Madi, approached her and a couple of girls. He wanted to interview the girls and invited Delisha to talk with him too.

Delisha had studied quite a bit about Christianity. Her parents had always encouraged her "to study out the infidels, that she may know the nature of the wolves in sheeps' clothing." Delisha was not only interested in learning about other pagan religions, but also was curious about their tenets. She knew that a Catholic bishop was an ordained minister who held the authority to officiate and rule in the Catholic Church. She knew some of them were called cardinals, archbishops, patriarchs, and that there was a lead bishop or a pope that ruled over the entire church. She was aware that the bishops claimed to trace their origin to the ancient apostles. She also knew that Mormon bishops were somewhat different than Catholic bishops.

When her friends introduced her to Ridge Southerland, who was a bishop and an FBI agent, she was overwhelmed with curiosity. Why would this man want to interview her? *Would my parents object?* she questioned. *I think not, since they have allowed me to come and associate here for some time now.* She determined to go through with the interview out of curiosity, if nothing else.

She knocked on Bishop Southerland's office door. As Bishop Southerland opened it, greeting her, she was comforted by his wide smile and the relaxed manner in which he received her. She thought, *This man is so unlike the holy men I have known who preached from the lectern and seldom stepped down. He is not even that serious.*

Delisha recalled how surprised she had been to see Bishop Southerland with his coat and tie removed playing basketball with the young men in the cultural hall in his socks. He had rolled up the sleeves of his white dress shirt, and sweat was pouring down his forehead. She was struck by the thought that this kind man had to use a gun for his job.

Bishop Southerland opened the door, smiling at Delisha, and invited her in, motioning to a chair in front of his desk. She sat down.

"Delisha, what a pleasure to finally talk to you one-on-one. My daughter, Madi, speaks so highly of you. You have been here quite regularly for some time now, but since I've been called as bishop, I don't think we have been able to say much more than hi." Bishop Southerland had a warm countenance.

"That's right, sir." It was still very uncomfortable for Delisha to refer to this man as "Bishop." "I'm only allowed to come occasionally. My parents are quite strict about that."

"But you have come off and on now for several months, Delisha. Why is it that you've never been baptized?" The bishop was obviously curious, making Delisha more than a little uncomfortable.

"Well, my religion is Islam, and as you may know, I've been raised by my parents to be Muslim. It really doesn't mean much to me, since we do not attend the local mosque. Practicing the worship of Islam is just a custom my family carries that we do not want to break."

Delisha's face reddened, as she lied regarding her regular attendance at the mosques with Rashid Siddiqui and the other imams who were instilling poison and hate for America into her and Lufti. She was basically honest in nature and hated having to lie to other people. Yet she knew that would be expected of her in

America in order to obscure her real reason for being there.

"Well, Delisha, the reason I wanted to interview you tonight is because I think you could possibly qualify to receive what we refer to in the church as the Young Women Recognition Award. It's for young women who have set high goals for themselves in their spirituality, service to others, and other important areas. Would you be interested in hearing more?"

Delisha had never received any kind of rewards or recognition because her parents had always stressed keeping her and her brother out of the limelight. She was excited about the prospect of receiving something based on her personal standards, even if it was from a church she could never join.

"Yes, sir, I believe I would like to know more." She smiled out of excitement.

"Delisha, the award is given to young women, not necessarily just of our faith, who participate in a goal-setting and achievement program within the Young Women organization of The Church of Jesus Christ of Latter-day Saints. The purpose of the program is to help young women progress in eight major areas of their life. It's designed to lead young women to their Creator and to help them focus on important values. Still interested?"

"Yes," replied Delisha. "Absolutely yes!"

"The program leading up to receiving the award teaches young women how they can know they are daughters of God."

Delisha drew a blank expression. *Who is God?* she thought. *Is he Allah? Is he the Christian god? Who is he, really? When the missionaries came and taught our family about their god, the Christian god, it seemed special. I felt something then that I have never felt before.*

The bishop continued. "The Young Women program helps you develop personal religious behaviors such as prayer, scripture study, and service."

Again Delisha was in deep thought. *I can't tell him that I pray five times a day to Allah. If word got out, I would be an object of suspicion in this country with the current concerns about Mideastern terrorists. And scripture study? There's no way I can tell him I spend as much time as I do reading the Koran. And my parents have made it clear that I am not to study the writings of any other faith, so how do I get by this part?*

Suddenly Delisha made a decision that she would never share with Lufti or her parents. *I'll begin reading the Christian scriptures. Why not? I'm a big girl. It can't change me or my destiny.*

"The program will also help you develop your talents and skills," Bishop Southerland continued. "This will help you to be a better wife and mother later in life."

Hints of tears began swelling up in Delisha's eyes. This last comment by Bishop Southerland took her off guard. *I will never have a husband or children!* she thought. This was the first time in her life that she had come to grips with the fact that she would never achieve the crowning glory of her gender: being a mother and a wife.

She thought, *What's wrong with me? I've never considered before that I would never have the privilege of motherhood or that I would never be a wife. Why now?*

Is this really worth it? Delisha asked herself. *Have I really been created to take life by destroying as many people as I can, rather than giving life to children and accepting love from a soul mate? Is this really my destiny?* She paled at the idea and again became lost in thought.

"Delisha? Delisha, are you okay?" asked Bishop Southerland.

"Oh . . . yes. I'm fine. I really am," answered Delisha unconvincingly. "Yes, sir. I'll work on these goals and I'll achieve that award." Delisha was serious. She knew her parents would believe her if she informed them she was only doing this to help disguise her real intentions.

Two years later, when Delisha was eighteen and Bishop Southerland was being transferred from his Florida FBI resident agency to FBI Headquarters in Quantico, Virginia, she finally completed the requirements for the Young Womanhood Recognition Award and received the special medallion . . . the first and only award or recognition she had ever been permitted to receive in her entire life.

At a special church service, Delisha was recognized. The bishop had this to say: "Brothers and sisters, many of you have known Delisha Ahmed and her family for years. They are in attendance tonight."

While Delisha's father squirmed nervously in his seat, her

mother seemed pleased they were being recognized.

"As most of you know, Delisha is not a member of our faith. However, I have learned from her example that her values compare favorably to our own." Upon hearing a Christian church leader articulate the worth of her values, Delisha became overcome with pangs of guilt that throbbed and stabbed her conscience. She looked down.

"Delisha has participated in service and activity with the youth of our ward over the past years and has complied with all the requirements of this reward. We hope that someday soon she will join our church, along with her family." That statement caused both her parents and Lufti to look away.

Bishop Southerland went on. "I was so pleased the day I discovered in the new handbook of instructions that this reward could be presented to worthy young women of other faiths. She's a friend and good example to all of us. It's a great honor for me to award her this. I commend her parents for raising such a wonderful young woman."

Upon hearing this, a smile actually appeared on Delisha's father's face, while her mother's pleasure was written all over her countenance. Lufti, however, was restlessly trying to determine the quickest way out of the chapel after the meeting so he could leave without having to talk to anyone.

As Bishop Southerland opened a small box containing the medallion, he motioned for Delisha to come forward to the stand where he waited for her behind the pulpit. She immediately sprang to her feet enthusiastically and walked briskly, excited.

The bishop handed her the lovely medallion, which was attached to a gold chain. She was stunned by the inherent beauty of this piece of jewelry. To her, it represented so much more. It was a beautiful gold color with an image of the Salt Lake City temple in the center with all its many spires of granite.

Delisha wasn't content with just placing it back into the box and walking away. Instead, she carefully placed the chain medallion around her neck. After assuring herself that the award hung down over her blouse where it was visible, she tucked the box into her pocket, shook Bishop Southerland's hand with both of hers, and walked off the stand, smiling enthusiastically at her family and those in the audience.

Delisha knew that the opportunity of wearing the medallion in full view of her mother and father would be short-lived, but she relished the moment. From that day forward, wearing what she eventually overheard her father call "a mark of the heathen," would definitely be forbidden in her home. However, when Delisha was outside of her home, she wore it with abandon.

Once she received the gold medallion, she carried it with her as much as possible, and when she was not around her parents, Lufti, The Twelve, or anyone else affiliated with al-Qaeda, she wore it proudly as a necklace. For the first time in her life, her self-worth had been recognized for something other than being a human sacrifice in the cause of a god whose motives she still didn't completely understand.

CHAPTER 18
SETTING UP THE JUDGE

NEW YORK CITY, NEW YORK
OCTOBER 1

US DISTRICT COURT JUDGE Clyde Alan Jeffreys, age fifty-seven, was tall and lean, had a bronze tan, and sported salt and pepper hair. Authoritative and condescending in nature, the judge knew he had set a new standard in becoming the storied "hanging judge," even though he had been appointed by a liberal president.

Judge Jeffreys walked with a bit of a "John Wayne" swagger and considered himself the nemesis of his pantywaist cohorts on the bench, who he considered "empty suits" when it came to hard and tough rulings. For Judge Jeffreys, their liberal outlooks, reflected in their court rulings, characterized them as hacks taking marching orders geared to the politically correct, far-left attitudes of a liberal administration.

Jeffreys felt indeed like a man among men in spite of his bisexuality. Being a closet "switch-hitter" never made it inconvenient for him to maintain a healthy relationship with his wife, Eunice, who was pretty in her advancing years as well as slim and a chic dresser. At age fifty-two, the judge's brunette wife displayed the radiance and vivacity of a much younger woman. In their twenty-seven years of marriage, Eunice had never even once suspected that her high-profile husband was meeting with gay men on the side.

The couple had two children. James Alan, twenty-five, had

just completed law school at Harvard and joined a Wall Street firm, wanting to follow in the path of his father.

Their daughter, Elsie Mae, at twenty-two, had just graduated from George Washington University in their pre-med program with plans to become a general practitioner.

Judge Jeffreys had several terrorist detainee cases on his docket to try before the end of the year. But he planned on vacating the bench for ten days—as he always did in October—for his annual deer hunt in south central Idaho near Stanley, a little town close to the headwaters of the Middle Fork of the Salmon River in the Frank Church Wilderness Area, the largest wilderness area in the lower forty-eight States. He enjoyed hunting deer in the area of Red Fish Lake near Pole Creek at the foot of Galena Summit in the jagged Sawtooth Mountains.

Judge Jeffreys again planned to participate in a guided hunt with his hunting partner/boyfriend, Jack Parsons, an attorney and long-time associate of the New York law firm of "Benson, Schultz and Goodrich," a personal injury litigation group.

In checking his court docket, Jeffreys noticed he had two cases scheduled during the special hunt period of October 14 –25 that could conflict. He picked up the phone and addressed his secretary, Joan Hansen.

"Joan, this is Judge Jeffreys. How goes your day?"

"Fine, Judge. How can I help?"

Joan had her suspicions about the judge's private side. She had worked for him for seventeen years. Some of his interactions with other men had become somewhat palpable and unordinary, as were some of the "off the record" callers. Nevertheless, the thought of losing her grade-in-pay and retirement because of her curiosity eclipsed the importance of pursuing or investigating her suspicions. She kept a low profile and had nothing to say about her job that was not said in court and in the judge's chambers. Her motto was, "What happens in court and chambers stays in court and chambers!" For Joan, anything else regarding His Honor's behavior was off-limits to her.

"Joan, I see there's a hearing on an old Gitmo case we're involved in again and one appearance to reduce bail on another matter during my October hunt. Would you clear those for me?"

"Absolutely, Judge . . . and I'll let Chris know also."

"You're an angel, dear!" The judge sighed with relief and cradled the phone.

Chris was Judge Jeffreys' court reporter. Christopher Reynolds Tomkins, a fifty-two-year-old bald-headed bachelor, who, at five feet six inches tall and two hundred and fifteen pounds, was a slovenly-dressed but very efficient court reporter . . . and an alcoholic with a gambling problem. Six years earlier he had been under investigation by the Securities Exchange Commission (SEC) for selling some valuable inside stock trading information in a pending criminal case that Judge Jeffreys was presiding over. The defendant's defense attorney was aware of Tomkins propensities toward alcohol and Las Vegas–style gambling. He knew from the courthouse rumor mill that Tomkins could be bought. For the right price, he would hand over tidbits of information regarding how the judge would most likely rule on certain evidence critical to his client's case—information that could deliver a huge advantage to the defendant.

Unknowingly, Judge Jeffreys had dropped Tomkins a few hints with some "off the cuff" remarks over lunch during a recess in one of his cases. This information could be very valuable to the defense. Such clues were dropped carelessly without Jeffreys giving it a second thought. From those comments, however, Tomkins could quickly figure out the drift of the judge's eventual rulings. The chubby court reporter had received fifteen thousand dollars on two separate occasions—directly from the defendant's attorney. He indicated to Tomkins that Tompkins' "assistance" might be needed again.

Judge Jeffreys heard through the court grapevine what his reporter had done, but it would have been dangerous for Jeffreys to fire Tomkins. Jeffreys knew Tomkins had far too much on him. He had unsuccessfully solicited Tomkins for sex on prior occasions, mistakenly thinking Tomkins was gay because of his single status. Not only that, the judge had carelessly mentioned to Tomkins something about past relationships he'd had with two other gay men outside of his marriage with Eunice.

Tomkins knew far too much and was indeed a dangerous man. So the judge chose only to severely reprimand him. Then he swept it under the carpet.

Good decision! Jeffreys thought. *Best keep him happy,* he concluded each time he considered coming down hard on the reporter. Nevertheless, Judge Jeffreys had recently had to confront his courthouse confidante.

"Tomkins, old friend, just received another DUI report on you. You promised me you would never drink and drive again. What's the deal?" Jeffreys had hissed.

"Sorry, judge. I don't know what happened on this one. I had a friend who was going to drive me home in my car and then take a taxi back to the bar, but we got in a rift over a few bucks I owed him, and he dumped me. I had no other choice but to drive home." Chris had looked shamefaced.

But Jeffreys knew what "a few bucks" meant to Tomkins, who ran up huge debts to associates while gambling when he was stoned. "That doesn't cut it, Chris! We had a deal. You've been cited and arrested for driving under the influence three times in the past year, and I've had to arrange to have the charges quashed every time. I'm running out of excuses for the police. I can't cover for you anymore. Was this another gambling debt?" The judge had had it.

"Only two hundred bucks this time, Judge. No biggie. I'm good for it in my next paycheck." Tomkins sensed that Jeffreys was not going to cut him slack on this one.

"Look, Chris. I want you to voluntarily submit yourself to alcoholic rehab. You can go in for a month, starting next week, and you'll come back to your job the same day I return from my hunting trip. I'll arrange to have it vouchered as additional annual leave and won't even register it as medical. That way there will be no official inquiries by the news. What do you say?"

What could I say? Tomkins had thought. *The old man has me right where he wants me. He'll go home gloating over this one.* Tomkins was reluctant to respond. He was incensed at Jeffreys' hypocrisy in forcing him into a health clinic while the judge was out cavorting around in the mountains with his male "companion," unbeknownst to his wife. Nevertheless, the judge had stood up for him on a much more serious issue when Tomkins had leaked that information on the insider trading case. He could have gone to prison. He knew Jeffreys would be totally justified in firing him if Tompkins did not at least make a token gesture at getting dried out.

"All right, judge. I'll do it if you feel that strongly about it." Tomkins was furious that he had to give in.

"Thanks, Chris. You're the man!" Jeffreys patted Tomkins on the shoulder. His condescension nauseated the court reporter.

*****

New York City, New York
October 3

Buck Bowen made a long plane trip to New York City. He drove from Hayden Lake, Idaho, to Spokane, Washington, where he boarded a flight through Atlanta, then on to New York City. There he rented a room at a Hilton near the federal courthouse.

The night before leaving, he had received a call from Abu Khan's residence in the Marriott Hotel in the Grand Caymans. Since his survivalist group had begun contracting with Abu Khan for delivery of high-powered explosives, there had been many such telephone calls between the two.

"Hello, is this Buck?"

"Yeah, Abu. What's up? Still worried about the timing on the explosive belts for your thing? Well, don't worry. We'll have them to your locations: signed, sealed, and delivered." Bowen did not want to be pushed but neither did he want to kill the "golden goose." *After all, this is big money, coming from those ragheads,* he thought.

"That's no problem at all," Abu responded. "What I need is very different. We need to do away with a federal judge."

"What? You've got to be kidding! A federal judge? Do you know how risky that is?"

"Five million, Buck. Two and a half now and the rest when we see the obituary."

There was a lengthy pause. "How soon?" Bowen asked.

After checking in at the Hilton, Bown went out for the evening.

Bowen approached Christopher Tomkins two nights after Jeffreys secured Tomkins's commitment to rehab. Tomkins was drinking heavily again at the Little Havana, a Cuban bar/café near the United States Courthouse—a favorite of Tomkins for getting soused. Rumors of Tomkins's vulnerability were widely-spread among the courthouse crowd, making it easy for al-Qaeda's people to pick up on it and pass the information on to Bowen. Having lived with hardcore white supremacist separatists from Hayden Lake and the revolutionary Freemen group from Jordan, Montana, Bowen had years of experience blending in with discontents like Tomkins. As he sidled up next to Tomkins at the Cuban bar, he was confident. He had been made well aware of Tomkins's propensity for a loose tongue.

As the two men became engaged in conversation, first about the New York Yankees' general manager, then about the failings of the current government, Tomkins was getting more and more "happy" . . . mainly because Bowen kept buying the drinks. By the time Bowen inquired about Judge Jeffreys future itinerary, Tomkins was ready to offer up His Honor's life history, in addition to what he would be doing the next several months.

When Tomkins mentioned Jeffreys' deer hunt near Stanley, Idaho, the week of October 15, Bowen's ears really perked up. He and several of his survivalist cronies knew that area well. They had contacts with a couple of the guides there. Determining exactly where the Judge would be that week was the most difficult part.

"Can you give me a photo and description of the judge, with some additional information as to what time he gets there and who he will be with?" Bowen asked.

As drunk as Tomkins was, he knew he was talking to someone who had something very serious in mind for Judge Jeffreys. The idea of his boss's demise instilled little pain in the drunken court recorder. His anger was currently rekindled at his employer, who was the catalyst for this week's drinking binge. "How much is this information worth?" queried Tomkins

"It will be well compensated," responded Bowen.

"How well compensated?" countered the drunk.

"Twenty-five thousand dollars, cash on delivery."

"Sold to the man in the plaid shirt!" responded Tomkins lustily. A meeting was arranged the next night at the same bar where Tomkins would provide all that was requested.

After spending a couple more hours with Tomkins and supplying him enough hard liquor to necessitate a taxi ride home, Bowen excused himself, patted Tomkins on the shoulder, and slowly walked away.

Tomkins realized he had never asked Bowen what the information would be used for, although he surmised that for some reason, probably based on a hostile verdict the judge had rendered, Bowen wanted Jeffreys dead. Tomkins couldn't have cared less.

Good! Tomkins thought. *That will mean there will be one less gay judge out there! And if these guys take him out, the judge can't hold that payoff I got over my head any longer. He's the only one that knows about it. I'll keep my job without having to go to rehab and I'll be twenty-five grand richer. Who can't do that math? Make room for me, Las Vegas!*

CHAPTER 19
THE HUNT

NEAR STANLEY, IDAHO
RED FISH LAKE AREA
OCTOBER 12

IT WAS DAYBREAK.

Judge Jeffreys was climbing a low-lying forested ridge near Pole Creek, just a few miles from Stanley. He had a .7 mm magnum rifle slung over his shoulder. His intimate friend, Jack Parsons, had introduced him to deer and elk hunting, which provided the judge a good deal of stress relief from his court calendar, as well as special time to be away with Jack. Even though Jack always accompanied His Honor on the hunting outings, he preferred to stay in camp, cook, and just help out when it came to dressing out the kill and processing the meat.

The judge preferred to hunt alone, enjoying the uninterrupted peace of mind this gave him. The beauty of the Sawtooth Mountains near Stanley and the cool crisp fall air seemed to invigorate his mind and spirit, giving him renewed energy for coming face-to-face with the grueling schedule of a federal court calendar. That, coupled with the feeling of fulfillment he received from participating in what he regarded as a primitive male ritual in obtaining meat for the table, seemed to balance out, in an odd sort of way, a lack of self-esteem he felt from secretly participating in his alternate lifestyle.

As it became light, the judge worked his way to the top of the ridge, where he sat and waited. He had the wind in his favor, coming in from the south and blowing uphill at him. He knew from prior hunts that the deer were moving up into the timber, possibly within view. There had been a full moon the night before, which meant the deer had been feeding throughout the night in alfalfa fields. At daybreak they headed up for higher ground. He took off his backpack, spread out his rain poncho over a pile of pine needles, sat down on it, pulled out his binoculars, and waited.

About 7:30 a.m. branches began crackling seventy-five yards downhill, and the sound of several pairs of bouncing hooves crashing into a shale slide below him were unmistakable. Judge Jeffreys brought up his binoculars and spotted several does following single file through the shale. Then looking off to his left, coming up near the edge of the timber was a four-point buck that he knew would be good for a winter supply of venison. Just as he brought up his rifle, thinking he could get a quick snap shot before the animal re-entered the timber, he lost sight of it. He figured the buck had seen him and crossed back into the thicker timber to come up past him. As he became captivated by the sound of the huge buck, he lost sight of the does that had now crossed the shale slide. He didn't care. He would hold out for the buck.

He could no longer hear the noise that had emanated from the woods behind him. He knew the buck probably saw him, so he figured pursuing him right away would not help the situation. He decided to wait. He could pick up the trail later. That way he wouldn't spook the big mulie. Jeffreys had learned about the curiosity of a mule deer . . . how they would sometimes stop, turn, and look at a hunter, even if the hunter had shot at them. They were so unlike their cousin, the elk, which would run for miles once they were spooked.

The judge broke out a ham sandwich and some chips that his partner, Jack, had prepared for him. He ate and waited.

Just as Jeffreys drew out a thermos of hot chocolate and began swigging it down, he saw the big buck, about one hundred and seventy five yards above him, on another ridge that fed into the low-lying ridge he was on. It was standing broadside at the foot of an outcrop of granite, looking right at him. The judge fixed his scope crosshairs on the buck, aiming behind the front leg and just over his back, knowing the round would drop a little as it progressed uphill. He slowly squeezed the trigger and heard the repercussion of the round leaving the barrel. He noticed the animal hump just slightly and start walking slowly away. He knew he had hit the mulie, but it still stood up. Suddenly the big deer bedded down.

Jeffreys grabbed his rifle and headed straight up the hill, knowing that he could waste no time, since the animal would move away quickly once it recouped its strength.

The judge's lungs were bursting for oxygen as he hastened up the steep ridge. He stopped a half dozen times for thirty-second intervals to get his breath and to decide whether to shoot again, just to make sure the buck didn't escape. He knew, however, that if he shot the deer in the flank or the front quarters, he would waste a lot of meat . . . a sloppy move for an experienced hunter, something not worthy of His Honor.

When Jeffreys got within twenty-five yards of the animal, he knew it was hit hard, although he observed no blood. He was aware the deer was looking directly at him with glazed eyes as he approached within twenty feet.

Suddenly the big animal got up on all fours and ran straight at him, groaning and blowing snot and blood from its nose. Its head was bowed as it charged, antlers first. Jeffreys released the safety off his rifle and pulled the trigger to no avail, realizing he had forgotten to jack another round into the chamber after his first shot. The deer was almost upon him. There was no time to reload. His only remedy now was to use the rifle as a club. As the big mulie lunged within a couple feet of the judge, he took his rifle by the barrel and lowered the boom on the deer's head, breaking the stock in two. The deer went down on one leg, stunned, and then rose up, yanking its antlers up from Jeffreys feet, ripping his trousers and leaving a superficial cut just under his knee.

The judge now realized that this sudden development could be a fight to the finish. The deer had been gut shot, but not in a vital area, and although it was temporarily stunned, it was still full of life. He circled behind the buck where he could control its antlers, turned it sideways by thrusting his weight in a semicircle, and bull-dogged the animal to the ground. Then he pulled out his knife and cut its jugular. He didn't loosen his grip on the base of the antlers until there was no more movement. Only then did Jeffreys place his hunting knife back into its sheath and lay there next to the four-point, exhausted. *Am I ever going to get mileage out of this story! I'll be the talk of the court community back in New York!*

As Jeffreys dressed out his kill, he had no idea that a pair of binoculars was trained on him from the opposite ridge.

Within an hour's time, the animal was field dressed. Then the judge began dragging it down the hillside toward the road he had walked up prior to sighting the buck. Once he landed the animal on the bottom of the canyon within two hundred feet of the road, Jeffreys stood straight up, cell phone in hand, and dialed Jack Parsons, who was involved in the preparation of a gourmet dinner.

"Hey, partner! You won't believe this one. I can hardly wait to tell you about it!" Jeffreys said. "This is a story for the century!"

"I can't wait to hear it, Jim! Where are you? I'll come help you load it up," Parsons said excitedly.

"I'm just four and a half miles up the main road and over on the west fork. The same place we scouted for signs yesterday."

"I remember. Next to that small creek we thought would make a good site for deer camp next year?" asked Parsons.

"That's it exactly! Hustle on down here, and bring some of that good stuff you're making for dinner. This may take us awhile." The judge was already contemplating his partner's famous "seven bean soup."

"I'm on my way, Jim. Hang tough!"

The judge cradled his cell phone in its belt holster

Suddenly a bullet from a .300 magnum rifle ripped through his back and slashed through his lungs and heart.

* * * * *

Buck Bowen grunted with satisfaction as he contemplated the lifeless form of a federal judge lying on the ground. This would bring him far more monetary compensation than anything he had been paid previously by Abu Khan.

Aside from the trigger man, Luke Johns, and his accomplice, "Bubba" Tilford, Bowen had not told anyone in his Mountain Patriots group about the contract he had negotiated with Abu Khan to do away with the pesky judge who was coming down hard on al-Qaeda's operatives. Overseeing the judge's assassination with the knowledge of only two of his survivalist constituents was a secret easily kept and represented a lot of money that he wouldn't have to share with the entire group.

Tilford and Johns had only asked for a thousand each to take down Judge Jeffreys. That left twenty-three thousand cold cash for Bowen. Tilford and Johns were experienced assassins who had been on the radar sporadically for years by federal and local authorities for various homicides, but neither had ever been arrested for anything except drunken driving. Bowen considered them great fall guys in the event any of the three were seen near the crime scene. Their records of past suspicion by law enforcement authorities would surely eclipse any possible notion of Bowen's own involvement. He had picked his confederates well.

As Bowen approached the dead man, he noticed the judge's torn trousers and the broken stock on his rifle. This would surely give the initial impression of a hunting accident . . . that is until ballistic experts and forensic investigators processed the scene. He knew he and his two hired men would be far away by then. He hiked back down past the judge's pickup, then walked another sixty-five yards further down the road where his Ford Bronco was parked out of sight in a grove of cedar next to the creek. The other two were parked farther up the canyon.

Just before Bowen left the logging spur he had driven up after leaving the main road, Jack Parsons passed him going the other way. curious as to the reason for the massive cloud of dust behind Bowen' truck. It was obvious to Parsons that the driver was making a hasty exodus out of the canyon. His curiosity heightened, Parsons took careful note of the driver in the black Ford Bronco and the numbers on the Idaho license tag.

Two minutes later Telford and Johns came barreling down the narrow dirt road in a white Ford crew cab pickup, creating the same kind of dust that Bowen had thrown up in his wake. These two had to slow down almost to a stop as they passed on the outside of a narrow, steep embankment. Parsons looked them directly in the eyes, taking mental notes of their descriptions. It was suspicious behavior and he worried about the judge. He wrote down the license tag of the pickup and proceeded further up the logging spur from where he calculated the judge would have called.

Three minutes later Parsons drove up next to his friend's pickup, noticed his lifeless body lying on the ground next to the big mule deer, and stumbled out of his own pickup. He stared in disbelief, feeling a damp chill enter his consciousness. Then he knelt down on one knee next to his friend, muttered the words, "Jim! . . . Jim!" and began weeping uncontrollably.

* * * * *

"Could you believe that shot, Luke? Right through the lungs and heart. Best shot I made since I took down that big grizz up in Alaska two years ago!" Bubba Telford was proud of his marksmanship. He would compare shooting a human being to breaking a clay pigeon . . . all in the same breath.

"Don't forget, Mr. Potshot, you had to have a spotter. And one hundred and seventy-five yards with that scoped .300 mm magnum with me leading the shot through binoculars wouldn't exactly qualify you for the Guinness Book of World Records, now would it?" Johns was not about to let Telford take full credit for the kill.

"Do you think we should have buried him?" Telford asked.

"Bowen made it clear that we had to get out of there quick."

"Yeah, but that guy coming up the road back there sure gave us some strange looks." Telford's nerves were getting frayed.

Meanwhile, Bowen had passed through the game checkpoint at the main road where the logging spur parted up the canyon with no problem. Fortunately for Bowen, Jack Parson's call had come in from Custer County Sheriff's dispatch to the fish and game checkpoint just two minutes later. Hearing Parson's emotional plea for someone to stop the two vehicles with the occupants who most likely had killed his friend, the three fish and game officers manning the checkpoint had immediately placed two of their vehicles over the spur to blockade it, drew their handguns, and awaited the white Ford pickup. They contacted the sheriff's office in Challis, Idaho, for backup, but knew the considerable distance between Challis and Stanley would probably preclude any help from that direction. The fish and game officers would have to deal with the situation themselves.

One of the officers drove a pickup fifty yards up the road and pulled off into the brush just seconds before Telford and Johns came speeding down the precarious dirt spur. That's when they saw the blinking blue and red lights of two state vehicles blocking their exit and another pulling up behind them, with lights flashing, blocking their rear exit. Adding to their dismay was the sight of two armed, uniformed state officers who had a shotgun and a semi-automatic pistol pointed at them. They knelt behind vehicles canted toward them, utilizing the full protection of the wheel wells and engine blocks of their vehicles.

Both men thought the same thing. *Not even a rifle shot is going to work. Not against that kind of cover. Time to throw in the towel.* The third officer behind them had a rifle trained on them, crouched behind his vehicle.

"Driver, out of the vehicle! First turn off the engine and throw out the keys with one hand."

Johns complied.

Bubba began blabbering. "I knew Bowen would get outta this and we'd be takin' the beef. I somehow just knew it!"

"Shut up!" Johns demanded. "And don't you dare say anything to these guys, Bubba. You hear?"

Telford just nodded.

"All right, driver. Open the door slowly, step out, and walk backward to us. Do you hear?"

"Yeah, I hear," responded Johns and began walking slowly backward toward the officers, one of which quickly stepped forward and handcuffed him.

The officer giving the commands continued. "You . . . the passenger. Open your door slowly and come back with your hands behind your neck, fingers intertwined . . . just like your buddy.

Do you hear?" The officer was going by the book in issuing all the pertinent orders.

Once both Telford and Johns were handcuffed and placed in the back of one of the fish and game vehicles, they were advised of their right to legal counsel, their right to remain silent, and other provisions of the Miranda statute. When the questioning started en route to Challis where they would be lodged in the Custer County holding facility, Johns continually nudged Telford when he began answering any question. Both men were furious as they realized they had done Bowen's bidding, yet had not yet received their money and were now headed for jail, maybe even life sentences, or worse yet . . . a death sentence.

In the meantime, Bowen suspected that his license tag may have been taken down by the driver on the road and was well aware that once the individual stumbled onto Jeffreys' body, the fish and game folks would have his license number. He took the plates off and replaced it with another set of stolen tags he habitually carried for such purposes. He also replaced his jacket, put on a different baseball cap, and took a different route out from the Stanley Basin than he had taken going in. He went back out through Lowman, then on to Boise, Idaho, and on north, rather than back up Highway 93 into Missoula, Montana, and over to Hayden Lake, Idaho . . . the way he had traveled down to oversee the assassination. The Custer County Sheriff and other local authorities totally lost track of him.

CHAPTER 20
THE INTERVIEWS

CUSTER COUNTY JAIL
CHALLIS, IDAHO
OCTOBER 18

BOWEN'S HAPLESS ASSOCIATES WERE not nearly as fortunate. The second day of his incarceration, Luke Johns was taken from the booking area of the Custer County Jail in Challis to a room where two FBI agents—Ken Grogan and Ridge Southerland—were ready to interview him. They had an extraordinary interest in Judge Jeffreys' case. It was Saturday, and although efforts had been made to obtain attorneys for Johns and Telford, none would be available until the following Monday. The FBI agents, upon being advised of the arrests, had requested that the two men be held incommunicado from one another until they could be interviewed, in order to prevent them from trying to coordinate their responses.

Once Johns had been advised of his Miranda rights, he was asked specifically why he and Telford had killed the judge. Johns refused to answer. The agents had reviewed Johns' history from National Crime Information Center (NCIC) reports, which indicated he had a history of never cooperating with law enforcement. In both of his prior criminal charges for burglary, he had taken the rap and served his time rather than accepting a plea bargain.

When the agents advised Johns they needed to determine whether Judge Jeffreys' death was in any way related to al-Qaeda operations in the United States, terrorist trials, and specifically the

133

Omaha suicide bombings, Johns remained steely-eyed and just grinned at them, signaling that he would not give them the satisfaction of revealing any information.

Johns knew the FBI would push him. He had resolved not to furnish any information regarding the judge's assassination . . . specifically any information regarding the Mountain Patriot's plan to arm terrorists. After all, he had taken an oath never to give up information to government authorities. His organization considered the United States government and their representatives the enemy. Nevertheless, Grogan and Southerland were going to make an attempt.

"Look, Luke," Grogan said, "this thing could pan out a lot better for you if you would just give us whatever information you have about Omaha and any other plans the terrorists have. That kind of information is about the only thing that could possibly water down the time you will have to serve for killing the judge." Grogan's southern twang and authoritative voice, along with the possible allegation that Johns had been the triggerman set Johns off.

"I didn't kill the judge!' Johns screamed, waving his arms wildly while banging the handcuffs together around his wrists. "And I'm not signing the friggin' waiver, so you guys can just butt out! You hear me? I ain't talkin' about nothin'."

"You know you're facing a life sentence, Luke?" Agent Southerland chimed in. Ridge Southerland had interviewed men like Luke Johns before. He knew they often displayed huge resistance in initial interviews, and then as time went on and the sentencing date drew nearer, they would often cave in. But there was something resolute and determined about Johns. *Maybe it's the years spent in prison before hooking up with the Mountain Patriots,* he thought.

"You guys can take that waiver and stuff it," Johns responded. "I ain't signing anything! I know you got federal holds on me. So what? I got friends outside that could break me out of this little chicken coop jail anyway!"

Johns then preceded with a diatribe, denouncing the government of the United States, including its imperialism, its abuse of human rights, and far-fetched criticism of its monetary and tax policies, all the while raising the pitch of his voice and waving his arms back and forth.

Agents Grogan and Southerland came to the conclusion that the interview was going nowhere.

* * * * *

As Agent Jim Flynn and Custer County Deputy Sam Grigg escorted Bubba Telford down the hall of the sheriff's office to the interview room, they passed the processing room where agents Grogan and Southerland were interviewing Luke Johns. Through the window of the door leading into the room, Telford was suddenly struck by the image he saw: Johns was talking incessantly and throwing up his arms. That meant only one thing to Telford—Johns was snitching.

That cotton picker is nailin' me! Telford thought sourly. *Sure 'nuf he's nailin' me good . . . layin' that whole shootin' on me . . . probably sayin' he was just there to drive or somethin' like that. He's layin' the whole thing on me. I know he is!*

As Telford continued down the hall, handcuffed in his orange jail fatigues and thinking about the ramifications of what Johns was revealing, he began to break into a sweat. His face took on a pallid appearance. His legs felt rubbery, and a slight trembling set in.

"Hey, guys!" Telford mumbled. "I gotta sit down . . . quick!" Both agents grabbed an arm, stabilizing the obese man whose legs were beginning to buckle.

"You all right, Bubba?" Flynn asked as he hefted the bulk of Telford's weight onto himself. "Set him down right there at the end of the table before he collapses," ordered Flynn. The deputy assisted Telford in taking a seat.

"All right, Bubba. You know who we are already. You've seen my credentials and you know Deputy Gregg here is with Custer County. You also know the FBI doesn't show up to issue traffic tickets. That kind of gives you a sense of how serious this is, right?" Flynn looked Telford in the eye.

"Yeah, okay . . . okay. I–I know," stuttered Telford.

"Now, how you feeling? You look kind of . . . you know, pretty pale in the face. You need anything?"

Flynn knew he had Telford on the hook . . . even before casting his first line.

"I . . . uh, I think I'm okay. Maybe a glass of water?" Telford was trying to compose himself. He was still sweating profusely, giving off a strong odor from underneath his arms.

Telford felt he needed to do something for himself . . . to strike some sort of deal with these guys before Johns completely sold him out.

"Sure, Bubba. Deputy Grigg, could you get our friend here a soda?" Flynn asked.

"It's coming right up, Bubba," responded the deputy.

Flynn waited until the deputy went out and the door closed.

"Okay, Bubba, let's talk! Here's the deal. I'm going to advise you of your constitutional rights as soon as Deputy Grigg gets back with your soda so he can witness it. In the meantime, bear this in mind and think about it before you decide to exercise your right to remain silent. Your fingerprints have been found on both the trigger and the trigger guard of that Remington magnum rifle you used to bring down the judge."

Telford felt a chill go down his spine and suddenly realized he was about to pee his pants.

"In addition, another hunter one ridge over from where you guys were when you shot the judge," Flynn continued, "described two guys coming out of the area where the shot was fired, and that description fits you and Johns."

Telford felt his pulse quicken and could actually feel his heart thumping in the carotid artery in his neck. He began shaking, feeling even fainter. He was sure he was losing control of his bowels.

Flynn kept talking. "Just wanted you to be aware of that, Bubba. You saw your friend in there with the other agents. Someone's going to sing! Whoever joins the choir first may get the best deal."

Deputy Grigg returned with the soda and handed it to the trembling Telford.

"Thanks," mumbled Telford, taking the drink in a quivering hand.

"Okay," started Flynn, "Now that the deputy is back to witness the waiver being read, let's proceed. But first I need to advise you that you are being accused of murdering a federal judge and conspiring with another individual to do the same. Do you understand the charges?"

Telford reluctantly nodded in the affirmative, saying "Ye . . . yeah. I do."

Flynn started reading the waiver, slowly and meticulously, most of the time citing it by heart while staring directly into Telford's fearful eyes.

"You have the right to remain silent.

"You have the right to have an attorney present. If you cannot afford one, one will be appointed for you."

"Anything that you say could be used against you in a court of law.

Telford could no longer control his emotions. "Hey, forget the attorney part! Let's get down to striking a deal! I want a deal, man. Let's get to that part." Telford had sensed an opportunity to help himself by spilling his guts.

"Hey, slow down, Bubba!" Flynn said. "You need to hear all your rights. Then we'll talk about that . . . after you've signed the waiver. Okay?"

"Okay . . . okay. But let's get to it, okay? I know that puke Johns is in there layin' the whole thing out on me 'cuz I pulled the trigger, but he's the one that scoped the guy out with his binoculars and told me when to shoot and . . ."

"Take it easy, Bubba! Slow up," warned Deputy Grigg. "Let the man finish reading the waiver."

Flynn finished reading Telford his Miranda rights. Once Telford indicated he understood them by signing the waiver, both Flynn and Deputy Grigg witnessed his signature by signing the waiver themselves.

After Telford had furnished a complete statement as to his role in assassinating Judge Jeffreys—naming John as an accomplice and a person called Buck orchestrating it—he made another comment that caught the full attention of the interviewing officers . . . the first comment since the Omaha bombing that would shed light on the OMAMALL investigation.

"The more information I give ya, the better chance I have of avoiding the death penalty, right?" Telford asked.

"That's right, Bubba," Flynn assured. "Although we're not authorized to promise you anything for sure, we will bring it to the attention of the sentencing judge, which could help you a lot."

Telford seemed okay with that assurance.

"That thing in Omaha's just the start." Telford stopped.

Flynn's heart missed a beat. This is just what they needed—the one piece in the puzzle that the agents hoped would relate the judge's death with the Omaha attack.

"Keep talking, Bubba. You're doing fine," Flynn assured. "Keep talking."

"All I know is the Patriots helped out somehow with that Omaha bombing. They don't tell me much, cause I ain't been around that long . . . I mean with the Mountain Patriot bunch, and I'm not privy to a lot of the information. But the Patriot boss, Buck, is in charge of the group . . . the same guy that was at Red-fish Lake, overlooking that shootin'. They got a place somewhere in Idaho up some big river where they hide out a lot and make some bombs. That's about all I know. They took me into their organization about a year ago, because before I deserted from the US Army, I was a sharpshooter, and they figured they could use me for some of their stuff. The other guy you got in here—that Johns—he has been with the Patriots several years and knows a lot more about what's going on than me."

Flynn interjected a question. "You said Omaha was just the start. What did you mean by that?"

"All I heard is that the folks that used those bombs in Omaha are going to hit a bunch more places some time later this year. That's all I know. Remember, it's like I told ya. They don't talk to me much. I'm way down the ladder. Now ole Johns in there. He knows a lot more." Flynn was convinced Telford had leveled with him.

CHAPTER 21
A CLANDESTINE CONFERENCE

COUER D'ALENE, IDAHO
NOVEMBER 10

NOW COVERED THE MEADOW, laden with fallen leaves from the surrounding stands of birch and needles falling from the giant pines nearby. The crisp late fall air signaled the advent of winter just around the corner. The hastily constructed outdoor conference center was put up in just a couple days a few miles outside of Couer d'Alene, Idaho. The site was nestled on the shores of a lake teeming with trout, wild fowl, and other wildlife of all kinds. The brisk winds blew without mercy on the two hundred wild-looking men, many bare-headed, who congregated in front of the quickly improvised wood platform, built just for that one occasion.

Things had become too heated for the motley bunch at Hayden Lake, where in the 1970s Reverend Richard G. Butler founded the far-right Aryan Nations white supremacist group, classified as a terrorist threat by the FBI. Staying away from the public eye and out in the woods seemed to be the wiser course for Buck Bowen and his associates who had set up the rendezvous.

Excitement permeated throughout the gathering, composed of radical extremists who had anticipated this time in history for decades. They had all been alerted that al-Qaeda was ready to strike. Those present could hardly wait to follow on their heels.

A mix of many factions hated America as she was. The laws,

economic structure, the way the US Constitution was interpreted and the integration of Jews and blacks into American society were highly disturbing issues to these malcontents . . . far more than they could tolerate.

After all, they needed only to glance in the mirror to determine who was really entitled to the fat of the land. They were the ones in tune with nature and God's abundance to mankind on account of their pure and noble race. They were the ones who were trained and equipped to survive when all else failed. They—and only they—could really understand the monetary system and how it should work.

It was this collection of castoffs from all the hate groups that were finally uniting . . . rejected by America who they believed was in its "lost and fallen state." By their definition, America had strayed too far left and was on a downhill path, accelerating each day more rapidly. This was the America they could no longer love. The America that had meandered away into what they believed was a state of decline and degradation . . . a condition brought on by mixing in the reprobates and their tax-happy inclinations and Stone-Age legal system into a society that should be "pure white without Jews and blacks."

The congregants included past and current members of the Ku Klux Klan, Neo-Nazis, Aryan Nations, Skinheads, the Freemen of Montana, and others who shared their views. Bowen and the Mountain Patriots had succeeded in uniting all these groups into a loosely organized confederation, based upon common convictions and goals, yet one where each faction could maintain its individual identity and commitments.

Once this gathering concluded, the wooden stand and podium would be torn down, stacked into a pile, and, for the finale of the conference, be ignited into a huge fire to warm the hearts and souls of all present . . . a fire in which a dummy made to look like the president of the United States would be burned in effigy.

Bowen was seated on the platform behind the podium with four other speakers. He glanced at his watch, noting it was almost 2:00 p.m—time to start. Rising to his feet, he approached the podium and pulled out his glasses, looking as authoritative as he could. He cleared his throat while staring from side to side, assuring himself that he was receiving the full attention of all present. He began speaking.

"Friends and associates, about two hundred of you are here today, representing your own organizations' interests, as well as to support all our common endeavors. You have traveled here from all over the country, upon our invitation. We, the Mountain Patriots, welcome you wholeheartedly. We exult with you in the forthcoming culmination of events that will reshape America . . . events we have eagerly and patiently awaited for decades. This is the same America that has ignored us and dismissed us as unworthy radicals. That America will be brought to her knees by the forthcoming developments. It will be soon . . . very soon."

Bowen knew he could only go so far. He would not specify the Christmas Eve date or where the attacks would take place. He had been specifically warned by both Bashir Sayed and Rashid Siddiqui that under no circumstance could he disclose the exact dates or places of the suicide attacks, nor any of the specific details, but that he was at liberty to speak in generalities. Bowen knew FBI informants and other intelligence sources habitually infiltrated at gatherings such as this one.

He continued. "When this event unfolds, the government of this country will fall into disarray, as it attempts, unsuccessfully, to find sufficient numbers of fingers to plug the holes in the dikes. The US economy will unravel. The people will fear to walk again into public areas. The mental effect will be devastating.

"At this point, we'll hear those from your midst. We should conclude in two hours at which time we'll break and dine upon twelve deer and seven elk that have been expertly poached and barbequed for us . . . snatched right out from under the eyes of our 'vigilant' government authorities who are taking such wonderful care of our fish and game."

Guffaws erupted everywhere, accompanied by lengthy applause.

Bowen continued. "Following the feast, several kegs of our favorite mountain brews will be available to sip on while we burn You-Know-Who in effigy."

Again huge applause mixed with coarse laughter.

"You'll first hear from Tex Kinkaid, representing the Free-man Organization. Tex, the time is yours."

Kinkaid was a tall, lean man in his sixties with a leathery, sun-worn face, void of any hint of a smile. He seemed a little retreating and tentative as he approached the podium, but his appearance was haunting and intimidating . . . the kind of person this crowd loved hearing from. Kinkaid slowly withdrew some notes he had scribbled on eight by eleven lined papers—which he had tucked into the inside pocket of his camouflaged jacket—unfolded them, and glancing quickly at his audience, began reading from them.

"Greetings, friends. Since June 12, 1996, the day me and my associates were chased out of our 'Justus Township,' thirty miles from Jordan, Montana, by the feds, the memory of that day has taken a real toll on me and burned deep into my heart. Not only that, it nearly destroyed my health.

"All we wanted was to expand on our God-given concept of 'individual sovereignty.' Sure, we rejected the authority of the US Government. Who wouldn't?"

More laughter.

"Especially after what they did at Ruby Ridge and Waco. The 'Whackos at Waco.' That's what we called them! The stupid idiots just burned those poor folks out!"

Once again, explosive applause came from all corners. It was obvious to Bowen that his guests were wild about this.

"So, on the basis of striving for our freedom, sure, we set up our own government, courts, and our own banking and credit system. We issued checks based on our God-given freedoms. So that's why they came after us. That's all we'd done and they honed in on us . . . for eighty-one days, mind you! Yeah! Eighty-one days.

"And all we were doing was protecting all the farmers and ranchers from the government's habit of building up the national debt and doing all that price manipulating . . . the two things that were bankrupting us as a people.

"Our leader at the time, LeRoy Schweitzer, kept holding out against the government, defying them at every turn. So Big

Brother responded by trumping up charges for bank fraud, mail fraud, making false claims to the IRS, interstate transportation of stolen property, threatening public officials, firearms violations, and even charged him with participating in the armed robbery of a television crew that was at the ranch filming stuff and going on without our permission. Can you believe that? Coming onto our land, making up stuff like that, and then driving us off our land!"

Kinkaid kept throwing up his arms, gesticulating wildly, and intentionally contorting his countenance with forlorn expressions of grief as he continued. "Then we started plowing our fields and they said we had no right to do that . . . on our own property at that!"

As Kinkaid looked over his listeners and listened to their booing the government, he knew he had a captive audience. They were shaking their heads and making fists at each of his remarks. What he had cleverly omitted was the fact that the property he and the others had plowing was leased property and they had no right to work on it. He also omitted LeRoy Schweitzer's involvement in all the crimes he had been charged for and later convicted of.

Kinkaid went on. "I was one of the few that weren't charged with anything . . . mainly 'cause the stupid feds didn't dig deep enough. They never do."

More laughter.

Kinkaid prolonged his rant for another half hour, outlining his beefs with the federal system and with the FBI. Once he had laid out most of his complaints concerning US policies and procedures, he ended with these words:

"Knowing that within a short matter of weeks the US government will collapse and have to humble itself and eat crow gives me more satisfaction than you could ever imagine!"

As Kinkaid walked down from the podium, he was met with thundering applause.

The next speaker who mounted the podium was Jimmy Deckert, representing the Aryan Nations.

"My good friends. Too bad we had to leave our home in Hayden Lake where we were appreciated and cared for by our dear deceased friend, Reverend Richard Butler. Bless his soul. We had twenty wonderful acres of Freedom before ZOG drove us out also. It was that dirty little snitch who turned out to be an FBI informant that brought us down. When the reverend died in 2004, he left something in each of our hearts—he left the truth and the commitment to form a true Aryan Nation comprised of white men and women from noble Aryan ancestry unpolluted by Jews and blacks. Once our friends, the al-Qaeda warriors, culminate their 'event' in the near future, that dream of Reverend Butler will begin to be fulfilled. Yes, that first wave of destruction will culminate in the demise of the ZOG government."

Deckert continued trumpeting the endless positives of a new all-white supremacist government, void of the presence of blacks and Jews, with the focus on what he kept referring to as "National Socialism."

Deckert was followed by a proponent of the Neo-Nazi movement who, dressed in the garb of a German soldier, spent another forty minutes extolling the virtues of Adolph Hitler.

The last presenter was a Ku Klux Klan member, dressed in full white robes, mask, and topped off with the typical conical hat. Blacks, Jews, Communists, and Catholics were the targets of his rants. He made several references to his ancestry of "Anglo Saxon" and "Celtic" blood, claiming his pure lineage dated back to the eighteenth century British colonial revolutionaries. He swore he would face damnation before having his blood or that of his posterity mixed with that of any black or Jew. Throughout the course of his rants, his rhetoric was punctuated by wild arm thrusts and vile pronouncements.

The crowd was feeding off it, almost in a trance of oblivious exhilaration.

The Klan man's tirade culminated in a staged frenzy of excitement regarding the forthcoming change in America's "complexion," once the Jews and blacks were eliminated.

After two hours of angry, heated rhetoric and exciting prognostications as to the future of America, given her coming demise, Bowen approached the podium for his concluding remarks.

"All right, friends. The question on everyone's mind must be this one: 'Once the damage is done and the country is in chaos, where do we fit in with our united coalition?' There is a special guest here with us this afternoon that has come to address that subject . . . all the way from Islamabad, Pakistan."

Bashir Sayed stepped forth with a determined gait, ascending the staircase and mounting the podium. His short, stocky frame and dark complexion, highlighted by an ominous, assertive expression, was neither striking nor really that impressive to the Mountain Patriots and their coalition of America haters. Sayed's accent was barely sufficient to make himself understood.

Seeing a man from a faraway country crashing this kind of party, especially being dark-faced and a minority was construed by those present as an awesome show of courage. However, Sayed was cloaked in security by his reputation that had come before him. He was, after all, the major link between al-Qaeda and the Mountain Patriot coalition in their great mutual effort to destroy America.

Sayed stood silently before the microphone on the podium. Once he knew his listeners were ready, he began.

"I will call you friends. It is, after all, our mutual hatred for this country that binds us together as friends . . . is it not? It molds us as one and galvanizes our objectives. It is our mutual disdain for the Jews and the Zionist traditions of this nation, and their government specifically, that weld our interests together."

Scores of heads, many bald, were nodding in agreement, fascinated by this dark-skinned little man that stood before them, obviously fearless.

"Although certain differences in my culture and yours will most likely prevent us from ever worshipping the same God and adhering to the same customs and traditions, we are nevertheless of one mind in achieving two distinct and specific goals: destroying the American government, stifling its economy, and making the United States accountable for defying and going to war against the followers of Islam."

A few in the audience shook their head at this statement. They couldn't care less about who went to war with Islam, but they liked the part about destroying the American government and

145

stifling its economy. *Who cares about the economy?* they thought. *We could live forever on poached venison and elk steak.*

"Second, ridding your country of its Jewish population," Sayed continued.

Yeah! Now he's talking! many in the audience were thinking. *And let's throw in those Blacks too!*

More clapping and cheering.

"How will you benefit, you ask," Sayed pushed on. "And what will your role be? My associates and I recognize that many of you have been instrumental in bringing Islamic jihad to America. Some have been instrumental in preparing and supplying necessary explosives, like those we used in Omaha. You will help in transporting many of our people to the destinations where they will culminate their events. The knowledge that we share the same disdain for our common enemy unites us. It's a great advantage knowing that we can depend upon you who have lived here all your lives and know the country so well . . . that we can call upon you and your 'tactics' as needed."

Heads kept nodding affirmatively.

"When the government fails, those principles you have espoused and fought for can be instituted. Your own monetary systems can be set up. You will be able to govern with your own laws as best you see fit. Your own leaders will rule those areas wherein you will dwell.

"As for us of the House of Islam, our Sharia law, derived from the Koran and our traditions, will still govern us, wherever we will settle. There is no reason that we cannot coexist peacefully in a conquered America. Nor is there any good reason we could not share the spoils obtained by the actions of The Ten, The Hundred, and the others who will go ahead—making the supreme sacrifice where necessary. The same who will bring to bear the might of Islam in all its majesty. Once those scores of martyrs have made their mark in America over the coming months, the infidels who remain will want to leave. They are far too accustomed to the placid lakes and rivers without the intrusion of waves. Then we will divide the land . . . you with your portions and we with ours.

"Carlos Quesada's Mexican organization, the Culebra Cartel,

will be given a part of California. He too has been instrumental in bringing all this to pass.

"There is the plan, my friends. With the blessings of Allah and your Christian God, within a few short weeks, a new sun will arise on America's horizon . . . one she has never before known."

As Sayed walked down off the stand, he was mobbed by those wanting to shake his hand, which he stretched forth . . . condescendingly.

Within fifteen minutes, dozens of men with wrecking bars and chainsaws began tearing down the wood platform, stacking all the pieces into a wood pile, topped off by a metal crossbar from which hung a stuffed dummy with a facial image resembling the President of the United States.

Once those present had consumed the barbequed deer and elk, the remaining bones were thrown on the wood pile. Two gallons of gasoline were spread over the surface of the wood, a match was thrown, and within minutes, flames leaped high into the dark night in the great meadow full of inebriated Americans content to sell out their country.

As Sayed sat in silence next to Buck Bowen, watching the celebrants drinking around the great fire, he was awed at the gullible nature of those present. They actually believed he and his al-Qaeda associates would share a portion of a conquered America. Al-Qaeda would never do that, not with such disgusting infidel reprobates as those who had gathered under the pine trees there in Idaho.

CHAPTER 22
THE KORAN

PLANTATION, FLORIDA
NOVEMBER 20

DELISHA WAS TORN.

What was that warmth that came over me when the Mormon missionaries were here? I still remember those feelings years after. Why don't I have those same feelings when Siddiqui and the other holy men speak?

As Delisha retired to her room, she pulled out her Koran and began reading pensively. She knew she was approaching a major crossroads in her life. In just over a month, she was scheduled to give up her life, and she had to know it was for the right purpose.

Why have Siddiqui's words rung so hollow lately? Same with the other holy men. Why? And these two young men who walked into our home those many years ago with their convictions of Jesus Christ —that Christ was more than just a prophet as I have always been taught. That he was actually the Son of God and the Savior of Mankind . . . a god in his own right! How could this be? These young men with no more than a year or two of college at most, making me feel something so comforting that I have never felt with the imams. Why?

Feeling a need she had never felt so powerfully before, Delisha fell to her knees next to her bed. "Allah, God, whoever you are? Please . . . comfort my heart. Help me! I must know before I give up my life! Is this really what you want of me?"

The longer Delisha was on her knees, the stronger the impulse came. It was for her to keep reading her Koran. She had both a

Bible that her friend, Madi Southerland, had given her, which she read occasionally, along with her Koran. A few years before, Madi had told Delisha that her father, Bishop Southerland, had indicated that she should first try to know for herself if Jesus was truly the Son of God before she learned more about the teachings of their church. This compelling impression surged within her again. It was like a small voice within her, "Read from your Koran!"

What is happening? she asked herself. *I feel God's hand in this.* She picked up the Koran, grasping for any possible solution to her dilemma, wishing that a solid answer would materialize. Opening the Koran, she began pouring through the 124 suras, or chapters, at random, starting from the front. She sought something— anything—in her own beliefs that could at least approximate the comforting sensations she'd experienced when the young missionaries had guided her through the Old and New Testaments in the Bible, as they talked about Jesus Christ.

Surely there is something here in the Koran just as powerful or even more so . . . and just as convincing as what Elder Brown and Elder Sterling told me, she pondered, again thinking about the young missionaries. *After all, my life is tied up in this!* she thought in desperation. In her mind's eye, she saw Elder Brown carrying Elder Sterling in his arms from the car to her door, so Elder Sterling could enjoy one more opportunity of what he referred to as "spreading the Gospel of love," which was just the opposite of following the course of death and destruction that the imams preached.

She opened the Koran to Sura II, "The Cow" and read on page six:

> *Verily, they who believe, and they who follow*
> *the Jewish religion, and the Christians, and the*
> *Sabeits—whoever of these believeth in God and*
> *the last days and doeth that which is right, shall*
> *have their reward with their Lord: fear shall not*
> *come upon them, neither shall they be grieved.*

Delisha was astonished! "How could I have missed this?" she asked herself. She turned a few more pages to page 14 of the same Sura.

*Say ye: "We believe in God, and that which hath
been sent down to us, and that which has been
sent down to Abraham and Ishmael and Isaac and
Jacob and the tribes: and that which hath been given
to Moses and to Jesus, and that which was given to
the prophets from their Lord. No differences do we
make between any of them: and to God are
we resigned."*

Upon reading these sayings, Delisha clearly saw a stark contrast between the inferred readiness in the Koran to recognize the Christian and Jewish cultures and accept them for what they were rather than destroy or annihilate them as the al-Qaeda clerics preached. *Why would I want to destroy people in the cause of Islam because of my religious convictions when the Koran clearly states there is mutual acceptance of one another, according to these readings?*

She turned to page 19, wondering why certain sayings seemed to be sticking out, trying to draw her attention. *Is this the way God is beckoning to me?* she wondered.

*And fight for the cause of God against those who
fight against you: but commit not the injustice of
attacking them first: God loveth not such injustice.*

THE INJUSTICE OF ATTACKING FIRST! Those words struck deep into Delisha's heart. So deep, she realized she wasn't ready for what lay ahead. She kept turning the pages, feeling as though God was guiding her fingers. "Which God?" she asked herself. "Is it Allah or is it the Christian God of the Bible?" Her fingers stopped turning at page 28:

Let there be no compulsion in religion.

Again, these words were jumping out at her. LET THERE BE NO COMPULSION IN RELIGION! *Isn't that exactly what Siddiqui and the others have trained us all our lives to do? To compel those who they call infidels to accept our religion or die? Of course it is! I can't do it! I have to get out . . . but how?* she asked herself.

Next Delisha felt compelled to open the Bible and the first

verse she saw was in chapter 5 of Saint Matthew in the New Testament. It read:

> *Blessed are the peacemakers: for they shall*
> *be called the children of God.*

The peacemakers!

She studied the words carefully and thought: *Peacemakers do not walk into public places and kill people . . . people they don't even know, let alone people they have no reason to hate.*

Delisha knew she could not possibly follow through with the suicide mission. Even though she was terrified at the prospects that lay ahead . . . at the obstacles she now had to face, she was grateful—grateful to have finally come to the conclusion of what she had to do. Grateful that God had revealed to her the answer to her pleadings. *Is this God's way of keeping me away from a cliff that I could have fallen off?* she asked herself. *Surely it is!* Then a terrible truth momentarily paralyzed her. *What about Lufti?* She reflected on her brother's absolute resolve to carry out his mission of martyrdom. She felt completely powerless to prevent him from a needless and terribly misled act against himself and against humanity. Tears began coursing down her cheeks as she contemplated the horrible death her brother faced while killing scores of innocent people.

She knelt and prayed fervently. "Oh, God, now that I know you and your will, please help Lufti! Please protect him from himself and from Siddiqui and the others . . . please!" Delisha had not realized her voice had been heard throughout the house, although her words had not been understood. Lufti and his parents had returned from a dinner with some friends. The crescendo of Delisha's voice in prayer had drawn Lufti's curiosity. He knocked on Delisha's door and entered.

"So, how'd your day go, sister?" Lufti smiled upon noticing Delisha had the Koran in her hands as she sat on the side of her bed. He appeared both proud of his sister and relieved that she was involved in her study of the Holy Book.

"I'm fine," responded Delisha. "I've been searching the Koran for remedies."

"Remedies?" Lufti asked suspiciously. Delisha quickly pushed the Bible under some things, away from Lufti's sight as she answered him.

"Yes, I'm trying to find the writings of the prophet Moham-med that will strengthen me for doing what we will soon do," Delisha answered evasively.

"I understand, sister. As our time draws close, I get the chills occasionally . . . not only from the fear of everything going right as planned, but also from the excitement of anticipating all the really wonderful things that await us once we do it."

Delisha wanted to grab Lufti and shake him. She wanted to tell him there was no way she would allow him to go through with it. She restrained herself, knowing that if Lufti and her parents knew of her change of heart, and if this information got out to the al-Qaeda people and their clerics, her entire family's security would be in danger. *No,* she thought, *not now! I have to wait for the right moment!*"

Still, Delisha was curious about Lufti—this older brother whom she had loved so dearly since they were little. The brother who had stuck up for her and fought her battles. The brother who was so sure he was doing the right thing—the thing Allah expected of him. She was curious to know if Siddiqui and the others had instilled in him anything special, like what the missionaries had instilled in her. She was so curious as to whether Lufti had felt anything from the Mormon missionaries similar to what she felt . . . and if he did, if he would ever admit it.

She couldn't ask him. She knew she couldn't. At this stage in al-Qaeda's Christmas Eve operations, Lufti would report any inquiry like that from her to his parents, who most certainly would alert al-Qaeda's operatives. She hated to believe that at this point her parents' zeal for their children's martyrdom eclipsed even their natural love and concern for their children's welfare. She was certain her parents would feel obligated to report any of her misgivings or a change of heart to Siddiqui, who would then have to find a way to deal with her. She knew it could even lead to corporal punishment or death.

No, I can't express a word more of what I really feel to Lufti or anyone else. Of this she was certain.

"Sister, you've been acting strangely. Have you been spending time with that Southerland girl? Do you think that is prudent as we draw closer to our meeting with Allah?" Lufti asked. "Sometimes I think Madi has some influence over you . . . you know, your thinking." Lufti waited impatiently for a response. As the day of their martyrdoms approached, Lufti had become increasingly more suspicious of his sister's activity with her friend, Madi, and her friendship with the Mormons.

"Madi Southerland and I are just good friends. No more than that, brother. Why? Is it wrong to have someone as a friend? Some personal enjoyments before doing what we have to do?" Now Lufti was on the spot.

"Let's see your Koran, sister." Lufti took the Koran and turned to page 34 in *Sura 3, The Family of Imran*. "Read here." He handed the book to his sister, and Delisha read.

> *Let not believers take infidels for their friends*
> *rather than believers: whoso shall do this hath*
> *nothing to hope from God.*

Delisha thought better of arguing with her brother over her friendship with Madi. She simply stated resolutely, "Look, Lufti, Madi is my friend . . . someone who has always befriended me and stood up for me. She has not questioned my religious beliefs and has always made me feel a part of everything. I love her as a sister, so don't question me about her."

Lufti got the picture. He thought better of pursuing the conversation further. "Good night, sister. Praise Allah!" he said as he walked toward the door of Delisha's room.

"Good night, brother," Delisha responded. "Praise Allah." An emptiness and lack of conviction alarmed her. Never before had she challenged her faith and convictions as she was now doing.

Delisha was cast down as she recognized that true happiness would always elude her . . . perhaps even in the afterlife. She came to the conclusion that her alternatives were extremely limited. *I could go ahead as planned,* she thought, *die in a blaze, taking many with me, and end it all. Then at least my anxiety and inner turmoil would finally be quenched.*

Then an extremely compelling question occurred to Delisha. *What of the innocents I would kill while fulfilling the demands of Allah? Then if I find that I have murdered in the eyes of the Christian God, who is probably the real God . . . then what? What if I suddenly realize I have died for no good reason and find my sins in the Christian afterlife to be unpardonable?*

Delisha's thoughts turned to her friend, Madi. *Sweet Madi— she's always there for me. Always good about listening to me . . . not pre- judging me because of the things that I have said that would make most people suspicious of me.* Delisha reflected on the conversation she and Madi had recently.

Delisha had expressed to Madi how she envied her ability to relish her love of life when it was often difficult for Delisha to do that, knowing what she had to face in her own future.

Madi had been particularly concerned with the comments Delisha made about often feeling like "a fattened calf" and her conviction that she would never be able to marry or have children. Madi hadn't pressed Delisha for an answer about these remarks, thinking these were personal matters that could be embarrassing for her friend to answer, but nevertheless, she had reported them to her father, who was also perplexed by what Delisha had said. Delisha had also alluded to Madi recently about how she would miss her.

"What do you mean?" responded Madi, "that I will miss you? Where are you going?"

Delisha had to respond quickly, suddenly realizing she had said too much. "No . . . only that I will have to return to Islam- abad with my parents soon. An uncle there is really sick, and we need to go see him before he passes on. That's all I meant by that."

Delisha hated to lie and was tired of having to cover up.

CHAPTER 23
THE "ENHANCED" INTERROGATION

BOISE, IDAHO
DECEMBER 14

SUBSEQUENT TO BUBBA TELFORD's interview with the FBI, both he and Luke Johns made their initial appearances in federal court in Boise, Idaho. Within two weeks of their arrest, Telford was arraigned, pled guilty to reduced charges, and was sentenced to thirty years of incarceration. He agreed to testify against Johns who had refused to cooperate with authorities. He promised to the FBI relay any information of value that he received while in prison, regarding the planned attacks by al-Qaeda.

On October 29, Johns was formally indicted by a federal grand jury convened in Boise. Johns was charged with being an accessory to the murder of Judge Jeffreys and with conspiracy to murder a federal official. His sentencing date was set for December 16. He was looking at life in prison. The FBI had interviewed him numerous times since his arrest in the presence of his attorney, trying to negotiate some kind of plea bargain in order to find out all he knew about the pending terrorist attacks that Telford had alluded to. Even though Johns's attorney encouraged him to take the government's offer for a reduced sentence in return for his cooperation and further information about pending terrorist attacks on the country, Johns remained stoic and unyielding. He seemed to have no qualms about a life sentence or even capital punishment for killing the judge.

Subsequent to the Omaha bombing and receipt of the intelligence indicating Johns could be the key to identifying terrorist suspects planning devastating attacks on the United States, the current administration had encouraged the passage of certain legislation permitting "enhanced interrogation techniques" to be used against high-risk individuals who, after being subjected to those techniques, could possibly deter the deaths of innocent Americans. The administration had seen the value in waterboarding in rare circumstances and had finally conceded that it was a mistake to have discontinued it.

The government's case against Luke Johns had provided the necessity for implementing waterboarding as an acceptable enhanced interrogation technique—one of the few times in the history of the country it had been used.

Johns's attorney was allowed to be present, along with a medical doctor provided by the court to oversee the procedure.

Just before the waterboarding was initiated, Johns was given one last opportunity to cooperate with the FBI. He refused.

They transported Johns to the Idaho State Prison in Boise, where the procedure was to take place. A specially designed gurney had been constructed for the waterboarding procedure.

Along with Johns's attorney, two US Marshals, and a federally-appointed medical doctor, Special Agents Jim Flynn and Ben Grogan were also present to witness the procedure and ask the pertinent questions.

Johns, who was wearing the standard orange prison jumpsuit, was immobilized by being strapped down on the gurney, which was tilted at a ten to fifteen degree downward angle, with his head at the lower end. A black cloth was to be placed over his face, and water, containing a saline solution, would be poured from a height of six to eighteen inches over his face. The saline solution was to minimize the risk of death from hyponatremia, a condition that dangerously reduced the sodium in the blood and occurred when too much water was inhaled. The gurney was tilted enough to facilitate the water being driven directly into Johns's nose and mouth areas. The marshals, who were administering the procedure, controlled the angle of the gurney carefully, so that it could be tilted up quickly, in case Johns ceased breathing.

The US Marshal who would be administering the waterboarding procedure spoke. "All right, Mr. Johns, this session will take two hours. Never at any time will water be poured over your face for more than thirty seconds. Those pours will occur only six times over the following two-hour period, which will constitute a total of three minutes maximum of pouring. No more than six minutes total of pouring will be administered over the following twenty-four hour period. If you supply the FBI the requested information, the pours will be discontinued immediately. Any questions, Mr. Johns?"

Johns shook his head to the negative. His eyes were opened widely, reflecting considerable apprehension, a state of mind the agents had not observed before in Johns.

"Okay, Luke," his attorney advised, "remember that at any time you want this treatment discontinued, you need only supply the FBI the answers to their questions and the treatment will be immediately terminated. Do you understand?"

There was another tentative nod from Johns.

The marshal placed the black cloth over his face, and each time Johns exhaled, he poured water into his mouth and nostrils. The marshal was careful to pour right after Johns exhaled to ensure he was taking in water and not air in his next breath. Johns immediately began choking, as the saline solution entered his nose and throat. The pouring continued from a height of about twelve inches. The marshals used their hands to prevent the runoff from spilling out of Johns' mouth.

Several precautions had been taken to prepare Johns for what he was going to go through. He had even been placed on a liquid diet, drinking large quantities of "Ensure Plus" prior to the procedure to keep him alive, in the event he began inhaling his own vomit.

Johns managed not to react much for the first ten seconds on the first pour. After fifteen seconds, however, he tried to turn his head to either side unsuccessfully. His eyes reflected terror and gave off the unmistakable impression that he knew he was drowning. Eighteen seconds elapsed, and Johns was brought back up to the flat position.

Johns's attorney began sounding off. "This is disgraceful! It's no more than a fine-tuning of torture and has no place in the ethics of American culture."

"We are at war here, counsel!" Flynn snapped. "Make no mistake about it. Your client is the only person in the world right now who may possibly save the lives of scores of Americans. Just keep that in mind. The government has legalized this procedure for this treatment. Until he talks to us, he will take in a lot more water, but don't worry . . . he won't die."

Johns glared at Flynn.

After twenty minutes had passed, the marshals lowered the gurney again and started pouring more water over the black cloth on Johns' face, this time at a height of about nine inches. This time Johns began sputtering and struggling nine seconds into the procedure, but still would not open and close his eyes three times— the signal he was ready to talk. Johns was tough and determined.

It was not until midway through the fourth pouring, approximately an hour and a half after the procedure commenced that Johns coughed and shook almost uncontrollably . . . then blinked three times. He was immediately brought to an upright position and administered a direct thrust below the sternum to clear any remaining water from his lungs.

Upon catching his breath, Johns exclaimed, "Okay, you win. I'll . . . I'll talk to you, as long as he's with me." He pointed at his attorney.

"You've got a deal," Flynn said.

Once Johns was given time to don a dry prison jumpsuit, he and his attorney were escorted to one of the interview rooms by the US Marshals, who waited outside the door during the interrogation.

"All right, Mr. Johns. You're here with your attorney. We'll supply you another Miranda waiver form just to be on the safe side, even though your legal counsel is present, and have you and him both sign it." Flynn handed him the waiver, while agent Grogan witnessed Johns's signature.

Johns was still a little shaky and pallid. Flynn asked, "Now, Mr. Johns, are you all right? Do you need anything?"

"No, man . . . no. I'm good. Let's get on with this thing!" It was obvious that Johns was embarrassed—humiliated that the government had gotten to him. He just wanted to get it over with and get back to his cell. If he cut some time off from a lengthy sentence, all the better.

"No problem," answered Flynn. "So you're okay? You didn't stop breathing, you have no sign of pneumonia, and you didn't breath in anything that is inhibiting you at the moment, right?"

"Look," answered Johns' attorney. "He's good to go. We've both signed the waiver. Let's get on with this."

Agent Grogan chimed in. "The floor's yours, Luke. We're all ears."

Johns swallowed. "It was Buck that set that thing up on the judge. He'd been out to New York and talked to some guy with a gambling and drinking habit that works in the judge's courtroom. I think Bowen said he did the recording or something. Bowen said he'd paid off the little twit to find out where the judge would be huntin' in Idaho and when. Bowen had his own contacts with folks from our organization in Idaho that knew all the hunting guides over in the Stanley Basin near Redfish Lake, where the judged like to hunt. Those guys passed the information back to Bowen, tellin' him exactly which areas he would be camped at."

"This Buck guy?" asked Flynn. "Are you talking Buck Bowen, the leader of the Mountain Patriots?"

"That's who I'm talkin' about," responded Johns. "The same guy . . . the honcho."

"Hold it a minute!" Grogan was perplexed. "If Buck is the main guy, why is he doing all the running around? Flying to New York to talk to Judge Jeffreys' court reporter? Being there on that ridge with you two when you shot the judge . . . ?"

Bowen's attorney interrupted. "You mean when *Telford* shot the judge. Remember, my guy was just there, all right?"

"Yeah, you're guy was there all right . . . spotting with binoculars for the best shot. Don't minimize this!" warned Flynn. "If we're getting a full, clean statement here, let's don't dance around the facts, okay? Telford already acknowledged he pulled the trigger when he sang. That's history. But let's don't frost the cake with your boy's favorite icing here, all right?"

Johns's attorney didn't respond. He sneered and kept listening.

"Bowen doesn't like to farm out assignments the ragheads give him that involve lots of cash," Johns continued. "I'm sure he took down beaucoup bucks for setting up the hit through the court reporter, or whoever he is. And I'm sure he got plenty of extra bread from them for making sure we took down the judge out there on that ridge. What he paid Telford and I was peanuts compared to what I'm sure he got. That's just the way he is. No job is too small for Bowen if there's extra money involved."

The agents knew immediately who the "court reporter" was. It would be none other than Christopher Tomkins. Agents Joe Fredette and Hank Duffin had interviewed Tomkins in New York City, and he had categorically denied any knowledge of the circumstances surrounding the judge's death; yet throughout the entire interview both agents had noticed that Tomkins eyes kept flitting away from them each time they asked him specific questions regarding his relationship with the judge. A records check had produced Tompkin's litany of DUI violations and references to his propensity for gambling. Both Fredette and Duffin suspected he was lying and had expressed reservations regarding whether Tomkins was withholding information.

"All right," said Grogan. "What's the deal on al-Qaeda's plans for their next hit? Our sources are telling us it's going down on Christmas. Talk to us!"

"I'm telling you what Buck Bowen passed on to me," said Johns. "There's going to be a hit on Christmas Eve. I don't know where it's going down. In fact, from what Bowen said, there could be several hits at the same time all over the country. People are going to walk into public places . . . like the mall in Omaha. I don't know who's going to do it or how many. I don't know where. Buck does. He's got this Pakistani guy, Abu Khan, who lives in the Marriott Hotel on the Grand Cayman Island. Khan's payin' Buck to make bomb harnesses and to transport them to wherever the attacks are going down by these suicide bomber people." It was obvious Johns didn't want to say any more than he had to. But he had already said a mouthful.

"Let's go back to this Buck fella. What did you say his last name was?" Grogan asked.

"It's Bowen. Buck Bowen. He's a big guy, nearly seventy, about six feet five inches tall, weighing roughly two hundred and thirty. He's been the head of the Patriots now for nearly six years," answered Johns.

"We know who he is," Flynn said. "But we also know he spends time at other locations. There's no bomb lab or storage unit at the Hayden Lake compound. It's been searched several times for illegal weapons and explosives that the Mountain Patriots were allegedly hiding. Never found a thing."

"He's never kept the stuff there. And I guarantee you, he won't be spending a lot of time in Hayden Lake since you found me and Bubba over at Challis. The word is out. I've met guys at the holding area here in Boise that have since been released and surely got the word out to him that you're going to be hot on his trail. He's got a lot of sympathizers in jails from around the Northwest." Johns actually seemed sincere.

"So where is he keeping the explosives and hiding out?" asked Flynn.

"It'll be hard to find . . ." Johns hesitated. "He's got a cabin up on the Middle Fork of the Salmon River at a place called the Parrot Creek drainage. It's down river quite a ways from the launching place at Indian Creek. You can't fly in there—no landing strip. The only way to reach it is by boat or raft. You got to know what you're doing navigating the Middle Fork or you'll never make it over Tappan Falls nor the rapids near Parrot Creek."

"Okay, so good . . . so far. What else you got for us?" asked Grogan.

"These guys are armed to the teeth. They got fully automatic M-16 rifles that they train with two or three times a week, tons of .223 caliber ammunition to go with them, and they aren't afraid to use them. Plus they all carry a sidearm, usually hidden: ankle straps or shoulder holsters. There's a real hard-core dude at Parrot Creek—Ike Grimsley—who's in charge of manufacturing the bomb harnesses for this guy Abu Khan. He's got the explosives lab in a cave about seventy feet from Bowen's cabin that has a real small opening. It's barely room enough for one man at a time to enter. You'll have to look real carefully to find it if someone doesn't point it out."

"Okay . . . what else?" asked Flynn.

"The wolves . . . I'm tellin' ya, there's a lot of them. The government allowed them to be transplanted from Montana and Alaska about twenty years ago, and now they've pretty well taken over. Most of the elk herds in that area are gone and they're takin' the deer down now too. The bad thing is that they're makin' swipes at some of the men out there at Parrot Creek now. They've had to shoot a bunch of them, but they keep coming back. Two of our guys have got bitten up pretty bad. Most of them don't even cross over to the tunnel into the cave without their guns anymore. Anyway, I've told you all I know about the explosives and the yahoos that are gonna hit all over the country. Most of them are tied in somehow with the al-Qaeda. That's all I know."

Special agents Flynn and Grogan believed Johns.

"So you guys are goin' to get me something out of this, right? I've given ya far more than what ya asked for. You keepin' your end of the deal?" Both Johns and his attorney were waiting for a positive response.

Flynn responded. "If what you have told us pans out, the court will cut you considerable slack as far as not giving you the death penalty . . . and your time will be reduced as much or even more than Telford's would be my guess. Especially if this leads us to identify where those attacks will take place and who is involved. And, for sure, you won't have to worry about any more water going down your nose. We'll get back with you about all this."

"We'll hold you to that!" Johns's attorney said.

CHAPTER 24
THE PAYBACK

LAS VEGAS
DECEMBER 16

AT 9:30 A.M. THE Pioneer Casino in Las Vegas was already humming with action as Special Agents Fredette and Duffin walked past the gambling machines, looking for the blackjack tables. The acrid smell of tobacco, alcohol, and human perspiration from folks spending a lot more time pulling the handles of slot machines than bathing, permeated the air. The two agents had little sympathy for the gambling set, many of whom were walking around half-stoned and bleary-eyed—few with smiles, more with frowns from having become the grim statistics of the house, losing far more than they had won.

Duffin and Fredette had enjoyed the $5.99 "Steak and Eggs" special, posted as a come-along out on the marquee in front of the casino. The house personnel knew Christopher Tomkins well. He was a "regular." The agents were informed he normally didn't arrive at the blackjack tables until around 11:00 a.m. They were advised he had been there three days and would surely return, since his room was booked for two additional days. The agents had been given a key to Tomkins's room and had searched it, but he was out, apparently having breakfast somewhere outside of the Pioneer.

The warrant for Tomkins the agents carried was for conspiring to murder a federal judge. Luke John's testimony was corroborated by two of Tomkins's confidantes at one of his favorite drinking haunts, who on several occasions had heard Tomkins brag when he got really tipsy that he had finally evened the score with the tyrant he worked for "who tried to force me into rehab."

"Hey, Duff," Fredette said, "let's advise the three Las Vegas agents to wait by the main entrance and we'll watch the blackjack tables. That way, they can grab him before he enters the main gambling area if he comes through the front door. If he comes in through the side entrances, you and I can identify ourselves to him, advise him of the warrant, and quietly walk out of here without creating any unfavorable publicity. Sound good?" Fredette was always in favor of avoiding the press and so was Duffin.

"Okay," responded Duffin. "I'll advise the head of security what our mission is here, so if there's a disturbance, we'll all be on the same page." Duffin hated undue publicity. He was the epitome of the low profile guy. Even when he was on the air, he hated using his radio, unless absolutely necessary. Drawing attention to himself was the last thing he wanted to do.

At 11:25 a.m. Tomkins walked in tentatively through the side door of the casino with a bottle of beer in one hand. He had started this binge early or maybe had just kept it going all night. It was hard to tell. Fredette and Duffin saw him immediately. He was the poster child for the adverse affects of drinking and gambling. He wore a sweaty tee-shirt with an Elvis figure on the front. The shirt looked like he had slept in it. Rolls of fat cascaded down his torso top to bottom, giving him the "roly-poly" appearance of one who would rather die than be caught in a gym. His hair was unkempt, and his Levis were way too tight for him.

Tomkins walked straight for the blackjack table that management had indicated he favored. Duffin and Fredette walked over to him, with Duffin in the lead.

As Duffin presented his credentials, identifying himself as a special agent with the FBI with a warrant for Tomkins' arrest, Tomkins turned pale and dropped the beer, which spilled over the richly-designed carpet.

"You're coming with us, Mr. Tomkins," Duffin advised with

a raspy but authoritative voice. "We know all the details. You are in big trouble! And you know why."

As Duffin advised Tomkins of his Miranda rights, Tomkins just looked at him as if through a haze, feeling like he was hearing the words from a tunnel, from far away.

"You have the right . . . . to . . . . remain . . . silent.

"You have . . . the . . . . right . . . to . . . a . . . . n a . . t . . t . . o . . r . . n . . e . . y."

Tomkins knew the drill. He'd heard the words numerous times before. But on this occasion, his mind was shutting down with not only alcohol, but cold, steely fear, the kind of fear one feels when it all finally catches up to them. All he wanted was escape, an unconscious escape somewhere . . . anywhere.

Tomkins was sure he was going to lose control of his bowels. Still drunk from the continuous drinking binge over three days, his head was reeling. *M-U-R-D-E-R!!! I think he said murder! I know he did! How did they find out? The plan was perfect. The guy said he'd keep me out of it and just give me the money!*

With Duffin on one arm and Fredette on the other, the drunk had no escape. The agents didn't bother to handcuff Tompkins until they had escorted him out the front door of the casino, where he was turned over to the three Las Vegas agents.

"Take him down to the holding area at the office," Fredette ordered. "Give him all the coffee he can drink and anything else to sober him up. Take accurate notes of anything he says while you're observing him. As soon as you're convinced that he's no longer under the influence, give us a call. Duffin and I will interview him."

"Right," replied the supervisory special agent who was there on the scene with two of his squad.

Tomkins was placed in the rear seat on the passenger side, next to a tall, dark-complexioned agent, handcuffed and strapped in. Another agent drove while the supervisor took the front passenger seat. As they observed Tomkins slumped way down in his seat, beginning to enter "La-La Land," they dismissed any notion of asking him any questions.

* * * * *

At 9:35 p.m. Fredette received a call from the Las Vegas FBI office from the same supervisor who had been on the scene earlier.

"Your boy's ready, Joe. He's stone cold sober and scared to death. No one's even spoken to him, but he's already screaming for an attorney."

"We'll be right there," responded Fredette.

Within a half hour, Fredette and Duffin were seated in an interview room in the Las Vegas FBI office across a table from Christopher Tomkins. Tomkins greeted them with a condescending sneer on his face, just daring the agents to violate his constitutional rights.

"Mr. Tomkins, we've previously identified ourselves to you, but you may not remember that. You were a little . . . shall we say, 'indisposed,' at the time." Both Fredette and Duffin showed Tomkins their credentials. "You were also orally advised of your rights; however, we are reasonably sure you didn't comprehend them at that time, so here's paperwork we refer to as the standard 'Waiver of Right' form."

"You can forget the form," responded Tomkins. "Do you guys really think that after twenty-three years as a court reporter in a US district federal court that I don't know my rights? And furthermore, do you really think that you're going to get me to say one word about anything without an attorney present?" Tomkins conjured up a toothy smile.

"No," Duffin replied. "I don't think you're going to say one word about anything. Nevertheless, Mr. Know-It-All, we're hear to advise you of your rights because the American system of justice says you are entitled to that. But, as for me, personally . . . you sad sack of cow dung, with all the goodies we have on you, we really don't need a statement from you. I'll proceed."

Once Duffin finished advising Tomkins of his rights, he was given a telephone and the opportunity of contacting his attorney. He was only entitled to one call before being transported to a holding area in the US Marshall's office. Nevertheless, the agents gave him three.

"What do you mean, you won't handle my case?" Tomkins screamed at the attorney on the other end of the line. "I've paid you good money for years for representing me on all those DUIs! What are you talking about?"

Fredette and Duffin looked at each other knowingly.

"So what if it does have to do with a federal judge?" There was another pause. "So what if I'd worked for him? You still have to represent me!" There was a click on the other end of the line. The next two calls were the same. No one wanted to represent Tomkins. The idea of orchestrating the death of a federal judge that Tomkins had worked for over a period of years was just too distasteful.

Tomkins was stuck. The only option he had was to have a judge appoint an attorney for him, but that would be at his initial appearance, which was still at least a day away. The agents stood up and were getting ready to turn Tomkins back over to the Las Vegas agents to transport him to the US Marshall's office.

"Wait! Hold up a minute. Who dimed me out? Was it Bowen?"

"So you are willing to make a statement?" asked Duffin.

"I'm willing to limit some remarks," responded Tomkins.

"Did you fully understand the waiver?" Duffin was going to be sure this was played by the book. "If so, sign the waiver. Then we'll talk."

Tomkins hurriedly signed the waiver. "Here's the deal. A guy by the name of Buck Bowen, who said he was some big muckety-muck from the Northwest, came up to me in a joint near my office where I was having a couple drinks. He asked me about the judge and laid some money on me for telling him what the judge's itinerary would be for the next few months. I told him about the hunting trip, who he would be with, and where he would be. The guy never told me what would happen to the judge."

Fredette weighed in. "So you just gave away all that personal data about your boss—knowing that he was a target for a lot of people that hated him—to a person that you didn't even know. Is that it?"

Tomkins didn't see any give in Fredette. He knew no matter

what he said, these two guys were going to come after him for the judge's murder. *Maybe I could deal,* he thought.

"So what can I get out of this?" asked Tomkins.

"Eighty-five years!" was what Duffin wanted to say, but he held back. "You're looking at a lot of time, based on conspiracy to murder a federal judge," answered Duffin. "But anything that you give us to bring Bowen to justice should help. At least, we'll bring it to the attention of the prosecutor."

Tomkins took the agents at their word and laid out the facts. He admitted figuring out that Bowen wanted to take out Judge Jeffreys. He also indicated that he was all for it, knowing of the financial rewards and peace of mind he would have, not having to go into rehab. In essence, Tomkins caved in.

Within a day, agents Flynn, Southerland, and Grogan had their warrant for Bowen, based on Tomkins's and Johns's statements, issued by a US district court judge in Boise, Idaho.

CHAPTER 25
CASING OUT THE MALL

SUNRISE, FLORIDA
DECEMBER 18

ANY FLORIDIANS CONSIDER THE Sawgrass Mills Mall, at 12801 West Sunrise Boulevard, the third biggest tourist attraction in South Florida, next only to Disney World and Sea World. To arrive there, one takes the I-595 exit off I-95 heading west, and then grabs the Flamingo Drive exit and heads north toward the mall. That is where Lufti and Delisha were to consummate their sacrifice in the name of Islam.

Lufti and Delisha had made numerous passes through the mall within the prior year in preparation for their final trip, familiarizing themselves with all the entrances, exits, and inner corridors, so that when they took their final steps on Christmas Eve toward their meeting with Allah, there would be no second guessing. Siddiqui, the holy man, had instructed all five sibling couples of The Ten to make five "target" orientations, one in each month leading up to the Christmas Eve event. This was the last pass through for Delisha and Lufti.

Delisha was just going through the motions. She had already decided there was no way she would be going through with the attack. Accompanying Lufti through the mall was only to allay any suspicions.

On this last trip, Lufti drove his red Camaro Z-28, accompanied by his sister. He parked the car on the third level of the garage across from the Burlington Coat Factory. Prior to entering the mall, the siblings passed a row of green hedges with white egrets, approximately two feet tall, perched on them. They noted that the birds had long, graceful necks. Their bright yellow beaks accentuated their whiteness.

A central plaza area came into view as the couple walked past the Royal 23 Cinemas movie theater on their left and a Gameworks store on the right. The plaza was lined with ten Royal Palm trees.

"These ten beautiful palms are standing like sentinels over this mall like we, as The Ten, are standing as sentinels for Islam, Delisha," Lufti stated proudly. "Do you see the similarity, sister?"

Delisha said nothing but nodded affirmatively.

They continued their walk through the plaza, Lufti straining to make mental notes of everything, as they had done many times before. They strolled past the marble benches with yellow umbrellas. Delisha had always been impressed by the tiled, multi-colored walkways with octagonal patterns, green on top and beige on the bottom, with salmon pink squares in the middle. She abhorred the thought of such a beautiful setting going down in flames

No way can I let this happen! she thought. *It is indeed a happy place. It must remain that way.*

Upon passing a seven-foot-tall hurricane simulator, they entered the indoor portion of the mall. There was a Target store there on one end and a J.C. Penney's on the other . . . both major anchor stores.

Delisha and Lufti had originally considered the Target store for their detonation. They had spoken about how appropriate the title of the store was. They were confident it was probably the biggest Target store of its kind. It had a huge yellow-tiled corridor with an octagonal-squared ceiling illuminated by four-foot-long black cylindrical light fixtures. Upon entering the store, customers were immediately engulfed in an ocean of the typical red with white bordered designs with the trademark of big red circles over little red circles.

Lufti had remarked on their first pass through, "We can't do it here. There has to be a better place."

The pair headed toward J.C. Penney's, which was on the other end of the mall. Then they turned right toward the Garden Food Court.

Finally, they approached the site they had chosen for their rendezvous with Allah. It was perfect. It was on Avenue Four, a seating area with three potted palm trees pointing up, located toward the center of an area containing six rows of tables with four chairs at each table. The area could seat at least 670 people. It was situated behind the Haagen-Dazs ice cream parlor, facing the food court.

As Delisha and Lufti walked between the Haagen-Dazs vendor and Green Leaf's Deli, Lufti exclaimed, "I've always thought this would be the perfect place!" In addition to the potential of a lot of victims seated and another fifty standing, Lufti had discovered that an "infidel" Christian choir would be singing on Christmas Eve at the designated time of the attack. That would bring the potential kill total to around 775, according to Lufti's calculations. Lufti smiled broadly as he realized there was a possibility of far more victims than he had ever felt possible.

Once Lufti felt the plan of attack was solidified, he put his arm around Delisha's shoulders, motioning toward the Ben and Jerry's ice cream concession. "Come on, sister, I'll treat you."

Soon the sibling pair was seated at a table facing the forthcoming attack site where, in just a few more days, they would sacrifice their lives for Islam. As Lufti shoveled in scoop after scoop of delicious butter pecan ice cream, he considered all the advantages of the location they had picked and was extremely pleased.

Delisha was very passive. It concerned Lufti.

"Are you going through with this, sister?" Lufti asked, worried.

"Of course I am, Lufti," came Delisha's response. "That's our destiny." She knew she wasn't convincing, but she couldn't tell Lufti the truth. She had to keep him satisfied.

Delisha was lost in thought, barely nibbling at the cone. She was transfixed, staring at the various people in front of her, walking through the future kill zone. Her attention was drawn to a middle-aged mother holding her Down syndrome son's hand.

The young man was in his early twenties. He was obviously fascinated by his surroundings, including a candy store, various clothing shops, and the numerous toy store outlets. He had stopped
in front of one toy store and held fast, pulling his mother back
and pointing at one vendor in particular, who was demonstrating
a remote powered helicopter. The whirlybird was launched first
vertically and was made to hover over one area, then made to
move sideways just as easily. The young man seemed mesmerized
by the flying toy. He continued to stand his ground as his mother
urged him to move forward.

As Delisha observed the handicapped young man enjoying the
helicopter's maneuvers, she asked herself, *Is he a threat to al-Qaeda?
An obstacle to the cause of Islam? Really?*

Something was happening with the young man. His outline
was screaming out, shining brightly, from those other people
around him. *What's happening here?*

Suddenly other images came into view for Delisha, illuminated
images like the young man's . . . obvious protrusions of certain
people from the rest of the crowd. There was a young mother,
pushing her twins in a baby stroller, heading for a children's
clothing store. Next came an elderly man, slowly shuffling along,
holding onto a walker. Then a group of eight- to nine-year-old
boys dressed in Cub Scout uniforms, led by a young woman in
her thirties, clad in a blue skirt and yellow blouse with the official
Scout handkerchief draped around her neck and fastened with a
metal slider.

Delisha noticed that each of these people were also encircled
with a brilliance that made them stand out just a little more than
the people around them.

They were all walking through Lufti and Delisha's kill zone.
Again, she had to ask herself, *Why is this happening to me? Why am
I seeing them so distinctly, even to the exclusion of dozens of people around
them? Are these the enemies of Islam? They all have to die?* Delisha
realized that none of these people could possibly present a threat
to Islam nor any other religion or organization. *Buy why?* she
asked herself. *Why is this being revealed to me in this way?* She knew
why. But Lufti didn't—and that was painful for her, very painful.

Delisha sensed that the kind of insight she was now experiencing was not coming from any supreme Islamic being that would have her slaughter these men, women, and children. Then that meant it was coming from another source. Perhaps the Christian god, deplored by the Muslims jihadists?

More and more people continued walking through the area designated for the attack, but Delisha seemed blind to all those except the elderly, the mothers with babies, the afflicted, and the young children. Those figures continued to shine out like stars on a dark night, to the exclusion of everyone else in the mall.

As another group of school children walked by, again into the anticipated kill zone, Delisha noticed that Lufti had consumed nearly all his ice cream. She had eaten little of hers. She pointed at the children, who were probably between seven and nine years old, and then to their teacher, a middle-aged lady in her late forties. "What do you think, brother?" she asked. "Cute kids, huh?"

Lufti answered unenthusiastically, "Oh yeah. Sure . . . cute." He knew something was wrong with his sister.

Delisha, meanwhile, was becoming even more overcome with deep-rooted anxiety, as she conjured up a vision of all these individuals being slaughtered . . . blown to pieces by Lufti and others of The Ten.

That was when a handsome little five-year-old boy broke away from his mother and siblings who were walking past the bench where Lufti and Delisha were seated just a few feet away. The little child ran over to them and stooped down to pick up three quarters, a nickel, and two pennies that had dropped out of Lufti's pocket. The child was full of excitement as he handed the money over to Lufti, smiling. His big brown eyes were set off with a tuft of brown hair that accentuated his Hispanic countenance. He waited, impatiently, for Lufti's response, continuing to smile.

As Lufti took the change from the boy, he said, "Thank you, but since you were honest enough to give me my money, why don't you just take it for some ice cream for yourself?" The little boy looked at Lufti, then at Delisha's ice cream cone, thinking it over. Without saying anything, he just smiled and shook his head and ran to his mother. Lufti and Delisha noticed how the mother proudly ruffled up her son's hair and smiled at him.

When Delisha had gazed down into the eyes of the five-year-old Mexican boy, it was confirmed to her yet again that she could not go through with it. No matter what the costs to her personally, she just couldn't do it.

She looked at Lufti, who was scooping out the last of his ice cream, nudged him, and asked, "Can you do it, Lufti? Can you kill them all?"

As Lufti jerked back and turned to Delisha, shocked, he dropped his ice cream cup with what little remained in it and exclaimed, "What?"

Again, Delisha repeated her concerns. "Look at the children, Lufti. That little boy. The old people. The children are like you and I were when we loved to ride the merry-go-round. What crime have they committed, that they deserve to die a horrible death at our hand? Where did all these elderly folks go wrong, that they have offended Allah? What about the boy with Down syndrome and his mother? Siddiqui wants them all dead, Lufti. Why do they deserve to die? Tell me, Lufti! Tell me! Can we really kill them?"

Lufti was speechless, wishing he could lash out at something. He was red in the face. He sprang to his feet, backing away from Delisha. He raised his arm slowly, pointing a finger at his sister, and remarked slowly and deliberately, "Don't do this, Delisha! Stop it . . . right this moment! Not now. Not at this point. Stop! Don't—just don't!"

Delisha knew she had said too much . . . way too much.

After staring angrily at Delisha for several seconds, Lufti composed himself and said, "Come on. Let's go home."

Lufti realized how far this could go if they debated about the merits of the mission. He knew Delisha's reticence and lack of commitment should be reported both to the holy men and to his parents, but deep down he knew he couldn't report her, especially considering such a report could cost Delisha her life.

The siblings arose and without further comment, headed back to Lufti's car. No one spoke on the way home.

Huge trees canopied the Ahmed home with branches flowing over the street in front of the house, creating a tunnel ceiling for the traffic. The neighborhood was a bedroom community, consisting mostly of one-story homes sitting on the edge of beautiful man-made lakes. It was an older, well-established neighborhood, populated mainly by the middle class. The homes were landscaped with lawns of Florida fescue grass and tall, gangly trees.

An elementary school and a small shopping center were just a few minutes walk away.

As Lufti pulled into the garage, he and Delisha exited the car and entered the living room, where their parents were waiting, apprehensively.

"It's okay," stated Lufti. "We've got it down. Close to eight hundred will die." He was smiling again, exulting in the proposed attack. Their parents smiled back, then looked at Delisha excitedly. With great concern, they noticed that their daughter, who had somewhat of a blank expression on her face, didn't share Lufti's enthusiasm.

CHAPTER 26

THE MIDDLE FORK BUST

**PARROT CREEK ON THE MIDDLE FORK
DECEMBER 18**

T HE FIVE AVON RAFTS glided quietly into the landing near the mouth of Parrot Creek. Four fully-armed FBI SWAT teams, five agents on each team—all clothed in camouflage, Kevlar vests, and the bureau insignia across the front—quickly jumped out of the rubber vessels and mustered under some trees near the trail leading up to the Mountain Patriots' cabin, a quarter of a mile inland. The location was exactly like what Luke Johns had described. It was getting just light enough to see the outline of the cabin. The agents had camped a mile up the river in order to carry out a surprise raid with the warrant for Buck Bowen based on his conspiracy with Luke Johns, Bubba Telford, and Christopher Tomkins to murder Judge Jeffreys.

The raft guides, river experts hired by the Bureau to ferry the men down the Middle Fork of the Salmon River to Parrot Creek, were instructed to land the rafts, then to quickly hike upriver far enough to be safely removed from any subsequent gunfire. The plan was for them to meet with three additional rafts, encamped a river mile upstream, that would be used to transport any prisoners downstream to a small airstrip. Several aircraft had been contracted to haul out all the agents with their prisoners and rafts.

Special Agents Jim Flynn, Ridge Southerland, and Ken Grogan were in charge of the impending attack on the Patriots.

Southerland and his five-man team were to advance to the rear of the cabin, while Grogan and his team moved to the front, where they would make a dramatic entry by breeching the front door, tossing in flash bang smoke grenades, and clearing the front living room. Once Grogan and his men had made entry, Southerland's group would force in the rear door and clear the kitchen, bedroom areas, and bathrooms.

Flynn's group of five agents would cover the front entrance and watch for anyone approaching the cabin from the outside, while the other five-man team would go to the entry of the cave, where the explosive harnesses were being manufactured. That team would include two experienced bomb technicians, who could defuse anything that could possibly present a threat to the agents. Those technicians would collect, bundle, and transport the explosives and their precursors.

Unknown to the agents, Buck Bowen and Ike Grimsley were the only ones left in the cabin. All the rest of the men had vacated the premises a week earlier in possession of the cache of explosive harnesses. They were delivering the explosives to The Ten in Los Angeles, Miami, Chicago, San Francisco, and New York.

Bowen had hung back because he was unsure how much information had been given up by Bubba Telford and Luke Johns about his involvement in killing the judge. He knew Bubba would be the first one to talk if pressured but had more confidence in Johns keeping his mouth shut. That was, until recently, when he'd heard word that Johns had brokered some kind of a deal with the feds to escape the death penalty. Bowen knew this might only be a rumor that his ex-con associate had presented; nevertheless, Bowen wasn't going to risk returning to Hayden Lake. Little did he know that Luke Johns had given up his location on Parrot Creek to the feds, rather than have another quart of saline water go up his nose.

Ike Grimsley was a man to himself and had little desire to be around the Hayden Lake folks any more than he had to— nor anyone else for that matter. The old government-hater was at Parrot Creek until he got snowed out. He was more than happy when Bowen appeared on a raft loaded with extra groceries and hard liquor, with the intention of laying low for awhile. That would mean lots of nights around the pot belly stove, drinking and playing checkers. *Bowen isn't such a bad guy,* Grimsley thought, *when he takes his mind off business and treats himself to a little hard stuff.*

Bowen and Grimsley were still sleeping soundly, having drunk until two in the morning. Bowen was on a cot set up in the living room. Grimsley slept in the bedroom where he had lived the entire summer and fall while working the al-Qaeda order.

Two of Grogan's men approached the front entrance to the rustic dwelling, an old cabin that had obviously weathered decades of abuse by Mother Nature. The streaks of pine sap running off the logs in downward patterns produced a pungent odor that attacked the nostrils of anyone entering. One of the SWAT team members hoisted a thirty-pound cylindrical metal device with two handles on it, called "the key." Taking a full swing to the rear, he slammed it within six inches of the door handle, the most vulnerable area in the door. Not only did the old door cave in, but the entire door frame went down with it. The second agent threw in a flash bang to the rear of the living room. Two seconds later the sound given off by the grenade gave the impression the world was coming to an end, as smoke bellowed from the device, causing the living room to fill up. Smoke immediately enveloped Bowen, then spread into the back areas and Grimsley's bedroom. Then both agents entered with their M-16 rifles, covering the living room where Bowen had, seconds before, been dozing peacefully.

"Buck Bowen, this is the FBI!" the first agent said. "Roll off that cot to your knees with your hands way above your head . . . and do it now!" Bowen, who was only able to halfway open his eyes, looked perplexed. "Whaaa-t? Wh-who are you?" he asked, confusion all over his face.

"You heard me!" responded Grogan's point man. "Down on the floor with your hands way above the head. Do it . . . NOW!"

"No! Not without that!" responded Bowen, pointing at a bottle of gin, three-quarters full, right next to his bed. "You let me have a shot of that . . . and maybe I can get my motor runnin'."

Grogan entered the room. "Go ahead and let him have some,

so we can get him up. But cover him good!"

Bowen pulled the bottle to his lips and drank deeply, brought it down to his lap, and held it there, obviously planning on a second swig.

"That's it!" hollered one of the agents, who took the bottle away. He discarded it into a garbage can. "Now stand up and pull on your trousers!"

Once Bowen was dressed, he was immediately handcuffed, while the other agents on Grogan's team cleared the living area and collected two rifles, a shotgun, and a .9-millimeter hand gun. Bowen was confined to one corner with two agents guarding him, while the rest of the house was cleared.

Ridge Southerland and his team were feeling a little uneasy behind the cabin as they waited for the signal from Grogan that the front door had been breeched. They had caught glimpses of several dark forms, flitting from one group of pines to another, closing in slightly about forty yards behind them. All the agents had been made aware of the unusually bold character of the wolves that thrived on the Middle Fork.

Once Grogan had radioed in the "Go" order to Ridge, his men made a similar entry from behind the cabin through the rear door and arrested Grimsley. They had Ike moaning, groaning, and cussing about the inconvenience of it all, before he showed even the slightest concern about being arrested. To Grimsley, being arrested from time to time was no more than an operating expense. He had spent so much time in jail for inciting riots, disturbing the peace, and petty theft, as well as a string of DUIs that covered several decades, that he couldn't get very excited about the early morning bust.

"What in the name of thunder do you fellas think ya need the entire FBI army here for? Ain't ya got any international terrorists ta follow around or some spies ta chase in the big cities? What in tarnation are ya doin' way out here on the Middle Fork?" The agents found it interesting that Grimsley appeared so casual about the whole thing.

Grimsley rolled from his bed down to his knees with his hands way over his head while he was searched, as if it was all scripted.

Bowen, on the other hand, was emboldened with that chug-a-lug of gin that he had swallowed. "Where's your warrant?" he asked repeatedly. "Let's see the friggin' warrant!" he insisted.

"Your time will come, Mr. Bowen," responded Grogan, "but not until you are secured and we are ready to advise you of your rights."

"I'm not talkin' to you guys!" Bowen shouted. "Ya think I'm a little squealer like those two guys back in Boise . . . the ones that had taken an oath . . . a sacred oath at that . . . to keep their mouths shut?" Bowen studied the facial response of the agents, hoping to know by their expressions that they would confirm his suspicions that their information as to his whereabouts and his involvement in Judge Jeffreys' death had come from Telford and Johns. He was convinced that the two people he'd commissioned to take down the judge had decided to take him down too.

Agent Flynn walked in behind Grogan. His men had secured the area surrounding the cabin. They were still out there, keeping one eye on the cabin and the other on the dark forms of the wolves that were moving around apprehensively, barking a little here and a little there, obviously communicating with one another. Flynn came in to report the cave entrance had been discovered, but that no one would enter until the command was given.

"Uhh . . . so what you are telling us, Mr. Bowen," said Flynn as he approached Buck, who was seated in a wicker chair in the corner, "is that you care not to cooperate? Am I correct?"

"You got that right!" responded Bowen, defiantly. "You got nothin' on me. And I'm goin' to call an attorney before I say one more word!"

Bowen was shaken by the smile that formed on Flynn's face.

"What phone you plan on using?" Flynn asked, his smile now stretching from one ear to the other. He turned toward the other SWAT agents in the room. "You fellas may want to continue with your search of the premises and the adjoining properties. By the way, plan on taking all the time you need. Agents Southerland, Grogan, and I will talk to this fine fellow and take all the information down that he's going to 'volunteer' to give us."

The agents in the room knew exactly what Flynn was saying,

between the lines. They preferred accepting Flynn's invitation to vacate the immediate area and not hear or see anything that they would have to testify to in court. Although the rules had changed since the Omaha incident, they were in favor of playing it safe by not witnessing the manner in which Bowen and Grimsley would be called on to "cooperate."

"Okay, Buck. We'll do this your way," Flynn muttered with determination. "Over three thousand people were killed in this country, which is also your country by the way, on 9/11 in Washington, DC, and in New York. Then last July 4, several hundred more were killed by the same group—al-Qaeda. Now, according to our information, several thousand more are going to die all over this country on Christmas Eve. And it's because of you, you scum bag! Do you hear me?"

There was something in Agent Flynn's eyes that was terrifying . . . a kind of fire that Bowen thought would flare out from the agent's nostrils and scorch Bowen at any moment. His stomach felt hollow once he realized that this time, Miranda rights were irrelevant for these agents. The stark reality set in that his interrogators were far more interested in saving American lives, and Bowen had that information. Indeed, the agents were intent on gleaning that information from Bowen any way they could, and he knew it.

Bowen stared at Southerland and Grogan, who were nodding their concurrence to everything Flynn was saying. At that moment he knew he was not going to win by merely shutting his mouth and waiting for the arrival of his attorney. *No, not with these guys,* he thought. *Not out here in the middle of nowhere, and especially not after what happened in Omaha.*

The fourth team leader entered the room and advised the three agents that they had found the entrance to the cave. They had searched it and located large quantities of acetone peroxide and other ingredients for making the bombs, as well as a large quantity of cloth fabric and leather straps, which could be used for harnesses, but had found no paperwork indicating where the harnesses were to be delivered.

Upon hearing this report, Grogan looked at Bowen

menacingly. His eyes were steely and cold. "Y'all are gonna tell us where that stuff went, arent'cha, Mr. Bowen? Cause if you don't . . . all those folks are going to die in those places you sent those bombs to! We're waiting, Mr. Bowen."

Bowen shuddered as the three agents stared him down.

As the fourth team leader began to leave the room, he advised, "Several of the men out there are expressing some genuine concern about the wolves. Apparently these two haven't left the house much in the last couple weeks, or they would have noticed it. There's about a dozen of those critters coming in real close to where the troops are."

"Tell them that once their areas are cleared and any logical evidence is secured from in here, the perimeter of the cabin, and inside the cave, they can head on back down to the river and set up a muster area," Southerland advised. "Tell them if those wolves get too close, to pepper 'em with a couple flash bangs."

"Sure thing," replied the team leader.

Flynn closed in on Bowen. He sat on a chair squarely in front of him, getting right in his face, inches away. Southerland and Grogan sat down on either side.

"Buck," he said, "where did those explosives go?"

Bowen's mind was made up. It was more than just a matter of snitching. Once the al-Qaeda determined who had betrayed them, it was a matter of dying.

"What explosives?" was his reply.

"Look at me!" snarled Flynn. "Do I look like I'm playing games here? Omaha was a game-changer, my friend! The rules aren't the same now. You don't squeeze out of this one, like you always have before . . . with your cozy defense attorney. You got it? People are going to die here. Americans . . . just like you . . . well, I take that back, not really like you at all. You couldn't care less about Americans."

Bowen sneered. Then he smiled condescendingly. "That's all I got to say to you guys!"

"No, it's not!" Southerland said.

"Really, so what do you guys have planned? You hot shots . . . the famous FBI! College policemen, right? Sure! Teethed on the notion of protecting human rights . . . remember?"

Grogan weighed in. "Hey, Flynn! I think it's about time to take this guy out behind the wood shed. What d'ya think?"

"I think you're right is what I think," muttered Flynn. He grabbed Bowen by the nape of his neck. Raising him from his chair and with the other two agents on either side, he ushered Bowen through the front door. Ike Grimsley, who had been listening carefully while sitting in handcuffs, gawked curiously. This was a police interview unlike any other he had ever seen.

"You can't do this!" Bowen yelled furiously as Flynn continued leading him outside to the creek in front of the cabin. "I got Ike Grimsley there as a witness, and when all is said and done, you guys will have to explain yourselves in court!"

"Yeah . . . sure," replied Flynn. "Tell that to all the people that your bombs are going to kill!" He brought Bowen to his knees, right next to the stream of icy water, approximately a foot deep, holding his head down only inches from the water.

"Did you know," commented Flynn, "that the rules have changed on waterboarding in exigent circumstances . . . like when American security is at risk? Like right now?"

Bowen's expression was blank. "What's waterboarding?"

"You're about to find out," declared Grogan.

Flynn kept talking. "Now, normally, a doctor's present when we do this, you know, just to make sure you don't drown. And in better times, on better days, we'd even tie you down to a gurney, reclined with your head down. But that sounds cruel and unusual . . . so we'll just take some short cuts, okay?" said Flynn.

"You're crazy!" replied Bowen.

"And you know," Flynn continued, "the sad thing is all you have to do is tell us where you sent the explosives, so we can stop some suicide bombers from killing your fellow Americans. What do you say, Buck?"

By this time, Ike Grimsley, who was being guarded by the two remaining agents in the cabin, was looking out the window and taking in the whole weird scene. *When did things change?* he asked himself. *Is it just cause we're out here in the sticks? Or can these guys really get away with this?*

"Last chance, Buck. Where are the explosives going?" Flynn had Bowen's head two inches above the surface of the swift icy stream.

"What explosives?" Bowen repeated. "I don't know anything about any expl—" Flynn submerged Bowen's head totally under the water. As he felt the portion of his arm under the water become numb with cold, he decided to keep Bowen under no longer than five seconds the first time.

When Bowen came up sputtering, vomiting out some of the water he had taken into his lungs, Flynn asked him again, "Where are the explosives going, Buck?"

There was no response. Bowen just continued sputtering . . . looking at Flynn defiantly.

Agent Southerland weighed in. "Give us some locations, Buck. You could go into protective custody. The terrorists would probably take you out eventually anyway, once they use you and your resources. They won't want witnesses around, nor will they want to share what remains of America after all the attacks, with some folks up in the sticks of Idaho that call themselves 'Patriots.'"

Southerland was trying to talk sense into a man that only cared about clearing his lungs, so he could take in enough oxygen for the next dunking.

"Forget it!" was Bowen's response. "I ain't talkin'!"

This time Grogan held him down and counted off eight seconds before bringing him back up. Bowen's face felt so numb from the bitter cold texture of the stream that it took several seconds before his eyes could focus on his interrogators and his hearing became normal. He immediately began coughing spasmodically and appeared to be going into convulsions, shaking violently.

"Can you help us, Buck?" Southerland asked. "You can see where this is headed."

Bowen tried to answer. This time it would take a while before his lips became nimble enough to articulate the words. After about fifteen seconds, came his response: "Go ahead. Better you kill me than those ragheads. Do it! Go . . . go ahead."

The agents all looked at each other. This wasn't going anywhere.

They pulled Bowen up. Southerland and Grogan each took an arm and supported him as he stepped forward tentatively and unsteadily, making his way to the cabin. There, he was placed on a cot. Flynn placed a blanket over him and advised the two agents in the room who had been with Grimsley to watch him.

Next, Flynn looked at Grimsley. "All right, Ike. Your turn."

Grimsley turned pallid. His eyes opened wide. "Wai-wait, gents. What would I know? I ain't the boss. It's the man on the cot there. He—he—he's the boss, not me!"

Southerland took Grimsley by the left arm, lifting him up. Grimsley tried to stay seated but didn't have a chance, as he was suddenly jerked up by the big man from Idaho.

As soon as Grimsley was outside of the cabin where Bowen couldn't hear him, he was ready to deal. "Look, fellas, I'm an old man, well into my seventies. I ain't lookin' to live forever. One thing I don't want is to have a cold drink right now, ya know what I mean?"

Flynn and Grogan, who were walking ahead of Buck and Southerland, turned slightly and winked at one another.

"What are you telling us, Ike?" asked Flynn.

"What I'm telling ya is there's a list of addresses inside a tobacco can down in the cave that ya might want ta take a look at." Grimsley pointed at the entrance to the cave.

"Okay, Ike. Now we're talkin'!" answered Grogan, enthusiastically. "Now we're talkin'."

When Bowen saw the four men turn from the direction of the creek to the cave, he began cursing Grimsley under his breath. He knew Abu Khan would blame him and Grimsley both for revealing the locations of The Ten to the FBI. Word would get out and sooner or later, their heads would roll . . . literally!

From his chair, Bowen searched the room, trying to figure out what was happening outside with Grimsley. He recalled the location of a loaded handgun, a snub-nosed .38 caliber revolver, that he had taped under the kitchen table chair next to the window as an emergency backup. Although it was only five or six feet away from him across the table, one of the agents guarding him was sitting right on top of it. Being handcuffed, he knew he couldn't get past the two agents and retrieve the weapon. *I've got to be patient . . . real patient,* he thought.

Grimsley and the three agents came to the narrow opening at the entrance to the cave. Grogan descended down through the opening first, then Grimsley and the others. The agents were amazed at how roomy the cave was once they made it through the entrance. They noticed all the empty shelves and the left-over precursors and paraphernalia for making the explosives and bomb harnesses.

"There it is!" exclaimed Grimsley, walking over to a coffee pot on the lower cupboard. He picked up a tobacco can next to it, plucked out a piece of lined paper, and handed it to Flynn, who began perusing it carefully:

Aadab and Fadwa Akhtar
1217 Blueberry Circle
Los Angeles, CA

Tahir and Safia Kauser
12445 Kensington Lane
San Francisco, CA

Yaman and Zakia Bibi
389 Knox Terrace
Chicago, IL

Baasim and Erum Hussain
1667 Apple Villa Street
New York City, NY

Lufti and Delisha Ahmed
14567 Lake Lure Court
Plantation, FL

"Bingo!" cried Flynn. "This is it! These are the addresses. We've got a satellite phone in my raft. I'm going to dig it out, point it south, and call headquarters with this info . . . right now.

We've got to get agents out there with search warrants right away."

"There's more," yelled Grimsley. "Don't get in a doggone hurry! Now you boys are goin' to see about cuttin' me slack, the more info I give ya. Is that right?"

Grogan responded. "Look, Ike. We don't have authority to make promises, but what I can tell you—and these other two agents also—is that in our experience, those that get on the bandwagon first and give us the best information are the ones that get the breaks in sentencing. Now the truth is, you've been shipping a lot of explosives to kill fellow Americans for a long time. You have a major problem. But if you can supply us information that will save other American lives, the judge that sentences you will give that a lot of consideration before he tucks you away."

"All right, then I reckon I'll take my chances with you guys. The one you really need to look for is a raghead by the name of Abu Khan, who's coordinatin' with al-Qaeda for a big time Christmas Eve hit against the country. He's a Pakistani. Bowen has been dealing with him for a long time, and his terrorist friends do what they want to do here in this country."

Grimsley caught his breath, hesitated for a few seconds, and then said, "Dang . . . this is beginnin' ta feel good, talkin' like this . . . and I don't really know why, cause I for sure don't like the way things are going in this country. Anyways . . . maybe I'm helpin' myself in more ways than one by tellin' ya all this. And . . . it's for sure that them folks out there do live in the same country that I do."

"That's good, Ike," said Grogan. "Maybe there's something still in you that has to do with 'mothers, the American flag, and apple pie,' eh? What do you say?"

Flynn and Southerland gazed at Grimsley and the slight change in his countenance. Both later commented they thought they had observed a hint of moisture building up in the corner of his eye.

"Anyway," continued Grimsley, "this raghead, Khan, has a place in Los Angeles with some family there, but spends most of his time living at the Marriott over in George Town, Grand Cayman, accordin' ta Bowen. This Khan gets lots of money from the ragheads over in Pakistan or Iraq or somewhere over there ta run their operations in the States. And in turn, Khan filters a lot of it over to us to supply them with their bombs and stuff. Dang! I'm glad to get this offen ma mind! And that's about it."

Flynn grabbed Grimsley's hand, shaking it vigorously. "You did good, Ike. When all's said and done, you did really good!"

A hint of a smile began forming on the old man's face.

"Okay," said Grogan. "Southerland and I will take Ike back in, get him and Bowen ready to transport, and, hopefully, we'll be heading down the river in time to hit that airstrip and our Cessnas before dark."

Ridge Southerland had only caught a fleeting glimpse of the names and addresses, but as he checked them out momentarily, before handing the paper back to Flynn, he became suddenly transfixed on the last names: LUFTI AND DELISHA AHMED! He couldn't believe his eyes at first, but then it all made sense:

> *Delisha being forbidden to join a Christian church.*
>
> *The conversations she had with him when he was a bishop about her struggles with comparing Islam to Christianity.*
>
> *Her conversations with his daughter, Madi, about never being able to marry and have children.*
>
> *The information she had shared with Madi about being gone soon on a trip to Pakistan to see relatives just before Christmas.*

Ridge pulled Flynn and Grogan over to the side, while two other agents took Grimsley back to the cabin.

"Remember when I talked to you two about my church work in Plantation, Florida, before I volunteered for this assignment?" Southerland said, somewhat anxiously.

"Yeah, Ridge," said Grogan. "You mentioned that you put a lot of hours in counseling the youth and trying to keep marriages together . . . stuff like that. After hours. Never could figure out how you could do all that, along with the Bureau work."

"Right on," Flynn chimed in. "Our hats were off to you, buddy."

"Well, those Ahmed kids on that list in Plantation—I knew them through the Church. They aren't members, but they and their parents would show up occasionally at church activities.

And now I know that for Lufti and his parents, it was to keep up appearances to throw us off on their real reasons for being in the country. However, with Delisha, I think she felt something. I think she's going to hesitate about going through with this plan. I just have a feeling. That address is correct. Let's get people out there."

Then another thought strafed Agent Southerland's memory like a hot bullet, searing through his consciousness. His family was scheduled to participate in a Christmas caroling session at the Sawgrass Mills Mall in Sunrise, just a few miles away from their home in Plantation, Florida, on Christmas Eve: the same night the suicide attacks were to take place. There would be more people in that mall that night than anywhere else in Southern Florida. *They wouldn't do that, would they? Surely not knowing Madi and the rest of us would be there. Or would they?* he asked himself.

"Jim, you need to get a message out to the Miami office right away! I think there's a good chance they'll hit the Sawgrass Mills Mall in Sunrise. That's where the big events are taking place on Christmas Eve, and that's where the most people will be, including my family."

"Will do, Ridge," answered Flynn. "I'll alert the cops down there to put special emphasis on security at that mall."

"I'm going to make a call home on that satellite phone also, to my family. They need to stay away from that place." Southerland waited nervously while Flynn tried to dial up the satellite.

"It's not working here," Flynn said. "Too steep. These canyons in the Middle Fork are some of the steepest in North America. We'll have to try again when we get to the airstrip."

Ridge was beside himself. Having to wait several more hours before he could warn Madi to stay away from Delisha and her brother was taking its toll on him. He was preoccupied and distracted.

As the agents entered the cabin, Bowen was red in the face, staring daggers at Grimsley.

"You told them, didn't you, you puke? You caved in, just like the sissy wimp that you are, didn't you?" Bowen had to be restrained by an agent as he tried to kick at Grimsley.

"Listen, mister big man honcho," responded Grimsley. "I owe ya nothin'. And I owe this organization of what we call Patriots nothin'. When it comes right down to the nitty gritty, it's me that put together more than half of them bombs myself, livin' up here in this dump, while you been rakin' money off on the side, killin' judges and stuff. Don't get high and mighty with me!"

The agent sitting at the table stood up to separate the two men who were screaming at each other. At that point Bowen lunged across the table to his chair, reached underneath it, and pulled out the loaded .9 millimeter. He shot Ike Grimsley twice—direct hits to the upper torso. Grimsley hit the floor motionless.

Bowen bolted to the door, with his hands cuffed, but with his right hand still pulling the trigger. A third shot flew wildly, making everyone duck. Everyone hesitated to return fire because of the agent between them and Bowen. As Bowen ran in front of the cabin, firing his last shots, two passed through the front window of the cabin. One hit the agent, who had been restraining him, in the arm, shattering it. The other entered Ridge Southerland's chest and lodged near his heart. He went down immediately, blood oozing from his mouth.

Bowen had one shot left as he ran behind the cabin into the timber. He began climbing a low-lying ridge up one of the fingers leading down to the Parrot Creek drainage.

As Flynn, Grogan, and the other agents in charge of guarding Bowen and Grimsley desperately sought a shot at Bowen, they were too late. About forty yards up the ridge, Bowen's final shot was heard muffled through the pines. They heard screaming, which was suddenly terminated, then eclipsed, by the satisfied howling of a pack of wolves.

CHAPTER 27
BOOTS ON THE GROUND

THROUGHOUT AMERICA
DECEMBER 19

WITHIN MINUTES FROM THE MOMENT Agent Jim Flynn obtained the addresses for The Ten, he was on a satellite telephone with Supervisory Special Agent Denny Campo, calling for 24-7 surveillances on each of the sibling pairs' residences. SSA Campo, in turn, notified the Special Agents in Charge of the San Francisco, New York, Chicago, Miami, and Los Angeles divisions to prioritize the OMAMALL bombing matter. Five two-man teams of agents were put together to watch each address. Next, Flynn immediately contacted his team leader, Joe Fredette, regarding the new development.

Fredette and Hank Duffin had coordinated contacts with informants along the East Coast consistently and painstakingly since the Omaha incident and had come up with the last name of Khan for a Pakistani-born individual the sources insisted was coordinating all major al-Qaeda initiatives in the United States. According to Fredette and Duffin's sources, Khan was a major player in the July 4 attack. The two agents had also received information that other extremely devastating attacks were planned and forthcoming in some major American cities by the end of the year, but they had no definitive information as to when or where.

Fredette and Duffin had a general description of Khan, but they had no other specifics.

The information that Ike Grimsley, Luke Johns, and Bubba Telford had corroborated the information from Fredette and Duffin's informants; however, until Ike Grimsley turned over the addresses for the suicide bombers, the agents had no idea who they were or where they resided.

Once Fredette and Duffin received the tip on Abu Khan's residence in the Cayman Islands, they chartered a plane to George Town, Grand Cayman, and made arrangements with local authorities to rent a car and meet at the airport the following day.

* * * * *

FBI agents in the five target cities throughout the country were assigned to maintain constant surveillance on the residences of The Ten. They worked revolving eight-hour shifts, assuring there were always five two-man teams on each shift.

Every vehicle appearing at each one of the homes was checked out for license tag registration information in an effort to identify the occupants. Descriptions were recorded of each vehicle occupant. Once the vehicle owners were identified, they were checked through all available FBI indices, including the National Crime Information Center (NCIC), for criminal history.

Detailed surveillance logs were maintained, together with specific descriptions of every person observed entering and leaving the target residences.

Agents on foot, dressed down as gardeners, plumbers, electricians, or just casual passersby, covered any back or side entrances not in full view from the street.

The following instructions had been passed down from SSA Denny Campo at FBI Headquarters to the Special Agents In-Charge of the Los Angeles, Miami, Chicago, New York, and San Francisco divisions of the FBI, via priority email:

IMMEDIATELY DETAIN ANY INDIVIDUALS, INCLUDING THOSE SUSPECTED OF DELIVERING TO SUBJECT RESIDENCES PACKAGES OR CONTAINERS OF SUFFICIENT SIZE TO CONTAIN EXPLOSIVE HARNESSES OR OTHER QUESTIONABLE MATERIALS. SAME UNKNOWN SUBJECTS (UNSUBS) ARE TO BE STOPPED AND

INTERROGATED FAR ENOUGH AWAY FROM SUBJECT RESIDENCES THAT THEIR DETENTION WILL GO UNKNOWN TO SUBJECTS AT THE RESIDENCES.

Further instructions were passed down from SSA Campbell that once those subjects were detained and their cars searched, they were to be held "incommunicado" by a federal court mandate until such time as it was ascertained that the same people could not possibly be back in contact with the residents of the target houses.

Days and nights continued to pass without incident, as every precaution was taken regarding each of the five residences identified from Ike's coffee can.

CHAPTER 28

THE JOURNEY

CHALLIS, IDAHO
DECEMBER 20

THE BULLET HAD BEEN removed from the flesh close to Agent Southerland's heart, but his condition was questionable. The raft trip from Parrot Creek down to the airstrip had taken a terrible toll on his body, with the bumping of the rapids and constant careening of the raft. Being strapped down on a wooden platform to avoid being jettisoned from the rubber boat added additional stresses. Nevertheless, the surgeon in Challis had been successful in removing the round and had stabilized Ridge to some degree. As Ridge tried to imagine where he was and what was going on, he vaguely recalled what his father had told him about meeting adversity.

"Just replace it, son. Replace it with something good and wonderful . . . something that makes you feel good inside." Ridge's father had been laid off from two jobs, went bankrupt once, and lost his first two children in a terrible accident. He knew something about meeting adversity.

Good . . . good and wonderful, thought Ridge. *Good and wonderful.*

His pain was diminished by the shots of morphine, and Ridge departed on a wonderful trip through sweet memories he was able to summon up. As those memories were unlocked, they infused his soul with warmth and strength.

The sedative kicked in and began insulating him from pain, fear, and apprehension. Ridge began to realize that he could handle this . . . that for Ridge Southerland, there was no problem without a solution.

He recalled the admonition from Church leaders that everyone needed their private, uninterrupted time to visit their own "Mount Sinai" where they could draw close to God and reflect on those things that were most important in life. The mountain flooded into his memory . . . the mountain near where he had grown up in Idaho. He had called it "Mount Hoolio" and had gone there often to pray and meditate. He recalled taking his problems up to the summit where he tried to find answers. He remembered that mountain peak was where he first envisioned what God might look like. He saw his Heavenly Father's face in his mind's eye as a perfectly sculptured visage with kind features, love reflected in His eyes, a long, flowing beard, and white hair.

As a young man in high school, he had worked in a service station, pumping gas. One day his boss told him he was out of money and couldn't pay him the eighty-five dollars he owed him. That was a lot of money in those days. He had his sights set on some new school clothes and some sports equipment that he had worked hard for. He didn't know what to tell his boss. He went to the mountain.

After taking forty-five minutes to ascend the peak, he watched the lights come on in the town below. Homes were beginning to glow on the landscape below.

The sanctity of the rocky peak with openings just big enough to kneel in always remained the same. The creek ran quietly below at the base of the mountain, bubbling away and carrying fall leaves—orange, yellow and brown, curled up in the front like miniature Viking ships.

He observed the house of his boyhood, across the dirt road from the creek, where he had slept out many moonlit nights on the front lawn, contemplating the universe, the Milky Way galaxy, and the North Star.

He remembered hunting ducks on the creek after school on

crisp, cool days in the fall and catching rainbow trout with worms on Wedding Ring spinners.

A black bear had once been sighted just at the base of the mountain across from his house.

Planks were nailed on a tree next to the stream, daring kids to climb up them.

As he prayed, he suddenly realized that his boss had a family with several children. He knew that he was thinking only of his own problems and not considering his boss's predicament. Business had not been good. He came down the mountain with empathy for his boss . . . realizing that he didn't need the things he had worked for as much as his boss needed to care for a family.

That was one of only several issues he had resolved on Mount Hoolio. *Mount Hoolio . . . wonderful Mount Hoolio!* he thought.

Next came a song—a beautiful song that had brightened his life each time he heard it. He had played its words back in his mind so many times.

He remembered spending leisurely days with his father, prospecting a mine claim up the Warm Springs canyon, near his home, and his dad singing this special song. The words brought carefree thoughts, a slower and relaxing tempo to his soul. It was an old and simple song, perhaps designed to put the skids on the frenzy of the twenty-first century:

Tra-la-la, twiddly-dee-dee
It gives me a thrill
To wake up in the morning to the mockingbird's trill
Tra-la-la, twiddly-dee-dee
There's peace and goodwill
You're welcome as the flowers on Mockin' Bird Hill
When the sun in the morning
Peeps over the hill,
And kisses the roses 'round my window sill
Then my heart fills with gladness
When I hear the trill
Of the birds in the treetops on Mockin' Bird Hill
Tra-la-la, twiddly-dee-dee

It gives me a thrill
To wake up in the morning to the Mockingbird's trill
Tra-la-la, twiddly-dee-dee
There's peace and goodwill
You're welcome as the flowers on Mockin' Bird Hill
When it's late in the evening,
I climb up the hill
And survey all My kingdom while everything's still
Only me and the sky—and an old whippoorwill
Singin' songs in the twilight on Mockin' Bird Hill

Ridge was amazed at how a song that came out in 1951, twelve years before he was born, was sung first by Patti Paige, then constantly by his father, could still have such a comforting, soothing affect on him so many years later.

He then recalled with awe the manner in which his dad dynamited the lead and silver outcrops at his mine to get to the accessible ore. He would watch from a hundred feet away as his dad walked among several sticks of dynamite with various lengths of fuse, lighting them one at a time, and then walking leisurely over to where he was, while Ridge waited nervously, praying that his dad would make it out before the sticks exploded.

Ridge felt a warmth in his belly, as he recalled the satisfaction of watching the sun's rays glistening down upon the small, meandering stream near the mine that tumbled down the side of the mountain through Indian Paint Brush flowers along walls of granite.

* * * * *

Ridge continued following the counsel of his father: "Good thoughts! Good and wonderful."

The sedative was working.

Ridge reveled in his recollection of the rerun of Rodgers and Hammerstein movie, *The Sound of Music*, specifically the voice of the saintly Mother Abbess.

Climb every mountain, search high and low
Follow every byway, every path you know
Climb every mountain, ford every stream
Follow every rainbow, till you find your dream

As Maria Von Trapp sought to find her life's compass, she had strengthened Ridge, as he re-experienced the warmth he felt when he saw that movie with his wife. He felt the kind of strength emanating from the Mother Abbess that he wanted to pass on to his consciousness . . . the kind of strength that he now needed . . . more than ever.

Ridge recalled with fondness the winters at home in Idaho when his family was snowed in and school days were cancelled. Sometimes that also meant Dad would be staying home from his work at the body and fender shop. It would become an automatic "family day." Popcorn was popped by the basket in the frying pan and covered with butter. His mother would bake fudge and the television in the corner became the family theater. He and his sister were still into trading comic books with their neighborhood friends. For that one overpowering purpose, snow could be waded through . . . snow that almost covered the windows and accumulated up to the eaves.

Ridge's father's counsel had truly proven to be a catalyst for his forays into the happy years of his youth. He reflected on viewing television for the first time and being captivated with the western series of *Bonanza* and *Gunsmoke* as a ten-year-old. In his mind's eye, he pictured Matt Dillon walking down the streets of Dodge City with his deputy, Chester. No criminal could escape them. As he reminisced over watching those reruns with his dad, his spirits rose up again and again.

He fondly recalled his admiration for Marshall Will Kane, upon seeing the rerun featuring the lawman in the movie, *High Noon*, whose role was played by Gary Cooper. He'd seen the movie four times. He recalled the many trips to Boise, Idaho, that he took as a boy. He would ride as far as Shoshone, Idaho, with his parents where they would put him on the train bound to visit his aunt and uncle for a few weeks of the summer.

He recalled simulating the excitement of *High Noon* for himself, as he paced up and down the railroad track in front of the train station in Shoshone while pretending that he was Marshal Kane—waiting for the notorious, recently-released prisoner, Frank Miller, who was coming back to even the score with the marshal who had sent him to prison. He remembered how courageous the marshal was under those circumstances, standing alone before a whole town that had "chickened out."

In remembering Marshall Kane and Matt Dillons' examples, Ridge wondered if those two lawmen had influenced his decision to become a federal agent. *Yes . . . could very well be.* As Ridge thought of his wife and children and their dependence upon him, he knew he must finish his race in mortality. He wouldn't allow himself to die now. *Finish the race, finish the race, finish the race,* became fixed in his mind. His memory reverted to other races in the past.

He reminisced running his first marathon at Seaside, Oregon, at age twenty-five, where he finally crossed the finish line in just under four hours after almost becoming delusional. He thought he was starving and hitting the wall at twenty miles, stopped to walk, then continued running on. The euphoric feeling of finally crossing that finish line defied all description. He felt again a portion of that feeling, which made his heart brim over with soul-satisfying accomplishment. He then reflected on another marathon he ran thirteen years later.

Ridge recalled the aftermath of 9/11. He had been training for a marathon to be run three weeks after the tragedy. He rigged a two-bottle water belt with duct tape, so that it would withstand the weight of the American flag pole that had hung in front of his family residence on holidays. After 9/11, he began carrying it on his training runs to rally the people of his community in the wake of the worst disaster that had ever occurred on American soil. He would shift the pole with the American flag from side to side and would carry it, while it waved in the wind, to all parts of the community. Drivers would honk with enthusiasm and onlookers would cheer upon seeing the symbol of America's resilience moving through their community. Once he had run eighteen miles with the flag, he decided he would attempt to carry it in the marathon.

One day at a Rotary meeting, one of Ridge's friends made the comment: "You know, Ridge, it's amazing how this attack on our country has begun to unify our people and create patriotism. I've even seen some guy running with a full-size American flag around town these past couple weeks. Can you imagine that?" Ridge looked at the man with an knowing grin and responded, "You don't say?"

The day of the marathon in St. George, Utah, onlookers gazed proudly at the flag, wondering if its carrier could make it the full 26.2 miles. After all, this was a real residential type flag with full-length pole, not just a one-handed waving flag. As Ridge ran down the highway with four thousand other runners, he ran with new meaning and a new sense of mission. Farmers lined along the country roads, farmers who saved their smiles mostly for when their daughters were married and their kids baptized, smiled unabashedly and cheered as the flag came by them. They raised their clenched fists and clapped their hands. The little children along the way all wanted to "high five" as Ridge weaved back and forth, trying to catch them all.

At the seventeen-mile mark, a woman from behind ran up to Ridge's side and remarked, "I have been watching this beautiful flag in front of me now for seventeen miles and hate the fact that I will now pass it. You, sir, have given this race a whole new meaning for me, especially following the attack on 9/11." Ridge thanked her as tears formed in his eyes.

Although the extra weight of the flag challenged his endurance, Ridge never once thought of quitting. Finally, as the finish came into sight at the 26.2 mile mark, the exhilaration and sweet sense of accomplishment Ridge felt upon hitting the tape was overpowering . . . something that he would never forget in this life. The medal placed over his neck for finishing the event meant little compared to the joy he was relishing from taking Old Glory through the finish with him, held high and waving majestically in the cooling breeze. This event galvanized his commitment with the FBI to fight the terrorist threat with all his heart, might, mind, and strength. It had led him to the A Teams.

Two days later, Ridge was awake. His fever had subsided and the bleeding had stopped, and he was assured by the attendant physicians that he could go home, as long as he would rest for a week before trying to perform any normal activities.

CHAPTER 29
LOOKING FOR KHAN

GEORGE TOWN, GRAND CAYMAN
DECEMBER 21

BASED UPON THE SATELLITE call from Jim Flynn two days before, Campo had decided to immediately dispatch agents Fredette and Duffin to George Town, Grand Cayman, to locate and hopefully arrest Abu Khan. Luke Johns's information had been corroborated by agents Fredette and Duffin's recent findings, culminating from their work with Pakistani and Iranian informants on the East Coast and in the Los Angeles area, where they had worked feverishly to identify anyone who might have been associated with the bombings.

Agents Fredette and Duffin struck gold in California. A highly-placed informant of Pakistani descent had obtained information from a person in Abu Khan's circle that it was Khan who had solicited the hit on Judge Jeffreys. Based on that source's information, corroborated by what Luke Johns had said, a federal warrant was issued by a US district court judge in Idaho for Abu Khan for "conspiracy to murder a federal official."

Coming up with the name of Abu Khan was the most promising development Fredette and Duffin could have wished for after five months hard work. They had come up with an Abu from one source and a Khan from another, along with other first and last names for suspects, but no Abu Khan. They had received information that an individual with the last name of Khan lived in the Cayman Islands and managed funds for al-Qaeda, but they had no idea where he lived. Johns had supplied the missing piece of the puzzle.

* * * * *

It was a typical December mid-morning in George Town, Cayman Islands. Five hundred and eighty miles south of Miami and a hundred and eighty miles north of Jamaica, the three Cayman Islands were soaking up the eighty-five-degree heat like dry sponges.

Most everyone lived on the big island—the Grand Cayman—about thirty-five to fifty thousand people. Nearby Cayman Brac, with three to four hundred thousand folks, and the Little Cayman with a few hundred more, plus a grass landing strip, were close but had little influence on what happened in George Town, one of the most popular tax havens and money laundering paradises in the world.

The area known as "Dolphin Cove" was bustling with excited cruise passengers, looking for glass-bottom boat rides and city tours. In an outdoor thatched-roof tourist information shop, hustlers were handing out tour write-ups and trip tickets. Another bamboo hut sheltered visitors who were busy boozing it up, as if they hadn't had a good drink since leaving their cruise ship. The Grand Cayman was shaped like a huge fish with a wide head, dorsal fin, and tail fin running from right to left.

The heat was beating through the streets as beads of sweat clearly emanated from the foreheads of passersby, clad in lightweight shorts and flowery shirts. Seven Mile Beach, located on the West end (tail fin) of the big fish-shaped island, just north of downtown George Town, seemed magnetized as most newcomers were immediately drawn to that part of the island.

Waste baskets stuffed full of water bottles and soda and beer cans testified to the intensity of the heat wave. Jamaican music, spewing out the sounds of Harry Belafonte, was activating the hot buttons of dark-skinned local residents clad in bright clothing, as they swayed to and fro with the beat.

As Joe Fredette and Hank Duffin drove their rented Camaro heading toward the Marriott Hotel on Seven Mile Beach, they noticed seven cruise ships anchored some distance out with tender transports filled to the brim with tourists pouring in. The busy little boats were the major link between George Town and the tourists, since there was no deep water landing. The Carnival Valor, the Carnival Legend, the Celebrity Infinity, the Celebrity Solstice, as well as three other ships too far away to identify, were all in the process of unloading shoppers with money burning a hole in their pockets.

As Special Agents Duffin and Fredette proceeded, off on the left was the Cayman Valhalla, a pirate ship, one of two boats used for the fall holiday when the "Gentlemen of the Sea" would conduct a fake raid on the city. Close into the dock, heads of snorkelers were bobbing up and down like misplaced coconuts in an aqua-green cauldron.

George Town took on at least several thousand tourists a day, seven days a week, bringing a multitude of new faces to the island, full of apprehension, excitement, and curiosity. As the two agents drove past the landing docks, they noted that before the visitors exited the tenders, the long tongue of a metal footbridge extended out from the pier to latch onto the tender, like a frog's tongue snapping up inordinately huge flies. The tenders' mate was barking out the refrain, "One at a time, please. No pushing!" as 325 penned-up tourists, acting as if they had spotted abandoned pirate booty, stood ready and poised to beat everyone else to the plethora of tourist traps.

Glancing back toward the massive cruise ships, the agents viewed a myriad of hues of sea surface dressed in aqua-green, light blue, and dark turquoise waves, dancing in succession on the incoming tide, rolling to the dock.

The two agents were practically intoxicated with the island environment, but they had work to do. Knowing Abu Khan habitually greeted a host of contacts who tendered in under the guise of cruise tourists in order to avoid suspicion, the agents had spent the morning comparing Khan's photo with the faces of the milieu of passersby. Abu Khan was no secret to the FBI. Numerous reports regarding his affiliation with al-Qaeda circulated, but the extent of these dealings had been obscure, prior to the agents receiving their tip.

They parked, exited their vehicle, and entered a square block area named "The Shops at Royal Walter." The first sign visible in front was a directory seven feet high, with the word: "Exit," "Info Maps," and "Pre-Booked Tours with Tickets." Black guides streamed through the square, hustling riders to Seven Mile Beach, the Governor's House, and the Old Homestead. The agents, dressed down in tourist apparel, each went separate ways searching for Kahn, with their cell phones tucked away in cargo short pockets to insure continuous contact. They were on high alert for Khan, who was now the last piece of the puzzle in trying to corral everyone involved in Judge Jeffreys' death. They knew Khan had registered at his normal haunt at the Marriott at the "Treasure Island Resort." They knew he was there—somewhere!

The agents believed Khan might be meeting his clients at the "Swimming with the Dolphins," a high-end tourist attraction in the Grand Cayman where it was easy to talk without being spotted and then disappear into a sea of tourists. Agents Fredette and Duffin entered the dolphin pools area through the gift shop, then to the changing area on the right. The aqua-green pools were surrounded by majestic royal palms. Fifteen to twenty swimmers in life jackets were lined up along one side of each of three pools facing their instructor, receiving some last-minute tips on how to max out their adventure. Six- to eight-foot long dolphins swam in front of them, teasing their future riders with a look at their dorsal fins and popping up their heads two feet out of the water, as they emitted a high squeaking peep . . . much like that of a bird.

Suddenly, some of the magnificent dolphins began jumping eight to ten feet out of the water, grandstanding, then cavorting back and forth across the pool like gray jets. Others were swiftly traversing the pools, pushing boogey boards on their snouts, waiting their turns to transport their onlookers.

Finally, the dolphins came up behind their passengers, who mounted the boogey boards. They would push the passenger rapidly across the pool to the utmost enjoyment of their riders. At the end of the ride, the mammal would ham it up even more by shaking their patrons' hands with their dorsal fin at the conclusion of the ride.

"This is perfect for Khan to meet for some official business . . . maybe to pass over a few thousand greenbacks or to receive a coded communication from one of his cronies in the Mountain Patriots," stated Fredette.

"Yeah, with this many people going and coming . . . not being able to take their eyes off these dolphins, it would be the ideal meeting place, but I don't see anyone here even coming close to Khan's description. We'd better head over to the Marriott." Duffin was becoming impatient. He had a warrant and wanted to serve it.

They walked cautiously back to the car, still hoping to spot Abu Khan, but to no avail. They walked past the outdoor café with the signs, "Conch Fritters and Margaritas: $12.00," then they turned back to the car, walking past the Turtle Farm. Someone was explaining to the gathering crowd that this was the site where thirty thousand turtles were bred and released into the Caribbean each year and that these turtles would eventually grow up to five hundred pounds in weight and live to be forty to fifty years old.

Fredette and Duffin continued searching for Khan, passing ancient cannons recovered from skirmishes with pirates and invaders from the seventeenth and eighteenth centuries. The two-hundred-year-old, eight-foot-long cannons were blackish-gray, covered with chunks of coral and solidified volcanic ash, and mounted on decayed wood bricks.

Spanish and broken English were heard everywhere except in the tourist circles. The agents got in their vehicle and proceeded north toward Khan's hotel. On Seven Mile Beach they passed "The Lord's Church," a dilapidated old building with iguanas scampering around on it. They heard a local Cayman guide pointing out the lizard-like creatures while explaining, "Look, folks! All them iguanas on top of church, tryin' to get their soul saved."

Directly across from the church was a stopover called "Hell," named for a jagged, formidable rock formation. With volcanic pointed rock resembling thousands of knife blades, it pointed straight up with dark green vines running through it. Three-foot-long iguanas were crawling around everywhere. A few small royal palms stood out defiantly amid the chaos. One black rock projecting outward definitely resembled the head of the Devil. Only a continuous mild breeze rescued an observer from the grasps of Hell.

The guide continued on. "You know what KFC stands for folks?" as he pointed down the road toward a "Colonel Sanders" fried chicken restaurant. "It means, 'Keep From Cookin'." Everyone laughed, and then the guide went on to explain how Columbus named the islands the Tortugas (the Turtles) because that is all he saw on the islands at first sight in 1493. He told the group that Sir Francis Drake later named them the Caymans in 1586, because the iguanas were so big they looked like caimans, a close relative of alligators and crocodiles.

Once the guide realized his comical rhetoric was striking home, he continued to pour it on his listeners.

"Look on your left, guys. It's a beautiful cemetery. People are dying to get in there!" He awaited the laughter and was well rewarded.

The agents drove past an average housing area, where a two-bedroom condo cost over $700,000 and a gallon of milk cost $5.50. They noticed men selling ice cold coconuts out of their pickup beds. They would lob off the top with a machete, cut one inch into the coconut, place in a straw, and sell it at a good profit.

As the agents entered the Seven Mile Beach area, they observed condos that started at the 2.9 million dollar range. It was an area where it was rumored that one of the world's wealthiest, Bill Gates, had purchased the top floor of the Ritz Carlton Hotel . . . not too far from where movie star Sylvester Stallone owned a home.

As they drove away from the area, Duffin said, "I don't know about driving on the left side. I always feel like I'm about to have a head-on!"

"I don't think we'll ever get used to that," said Fredette.

As they passed Heritage Square on the right, they observed a rather obese middle-aged man eating a huge plate of chicken legs. Duffin remarked, "Obviously, that guy couldn't wait to get back to the cruise ship for one of their six square meals a day."

Gas on the Grand Cayman was $4.93 a gallon in local exchange. One United States dollar equaled eighty cents in Cayman currency, so the gas cost $6.10 per gallon in US currency, but that did not keep the island from humming with the sounds of thousands of vehicles. The gas prices seemed appropriate on such a high-priced island.

The agents passed splendid rows of multi-colored bougainvillea flora, next to rosemary plants and Poinciana trees.

They passed another area that bore the effects of a massive hurricane. Numerous buildings, including hotels, had been flattened.

"What in the devil is this?" Fredette could not believe his eyes, as his took in the damage.

"I asked that same question back in town," Duffin said. "It was Hurricane Ivan in 2004. Hit the island head-on. Every building on the Grand Cayman was either destroyed or damaged by two-hundred-mile-per-hour winds. One-fourth of the inhabitants left the—"

Hey! That's him!" Fredette was signaling frantically toward a car.

It was Khan, accompanied by a pretty blonde-haired American woman, approximately thirty-five to forty years old. Khan's white late model Mercedes Benz was a stark contrast to the poor fishing village huts that were constructed of bamboo and thatched palm roofs and occupied by the poorest of the poor.

"Let's hang back, so he doesn't see us!" Fredette warned. "This guy has been followed before. He's pretty savvy to people like us."

They allowed two other cars to get ahead, between them and Khan. They passed the Tortuga Liquor Store on the right, with the Caribbean Sea on their left. Only about two minutes remained of the eight-minute drive from the dock. George Town, with its 567 banks, was twenty-two miles long by eight miles wide, but most of the tourist action, lodging, and meals were located on the western island edge of the Seven Mile Beach, where Khan lived at the Marriott.

"No wonder al-Qaeda loves this place," said Duffin. "No one can even identify their money, let alone seize it. Abu Khan's got a 'cushy' job, just keeping the piggy bank full, putting it in and doling it out. Nice retirement job for you, Fredette."

The Mercedes finally came to a stop, and Khan got out and walked into the Marriott with the woman on his arm.

The agents notified the local contingent of police.

"This should be a piece of cake," said Fredette. "We'll have the locals put men on all four entrances and exits of the hotel and request one of their four-man teams to back us up.

When the agents observed the police get out of their car and begin to secure the entrance and exits, they parked their car and entered the hotel.

Upon entering the hotel, the two agents looked in every direction for Khan. They were sure he had gone to his room but had no idea where it was. They went to the hotel clerk, identified themselves by show of credentials. and asked for a Mr. Abu Khan. The clerk shook his head with a puzzled expression and advised, "There is no one by that name here. But the name Abu seems familiar. Here's the guest register."

The agents searched rapidly through the pages of current residents.

"Now remember, he may be using an American name or Pakistani name," advised Duffin, "and if it is a Pakistani name, it may or may not be Khan for a surname. They don't always do that in Pakistan. What they usually do is add the most commonly used given name of the father after their own given name, but they can also use a title like Muhammad before their own given name, and the name Khan will not even appear. So look for Abu or Khan somewhere separately, or maybe even mixed with another name, and we'll probably come up with our guy, unless he's using an American name and surname."

"Sounds complicated," responded Fredette. "Nothing can come easy, can it?"

The name search took about five minutes. Finally, Fredette stumbled across one "Muhammad Abu" in room 5409. The agents were furnished a duplicate key, and they quickly entered the elevator. After arriving at the floor, they stepped out with guns drawn and knocked on the door. Ten seconds passed without a response.

"You open the door, Duffin," Fredette instructed. "And I'll enter first. You clear right. I'll clear left and we'll have the two locals follow."

"You got it!" Duffin said. As he keyed the door, Fredette entered in from right to left with his Glock 40 semi-automatic pistol, loaded with 10 millimeter rounds. Duffin followed immediately, armed with his own Glock, with the local police behind him.

Fredette and Duffin went from room to room, clearing each one, as the Caymanian police followed, occupying the cleared rooms.

As they entered the master bedroom, Khan's blonde-haired girlfriend jumped up and screamed at the agents. "Who are you?"

"Where is he, lady? The man that just drove you here?" Duffin demanded. "Who are you?"

"Ann Whidley. What man? What are you talking about? I've been here by myself all afternoon!"

"Right, lady! And I can hear a duck pass gas under water," responded Duffin. "Now where is he?"

Whidley remained silent.

"We're the FBI, ma'am!" Duffin said. "Under the provisions of the Harboring Statute, you could be prosecuted for lying to us."

"You best listen and listen well," warned Fredette. "We know you were with Abu Khan, because we saw you drive up with him. You can cooperate and watch after your own interests here, or you can lie to us and risk going to jail. Your choice, ma'am."

"Easy choice for me, boys," said Whidley, shaking her head. "I'm just his overnight 'escort,' if you know what I mean. Just a convenience. He spends money on me from time to time when he's here . . . lots of money, in return for 'favors,' but he has many other women. He means little to me. He took off as soon as he got a few things out of his room, including a handgun, which he put into a duffel bag. Then he changed into a pair of Levis, a long-sleeved blue shirt, and some military-looking boots and booked out of here like the place was on fire. Wouldn't tell me anything about what was happening. What'd he do? Rob a bank?"

"It's a lot worse than that," said Duffin. "You need to call us if you see him. If you do come in contact with him and we find out about it, and you haven't contacted us, we'll be back!" he warned with an ominous expression. "And that might be with a warrant for you for harboring a fugitive."

"Listen, I told you, he's no more than a passing moment. I'll call." The woman appeared sincere.

"Did he tell you where he was going?" asked Fredette as he passed the woman his card and contact number.

"No, he just took off," answered Whidley. "He left just three or four minutes ago. In a real hurry!"

Upon hearing this, the two agents hustled out the door, again with guns drawn. Motioning the local police to follow, they noticed an open hatch-type roof exit. They pulled themselves up through it, burst up onto the roof, and began searching. Suddenly, to their dismay, they discovered a nylon rope, about a half inch thick, wrapped around an air duct, neatly tied together with a bowline knot. The rope ran off the edge of the building five stories down to the ground. Next to the rope, lying on the ground, was a rappelling harness. They observed tire marks left behind from a vehicle that had probably squealed across the pavement of the parking lot in an obvious attempt to move out "post haste."

It was then that the agents remembered that Khan had trained with the al-Qaeda special forces units on numerous occasions during his younger years. Rappelling was only one of many tactics that he had mastered, not only off buildings, but out of helicopters.

Khan was gone!

CHAPTER 30
ESCAPE TO LABADEE

LABADEE, HAITI
DECEMBER 22

As THE CESSNA AIRCRAFT landed on a remote country strip on the island of Labadee, Haiti, a private island just off the north coast of Haiti, Abu Khan, seated next to the pilot, breathed a sigh of relief. He had narrowly escaped the FBI in George Town and knew it would be a long time before he could return to his comfortable apartment there and to his many women. He also knew the FBI agents had not come just to visit. *And what was their purpose? A warrant? Had the feds been made aware of his participation with the imam and the al-Qaeda leader in Islamabad? Did they know anything about the planned Christmas attack by The Ten? Or about his involvement in setting up Judge Jeffreys?*

Abu was well aware that whatever the reason was for the FBI visiting his apartment, the end result of their visit would not have been beneficial to him. He had been lucky to have the rappelling gear stashed in his closet and to have a friend he could quickly call as a get-away driver. That same person had shuttled him directly to the airport.

Labadee was a private paradise for guests sailing on Azamara, Celebrity, and Royal Caribbean cruise lines. Khan had a personal contact there, sympathetic with al-Qaeda's mission, who had provided him temporary lodging before when he had flown in either on an "emergency" basis or for a little much needed rest and recuperation. The island hosted a landscape composed of beautiful mountains, exotic foliage, and pristine beaches. The scenery was breathtaking, and the water activities were spectacular.

Lush green rain forests blanketed the volcanic mountains that rose straight up, then eventually plunged down to the white beaches. Deep aqua-blue waves nestled up against the white sand, usually thronged by tourists from all over the world.

Labadee had that distinctive charm capable of delivering in one secluded location some of the finest beaches in the storied history of the Caribbean . . . beaches reflecting the ultimate in natural beauty.

Khan got in the white, four-wheel drive jeep that he had requested his contact deliver to the airstrip. While driving en route to his friend's residence on the island, he passed by "Nellie's Beach," home to most of the stores, tourist traps, and one of the longest zip lines in the world. He noticed scores of lazy tourists lying under blue canopies, each covering two rows of six seats each. Other island visitors lined up to board the *Nina*, a shuttle boat hauling passengers from Nellie's Beach to "Columbus Beach," renowned for its luxurious beach cabins.

Khan watched carefully for any individuals that looked like federal agents. Scores of people waited on the cruise ships that had pulled into dock against a cement approach pier, which was approximately one thousand feet long by fifty feet wide. Many of the visitors were becoming restless, anticipating excitement riding the zip line and participating in parasailing and power scuba diving.

Like Khan, the tourists were finding themselves fully saturated in Labadee's omnipresent charisma, as they soaked their toes in the cool water lapping up onto the shore.

Khan loved this refuge, so hidden and out-of-the-way, which was by no means an ordinary island—it was an island where someone like himself could easily hide in its secret coves and inlets, while evading unwanted visitors. He continued heading for his friend's bungalow, passing bright red-roofed houses on both sides of the road.

Khan finally arrived at the fashionable residence in Buccaneer's Bay on the southeast side of the island. Al-Qaeda money had purchased it. And there he paused . . . for now.

CHAPTER 31
THE PEP TALK

THE EXCITEMENT IN THE old mosque was electrifying as The Ten, along with their parents and the imam Rashid Siddiqui, gathered for the final step in launching the five sets of siblings into martyrdom in the greatest attack ever on America.

The young people sat quietly and stoically, realizing their rendezvous with Allah was less than fifty hours away. Travel from San Francisco, New York, Miami, and Chicago to Los Angeles for this meeting with Siddiqui represented yet another form of obeisance to the man whose inspiration had convinced them to remain on their path to ecstasy in Paradise.

They would spend two final hours with the imam, then return on red-eye flights through the night. They needed to prepare themselves for the following night on Christmas Eve, when they would commit mass murders of thousands of Americans all on the same day . . . even at the same minute. America would never recover!

Siddiqui had planned this last-minute gathering to be timely and unrelenting. He would stoke the passions of his followers to the point that they would not even have time to think of turning back. They would leave the mosque in a frenzy of commitment. That heroic purpose would abide with them throughout the night and the next day. The Ten would totally be involved in saying their last prayers, reviewing their routes and fitting the harnesses to their bodies. They would be in a virtual trance, without even the slightest thought of backing out. Their parents would say good-bye to their children and would board airplanes with tickets for the entire family, but there would be two empty seats next to them . . . all to avoid suspicion. These young people would be the last to be suspected of the horrendous havoc they were about to bring to pass.

All present were quietly reverent as Siddiqui took to the podium.

Looking slowly into the eyes of each of the young people and their parents, and smiling profusely, Siddiqui started his speech, gesticulating wildly and emphatically whenever he wanted to emphasize a point.

"This is a time of celebration, my young friends! On July 4, the American day of celebrating its independence, two of us, Ghani and Kareema Hussain, successfully struck at the heart of this blasphemous nation at a mall in Omaha, Nebraska. Hundreds of the souls of the infidels were turned to ashes. Praise Allah!"

"Praise Allah!" came the retort in unison. The enthusiasm and fervor from those who would follow the Hussains' footsteps was obvious.

"From a very young age," Siddiqui continued. "Ghani and Kareema, with their parents, prepared well to offer their sacrifice in blood and spirit, as all of you are also about to do."

Heads were nodding in affirmation.

"Our holy Koran speaks specifically of those who will soon be in your hand. Permit me to quote the nineteenth verse from the eleventh Sura:

> They are they for whom there is nothing
> in the next world but the Fire: all that they
> have wrought in this life shall come up
> naught, and vain shall be all their doings.

"At this moment in time, 7:00 p.m. in the city of Los Angeles, California, in the infidel land of America, I am witnessing the courageous faces of a group of young heroes, who we in the clergy proudly refer to as 'The Ten.' Ten young martyrs, who through their training and their dedication to Allah, have volunteered their mortal futures; yes, even their earthly lives, to take on a much higher purpose.

"I honor them. I honor their parents. You have chosen the higher road . . . the eternal course. Through your love of Allah and your personal sacrifice, you will soon be in Paradise, feasting on the rewards of the martyr . . . the bounties of Eternity. I promise you that your greatest expectations will be fulfilled."

Siddiqui went on and on, postulating on the rewards of killing oneself in a greater cause. Those attending became enraptured in a state of mind that seemed almost hypnotic. Their eyes turned a little glossy as they began whispering affirmations in agreement with the spirit the imam was bringing upon them. This lasted for close to an hour.

Delisha noticed that her brother had fallen into this state of semi-hypnosis. She could not feel the same. She knew she never would. Nevertheless, this was the first time she had seen her young peers become this enchanted with the words of Siddiqui.

The imam continued. "The infidels will always underestimate your commitment and your motivation. They would have the world believe that all you are is a cluster of misled, misfit fanatics . . ."

There was a response in unison from the congregants. "No . . . No . . . No!" that became louder as the imam continued.

" . . . losers in every sense of the word: emotionally disturbed, poorly-educated young men and women who can't fit in anywhere, so you, as fanatics, sacrifice yourselves just to make a statement to measure your own relevance."

"Dogs!" came a response from a young woman. "Imperialistic dogs!"

A trancelike repetition followed almost in hypnotic unison. "Imperialistic dogs!"

Delisha was becoming more unnerved by all this as she observed Lufti in the same state as the others, repeating the same words.

"The people of this country pollute your reputations and impugn your character and dignity," Siddiqui said. "They allege that your passion eclipses your ability to think for yourselves. They say that you will always obey blindly without reasoning and will always follow ignorantly like sheep.

"They have referred to the sacrifices of your brother and sister, Kareema and Ghani Hussain, as the work of young hoodlums obsessed by a pseudo-religious fantasy of a killer's self-motivated martyrdom leading to Paradise. They scoff at you and demean you."

Then it happened.

A quiet chant emanated from a young man on the second row. "Kill the American dogs! Kill them all!" The rest of the group, now appearing to Delisha to have entered almost completely in a trance, joined in with the person that initiated it. Delisha had never seen The Ten like this. It was obvious to her that Siddiqui had saved the strongest poison for the last. She was nauseated by what was going on around her and felt a terrible spirit in the room.

"They call you baby killers who prey on the innocent. They are completely blinded to your higher purpose. They disrespect you and deplore you."

Siddiqui wasn't holding anything back, knowing he had The Ten right where he wanted them. He finished with one last refrain, which he knew would easily carry over to the growing bloodthirsty chant.

"For this, they must die!"

The chant erupted anew. "They must die! They must die!"

Suddenly, a new voice broke the silence.

"I have just one question, Master Siddiqui."

It was Delisha, who was seated on the front row between Lufti and her father. She stood to address Siddiqui. Eyebrows everywhere turned up as the young people and their parents focused on this irreverent young woman who dared interrupt the holy man.

"I just wanted to ask you regarding a *fatwa* issued recently by the supreme religious leaders of Saudi Arabia, some of our fellow

Muslims. Sheik Abdul Aziz bin Abdullah al Sheik issued it. In his edict, he advised suicide bombing was the same as suicide, which he said was not allowed in Islam. I am confused by this."

The trance interrupted, eyes were scornfully cast toward this young woman. The hypnotic influence in the room diminished as Delisha waited for a response.

Lufti was mortified and just stared at his sister incredulously. Surely her naiveté in asking such a question would draw unwelcome suspicion to her commitment and toward him and their parents. Delisha's father wanted to get his belt out right there and then and whip her. The frustration he felt knowing he could not do that in public was drowning him.

Siddiqui frowned disdainfully at Delisha but knew he had to answer her question. He certainly could not allow anyone to challenge his authority or the veracity of his rhetoric, much less this young woman who should know better than to pose such a question . . . especially at this important juncture. He had to answer, and answer well, to preserve his posture before the group. Their concept of the glorious mission ahead of them must not be compromised in any way, and not by Delisha's outburst.

Siddiqui's voice was stern and impassioned.

"Delisha, you of all people should know the answer. If you have studied in detail, you will recall it was Mohammed Sayed Tantaivi, a leading doctrinal authority in the Sunni Muslim world, who wrote that if a person blows himself up in a righteous cause, then he or she is truly a martyr. Another noted cleric, Sheik Yousif, stated that bombings are not suicide operations, but heroic martyrdom operations, and the heroes who carry them out are driven by an overwhelming desire to cast terror and fear into the hearts of the infidels . . . and that, Delisha, is a good thing. Any more questions?" Siddiqui was sure he had ended the debate.

But for Delisha, the debate had not ended. She continued, catching Siddiqui off guard.

"The Koran states:

And do not kill yourself, for God
is indeed merciful to you.

There is also a statement from the prophet Mohammed, who forbade suicide and decreed:

He who drinks poison and kills himself will
carry his poison in his hand and drink it in
Hell forever and ever."

The imam scowled at her again, eyebrows raised. He was not to be out-done by this upstart young woman, to whom he directed his remarks. "Delisha, according to the Koran, martyrs in the cause of Allah slain in his holy cause are alive in the presence of God and are granted gifts from Him. Also, for your information, pertaining to your own individual position as a female martyr, in 2001 the High Islamic Council in Saudi Arabia also issued a decree encouraging Palestinian women to become suicide bombers. The Koran states that *jihad* or holy war, can be accomplished by women as well as men."

Again, Siddiqui was sure that he had won. Delisha seemed to have nothing else left to say.

Siddiqui continued with great pride. Again, he directed his remarks to his entire following, turning away from Delisha, trying to make her appear irrelevant.

"Remember. You are not puppets, pressed into service against your will, nor are you products of unquestioned obedience. The truth is that each of you will become martyrs in the high and holy cause of spreading Islam throughout the world with your sacrifice. You will transform the public gathering areas of the infidel dogs into boiling cauldrons of terror!"

Delisha noted that the hypnotic feeling of trance—a stupor of altered sensitivity—was returning. Heads began to nod again in affirmation as Siddiqui continued.

"Never before have the youth of Islam taken on such a monumental challenge. Then again, never before have youth of your caliber been trained up for such an exalted mission. The beautiful sisters among you will add a new and amazing dimension to this mission by helping to provide the element of surprise. It has always been the young men up to now who have drawn suspicion to impending attacks. Women are always more revered and less suspicious. The American security officials will be prone to more easily ignore you as you enter your targets when you are with these fine sisters. There will be much less scrutiny.

"In closing, I would quote the Koran from the eighth Sura, 'The Spoils':

> *Twenty of you who stand firm shall vanquish*
> *two hundred: and if there be an hundred of you*
> *they shall vanquish a thousand of the infidels,*
> *They are a people void of understanding.*

"This is surely the most effective way ever devised to seek revenge against our enemy. All that is needed is a bomb to detonate and the courage to do it. Success is assured. It is inevitable."

Easy for you to say! thought Delisha, who was increasingly more convinced she should not allow Siddiqui to lead her to her death.

"So, my fine brothers and sisters, you are on your way to the greatest of days . . . the magnificence of eternity and the joys of Paradise. In carrying out this *jihad,* this war against the unbelievers, the enemies of Islam, in fulfilling your religious duty, your blessings will be innumerable.

"My friends, we will be successful. The Christmas Eve attack will make the Americans forget about September 11, 2001. Praise Allah!"

Siddiqui raised his arms to the group, gesturing for them to join in as he repeated the words, "Praise Allah!"

Applause broke out within the mosque as a rejoining chant of "Praise Allah!" filled the mosque. The young people pushed forward to hug the holy man and kiss his hand.

Some approached Lufti and asked, "What's wrong with your sister? Is she becoming crazy? Is she backing out?"

"No!" Lufti responded unconvincingly. "No. She's just always needing reassurances. Tonight she got those from the holy man."

Delisha knew what was waiting for her if she stayed to speak to Siddiqui. She knew that she would hear from him and possibly others in the Muslim clergy. She exited immediately without saying a word to the other young people there, feeling totally isolated. She just wanted to vanish immediately. Instead she waited for Lufti and her parents to take a taxi to the airport for their flight to Florida. As Lufti and her parents excoriated her all the way to the airport, she said nothing.

Rashid Siddiqui was consumed with anger.

CHAPTER 32
THE DEMISE AT NASSAU

NASSAU, GRAND BAHAMA ISLAND
DECEMBER 24

NASSAU IN DECEMBER WAS beyond wonderful. Agents Fredette and Duffin were still on the trail of Abu Khan. Their informant's call—indicating Khan had left Labadee, Haiti, and was in the vicinity of the Atlantis Hotel on Paradise Island, possibly renting a room there—was the best news the agents had received in weeks of prolonged searching.

The pre-Christmas crowds in Nassau were streaming through quaint gift shops, stocking up on gifts from Santa. From the pier, one half mile walking distance to the "Festival Place," was the first of the shopping areas. Looking south was the Paradise Island Bridge, a long bridge crossing over onto the island containing the Atlantis Hotel. As the agents led a convoy of a dozen Bahamian police officers over the bridge, the hotel came into view, with its pink-and-green-trimmed windows. The island could only be reached by ferry, a long walk, or a short car ride.

Upon arriving at the Atlantis, the agents noticed pink pastel-colored government buildings on both sides of Bay Street, which was lined with discount clothing stores and various other storefront businesses. Small boats for passenger use were seen throughout the area.

Fredette and Duffin entered the Atlantis, one of the world's most exclusive hotels. Everything spelled "money." Plush

European-style shops graced both sides of the long corridor with marble floors, including the John Bull jewelry store, the Havana Humido tobacco shop, the Faconable men's clothing, and the Cartier jewelry outlet. The agents entered the hotel through the exit leading to the marina called "Mariner Village." It was on the Coral and Beach Towers side. They then continued, proceeding through the entrance to the casino, and on to the "Royal Tower," where Michael Jackson had rented a suite for $25,000 a night while he performed for several days.

Duffin was particularly impressed by a spectacular glass fountain located just in front of the rest rooms. It was approximately fifteen feet high and eight feet wide with spears of thin glass sprouting in every direction. As he entered the men's room, he observed that not a hint of elegance was lost. The marble floor sparkled, and flower bouquets separated the wash basins. He noticed that even the urinals were cased in rich-looking white and tan marble. These were highlighted by a green leaf planter mounted on a white sculptured base.

"This is almost worthy of me!" he commented to Fredette.

The agents next proceeded through the casino, which was much like those in the Las Vegas' Venetian Hotel or MGM Hotel mode. The gaming tables were lined with tourists who appeared more than ready to give up their spare change to the house's superior odds. The tables and machines were like magnets. A magnificent blue and white crystal sphere comprised of large plates that was melted into a multitude of exotic patterns—gorgeous beyond description—was mounted directly over the ticket counter.

The blackjack tables in front of the elite "Nohu Club" were humming with "takers" with unrealistic expectations.

The agents kept walking, past the golden horned bulls statues in front of the entrance to the Royal Tower. Black women hugged the horns and hooves while their friends were snapping photos. Another woman was having her picture taken on Atlantis's throne of gold. The agents proceeded through the corridor to the lobby, where there were more elegant jewelry and clothing stores, including Solomon's Mine and Le Coultre.

Fredette inquired at the Royal Tower desk and confirmed

that Abu Khan had not registered there, although he knew Khan wouldn't have thought twice about paying the obligatory thousand dollars a night rent.

One floor down, the agents observed the Aquarium Wall. The wall was twelve feet high and encircled the bottom floor of the hotel. Among the fifty thousand fish were sting rays, angel fish, grouper, gray snapper, pork fish, bonefish, and yellowtail. The water came from the ocean: sixty-three million gallons of ocean water pumped through four times a day during high tides. Walls of what appeared to be glass running half way around the lower floor for observers to view the fish were really six inches of acrylic that could easily stop a bullet.

Suddenly, Fredette caught side of Khan approximately one hundred and twenty-five feet away from the two agents. He had been playing the "Ten Times Gold" dollar slot machine located in front of the Atlas Grill & Bar. Khan walked away from them without taking note of the agents' presence. Finally he stopped and stood in an enclosed circle with a sundial formation. Twelve blades emanated out from the center between two plants supporting potted foliage. Smoking and leaning over the railing, he looked east over a rectangular, descending pool of clear water leading into a display of green flying fish, then out toward the open sea.

The agents closed in. Khan spotted them and jumped over a fence in front of the Royal Tower desk onto the aquarium ground floor near a pool of water. As Fredette and Duffin approached him, Khan hurdled the four-foot-high black ornate fence. The Bahamian police tried to surround him from the other side, opposite the agents. Khan took notice of the two FBI agents rapidly descending the staircase behind him that was twenty-five feet to his right.

Khan fired two shots into the aquarium wall, hoping to create a diversion and aiding his escape, but it was to no avail. The rounds barely embedded in the acrylic surface. He stopped, displayed a round device to the police, and swore it was a grenade. Upon recognizing it was actually a hand grenade and that Khan had pulled the pin and had his finger on the depressor, the local police backed away a little but refused to leave him alone.

Khan exited the hotel, desperately heading for his Mercedes parked fifty feet away. But in his excitement, he tripped on the curb in front of the hotel entrance and dropped the grenade.

When the cloud and dust from the blast cleared, very little of the fleeing man remained on the pavement.

CHAPTER 33
THE EVENT

PLANTATION, FLORIDA
DECEMBER 24

DELISHA WAS OVERPOWERED EMOTIONALLY. She felt as though her heart would rupture. It was 4:50 p.m. The planned bombing was to occur in just over two hours. She felt totally alone. She knew she could go ahead, die, and end it all. Then at last her anxiety would be squelched. But again she thought, *What of the innocents I would kill while fulfilling the demands of Allah—a god that I now question? What if I were to find that I have murdered and have to suffer the punishment of a just Christian god? What if I die for no good reason and find my sins in the Christian afterlife to be unpardonable?* She knew she could not possibly go through with the assault. How could she tell Lufti? Or, of even more importance, how could she stop him?

Two men had just delivered the explosive harnesses for her and Lufti. Lufti was outside in the front yard, saying good-bye to the bald-headed men in the pickup with Idaho license plates. Lufti had anticipated them, so when they rang the doorbell, he met them at the door, invited them in briefly to deliver the box of explosive-laden harnesses, and then advised them they should leave immediately to avoid suspicion. The men didn't want to stay. Once they had handed over the box of harnesses in the brown cardboard box, they were anxious to leave.

Delisha noticed that as the two men were visiting with Lufti, they nervously glanced around the neighborhood, checking out every car being driven down the street.

Within just a few minutes, Delisha heard the car drive away and Lufti re-enter the house. He was heading to his room where he was intent on readying himself for his last trip to the mall.

When Lufti had given Delisha her harness, he said nothing but could sense that his sister was nervous.

"Don't worry, sister!" Lufti exclaimed. "In just a couple more hours, we will have achieved our life's purpose."

"Yes, Lufti. I know," answered Delisha. "I know. I'm all right." She took her harness and closed her door as Lufti returned to his room.

How could they have done it so matter-of-factly? Delisha asked herself, recalling how her parents had departed at 8:00 a.m. that morning to board an 11:45 a.m. flight to Islamabad. They left with four tickets, including passage for Lufti and Delisha. It was all a guise to throw off investigators or nosy acquaintances who might equate their children with the destruction that would occur later that night.

Delisha was hurt by the brief hug and fleeting smile from her mother, who didn't utter a word before leaving. Her father was just as non-communicative, just waving at her and Lufti and departing quickly. *Of course,* she assured herself, *this has to be so hard for them . . . losing their own flesh and blood in this way. They had to leave quickly to keep from breaking down. That has to be why!* Delisha struggled to ensure herself of that.

Again Delisha questioned why a wise and just God would want, or allow, all of this to happen. Killing innocent people? Sacrificing one's own children? Living a life of deceit?

The phone rang. At this point, both Lufti and Delisha were reluctant to answer it, but Delisha's curiosity was overwhelming. She picked up the phone. "Yes?"

It was Rashid Siddiqui.

What's wrong? Delisha asked herself. *Why is he calling here? Someone has warned him that I have misgivings! Lufti?* Delisha's stomach did somersaults.

"My child, Delisha," Siddiqui spoke condescendingly, trying to gush pleasure at having contacted his devotees prior to the big event. "I am near. May I visit with you and Lufti for just a few minutes? One more time?"

Delisha had absolutely no idea why Siddiqui would come to Florida just to see her *and* Lufti. She was the only one who had questioned him or the al-Qaeda's motives at the Los Angeles gathering the day before.

"Yes, Rashid. Lufti and I are both here. We'll await your arrival."

"At 5:30 then," came the response. "I'll see you then."

"All right" answered Delisha. "We'll be here." She hung up the phone, as a chill spread through her.

"Lufti . . . come! Come fast!" she yelled.

Lufti ran into the living room from his bedroom, located on the other side of the spacious, three-bedroom house. Upon seeing Delisha, he took instant note of her pallid expression. He had all ready put on his explosive harness and wore a loosely-fitting, extra large guayabera over it.

"What do you think, sister? Does it fit well?'

"Fine, Lufti . . . fine." Delisha felt unwanted emotion rise in her again as she stared at the death and destruction hanging from her brother's shoulders.

"Lufti . . . listen. He's coming here." Delisha's countenance broadcast the turmoil within her.

"Who, sister? Who's coming?"

"Rashid . . . the imam, in a half hour. Why, Lufti? Why is he coming here? Did you say something to him about me . . . that I wasn't committed? He must be upset with me, brother, and you know what that could mean!"

"I've said nothing to anyone, Delisha. Not one time, ever," Lufti said.

Delisha looked closely into her brother's handsome brown eyes. They were sincere, truthful. He seemed so hurt that she would accuse him of betraying her.

"I'm sorry, brother! Forgive me. I'm so confused right now. So conflicted. And I have no idea why the imam is coming here, especially when he must know you and I would be preparing now. I'm afraid of him, Lufti."

As Lufti looked pensively into his sister's countenance, he sensed genuine trepidation. He searched within himself for a way to comfort her. He was at a loss for words as he took her hand, trying to absorb some of her burden.

"Remember the kites, sister?" he asked Delisha.

Suddenly, Delisha's expression changed as a smile began forming around her lips.

"Oh, yes, brother. Yes. I could always cut your lines first," she answered.

The two reflected back simultaneously upon the heartwarming visits to Islamabad as youths when they, along with their cousins, would compete with one another in the famous Pakistani tradition of kite flying, where all the participants would endeavor to cut the other's kite strings once the high-sailing homemade contraptions achieved a certain height.

"You had no mercy on me and your cousins, sister! You should be forever ashamed." Lufti's smile was contagious. Delisha joined in with one of her own. *He has been such a good brother,* she thought, *always so supportive of me and always offering a listening ear.*

Delisha squeezed Lufti's hand. "I love you, brother!"

"And I you, sister."

The kite-flying recollection was the catalyst to opening a box of sweet childhood memories for Delisha and Lufti that for far too long had been obscured . . . drowned in a boiling cauldron of poison foisted upon them by Siddiqui and the other imams. Delisha suspected she and Lufti had been deprived of their agency by being embroiled in that cauldron. Her heart went out to Lufti, knowing that he would probably never believe he also had been duped. She knew she could not convince him of that.

Other fond memories were recalled as the siblings passed them back and forth from one to another, sometimes laughing . . . sometimes shedding a tear. They discussed Lufti's track meets and basketball games that Delisha had followed so closely . . . so proud that she had a brother possessing such athletic prowess. She had been Lufti's most loyal fan and follower, as he dribbled down basketball courts and sprinted to the finish in track.

Lufti grasped his sister's hand a little tighter, recalling her loyalty to him. She had always been there for him, even as his parents shied away from social settings and the public arena, where they felt they would be brought into too much contact with people they had no real interest in fostering social relationships with.

Suddenly, a light came on. *My parents! They told Siddiqui!* Delisha remembered her father's blunt accusations regarding her interest in her friend, Madi Southerland. He had always been particularly nervous about the fact that Madi's father was a special agent with the FBI. He would get upset about Delisha attending too many church activities with Madi and would badger her frequently about questioning her roots in Islam methodology. He was personally offended that his own daughter had questioned the imam Rashid Siddiqui.

Delisha was aware that both her parents had withdrawn from her in recent weeks, after she made a couple of comments that questioned her commitments to her pending martyrdom. More comments had been made by both parents regarding the need to "bring honor to the family and the ancestors" and to not "blacken their name."

The doorbell rang. Lufti opened the door, and Siddiqui entered, followed by two sinister-appearing men of mid-eastern descent, wearing stern expressions. All three men were clad in typical American attire: dressy shirts, open at the top, with nice slacks and sport jackets.

Lufti immediately took notice of the shoulder holsters that Siddiqui's associates were wearing, which protruded from underneath their jackets.

Lufti invited the three men to sit down in the living room. He and Delisha sat on a couch across from the sofa where their visitors were seated.

Siddiqui spoke first. "What a lovely location!" he said, sweeping his hand toward the window behind Lufti and Delisha. He pointed at a huge, open field of pasture of approximately two acres, bordered by a small orange grove. The Ahmed home was the last house on the street, perched on the edge of the orchard land, neatly contained within a sprawling urban development.

Siddiqui continued. "You've been furnished a beautiful home

here . . . nice furnishings, air-conditioned, near some excellent fruit orchards. But let's talk more about you two, both so close to your meeting with Allah. Are you doing all right?"

By the condescending tone in his voice and his intimidating demeanor, both Delisha and Lufti had received the same impression. Siddiqui was not here to comfort them. He was probing. But why?

Lufti asked with a slightly suspicious tone in his voice, "Rashid, with all that is happening throughout the country on the night of the event, why have you come here?"

Siddiqui knew they knew something wasn't right. The two men accompanying him stiffened at Lufti's briskness and were put on full alert.

"Bashir Sayed and I have coordinated the attacks with all of The Ten during the last three days," Siddiqui answered. "I have been to San Francisco, Chicago, New York, and finally here . . . just to make sure that there is no faltering . . . if you know what I mean?" He looked directly at Delisha.

"We need to know that after so many years of preparation and expense, that everything goes exactly as planned. We need to be here to ensure that you have everything you need. You have received your harnesses, I presume?" Siddiqui asked, already knowing the answer.

Lufti unbuttoned the two top buttons on his guayabera, revealing the harness underneath. "Yes. The two men from Idaho brought them just a short while ago, as you must already know. We both have them."

Delisha and Lufti both found it difficult to believe that Siddiqui and Sayed would actually be visiting each of The Ten in person just before the event, rather than calling them, especially with all that the brothers and sisters had to prepare for before their attacks. They both knew something was not right about this visit.

The armed men with Siddiqui added to Lufti's suspicion regarding their motives. *Do they have something planned for Delisha?* he asked himself.

Siddiqui looked at his watch, realizing that what he had come to do, he had to do now. He looked directly into Delisha's eyes with an icy stare, as if he was daring her to not tell the truth.

"Delisha, your parents called me yesterday morning with some very disturbing news. They indicated they weren't sure if you were prepared to carry out your mission."

Delisha's stomach muscles tightened. She fought back the need to throw up, as a cold chill emanated from her ears into her stomach, then throughout her entire body. Upon hearing that her own parents had betrayed her to the al-Qaeda, her heart felt as though it would split in two. She felt the impulse to run. *But how? To where?* she asked herself.

Siddiqui's words also sank into Lufti's conscience like searing nails. *My mother and father did this to Delisha?* Lufti thought. *To my sister . . . their own daughter? How could they? She's their own flesh and blood.*

"Yes, my child," Siddiqui continued, staring at Delisha. You have been given all this." Again he signaled from one side to the other throughout the house and the surrounding landscape. "You have had wonderful food and nice clothing all your life, much finer things than what are in Islamabad. You have your own car to drive. You have been afforded every consideration in obtaining fine schooling and a wonderful college education. You have even been able to make many of your own decisions."

Delisha was nauseated by Siddiqui's remarks. *Oh yes, and all I have to do to pay you back is blow myself up!* She knew she couldn't listen to much more of this. She looked at Lufti. For the first time ever, she could tell by his expression that he had also had it with the imam.

Siddiqui's rant continued. "The al-Qaeda, your brethren, have paid for all this. They have flown you back to Pakistan often for special training to prepare and educate you for your meeting with Allah. They have withheld nothing from you . . . and now, after all this, you are considering abandoning their trust? Deserting the cause of Islam? Running out on your sacred commitments?" Finally, Siddiqui became silent, awaiting Delisha's response.

Lufti's anger was mounting. Now he understood why Siddiqui had come with the armed men. He also felt betrayed by their parents and understood why they both had cowered away so quickly . . . so shamefully.

Lufti studied the expressions of fear and intimidation in his sister's face and noticed her trembling, following Siddiqui's accusations and badgering.

Delisha slowly composed herself and prepared to respond to Siddiqui. Lufti was surprised by the sudden change in his sister's demeanor. There was a conviction and certainty there that he had not seen previously. The color returned to her face, and her eyes became steely and determined. She arose and walked across the room to where Siddiqui was seated, stopped within a few feet of him, and asked, "Do you really believe that by browbeating me because I am a woman that you can win my obedience and my respect? Do you think that the money your al-Qaeda associates, who you call 'my brethren,' have spent in my behalf for this home, our food, our education, and our cars, plus whatever else you have expended could possibly equal the value of my life? Of Lufti's life? Or for that matter the lives of any one of The Ten? You want me to feel guilty because I have questioned the purpose of my death, because I have been paid so handsomely for giving up my life for you and the others, don't you?"

"Delisha . . . stop this! Say no more." Lufti walked over to his sister and said, "It's okay, sister. You've said enough!" Lufti knew Siddiqui would never tolerate this kind of rebellion.

"No, Lufti! Let me finish!" Delisha turned back to Siddiqui.

"No, Rashid. I'm not comfortable any longer with what you want us to do. We, The Ten, have been raised to further your purposes, your political goals, goals that you have disguised as the objectives of Islam. I read the Koran differently than you. I ask you again. Does my life have no more value than this . . . as you see it?

"And what of all the lives of those you would have us annihilate before this day is over?" Delisha continued. "We are no more to you than fattened lambs, sacrificial lambs, doing the bidding of you and your radical counterparts in the al-Qaeda organizations, walking like dumb animals into the jaws of a flaming hell. This is all about you, isn't it? You and your jihadists, right? It's all about you wanting to flex your muscles by shedding the blood of people that don't believe the same as you—people that don't agree with you on every issue. You can't stand the thought of someone not having your own convictions, can you?"

Lufti knew that Delisha was out of control and that somehow Siddiqui would exact a price for her outbursts. Lufti also knew that Delisha was unaware that the two men were armed.

Siddiqui's voice cracked. "You have decided to side with the infidel dogs with whom you have been associating all too much, Delisha! Haven't you, you ungrateful woman? And here I have always looked up to you for your dedication to Islam's destiny, for your education, and for your leadership and example among The Ten.

"Your kind of rebellion and lack of gratitude is foreseen in the holy writings of Muhammed, who states in the eighth Sura:

> *The worst beasts truly in the sight of God*
> *are the thankless who will not believe.*

"He is speaking of you, Delisha!" Siddiqui shouted.

Delisha was prepared for Siddiqui's hypocrisy. She walked across the room to the end table where she kept her Koran. She pulled it out, turning to the twenty-eighth verse of the tenth Sura, brought it back, and faced Siddiqui. She spoke. "My great regret, sir, is that it has taken me this long to discover who you really are. You and your destiny are described in this verse:

> *And as for those who have wrought out evil*
> *their recompense shall be evil of like degree*
> *and shame shall cover them—no protector*
> *shall they have against God: as though their*
> *faces were darkened with deep murk of night!*
> *These shall be inmates of the Fire: therein they*
> *shall abide forever.*"

Lufti was on high alert, knowing his sister had now crossed over into deep waters, with the bridge collapsing behind her. He knew he would have to defend her. His mind raced to figure out how that would be possible.

The imam was red in the face. "You have, indeed, betrayed us! But hear me well. You will never be permitted to betray Lufti and his mission here in Florida. He will go ahead."

Siddiqui looked quickly at Lufti and suddenly realized that Lufti was no longer in agreement with him. Then he looked over again at Delisha and demanded, "You will come with us!" He motioned to one of his men to help him restrain her.

"Lufti," Siddiqui said, "my other friend here will stay with you and will accompany you to the mall and will help you anyway he can."

As Lufti witnessed Siddiqui and the other man dragging his sister to the door, he knew that Siddiqui was leaving the other man behind to make sure he followed through with his self-sacrifice. That meant that the gift of his body to Allah would now be enforced, not voluntary. To Lufti, this changed everything about his life's purpose—an adulteration of his final act on earth. He was also keenly aware that once Delisha was taken from his presence, he would never see her again. He knew she would most likely be strangled in retribution for her rebellion. He had heard of other instances where people had defected from al-Qaeda initiatives and had suffered such retribution.

Lufti had to do something quickly.

But it was too late!

Delisha succeeded in shaking off Siddiqui's and the other man's grasps. She escaped through the front door out into the open field, running toward the orange grove. Lufti was stunned as he observed Siddiqui—the holy man, the imam—draw a weapon from beneath his jacket and join his armed accomplice, leveling semi-automatic pistols at his sister.

Delisha had a head start, and she was fast and gaining ground quickly. The third man stayed back, watching Lufti closely. The man was confident Lufti would not intervene for Delisha. After all, all of The Ten had been instructed that death would be the sure penalty for backing out on their commitments for martyrdom, once they had chosen that path. The man was sure that Lufti understood that.

But Lufti didn't.

Summoning all the strength and quickness he had acquired from years of competitive sports, he broke past his guard and hurled himself into Siddiqui and the other man. Both men misfired their weapons as they fell to the ground. Lufti was on top of them, pressing the two men down heavily with the added weight of the explosive harness hanging from his shoulders.

Meanwhile, Delisha gained more ground toward the safety of the orange grove.

That was when the man who had been guarding Lufti approached from behind and put Lufti in a choke hold, depressing the carotid artery so that the blood supply to his brain was restricted.

By now, Delisha was almost fifty yards away, sprinting for the cover of the fruit orchard. But she turned back to look and saw that Siddiqui and one man rising from the ground with guns leveled at her. The other man was choking her brother. She suddenly stopped.

"Lufti! Brother!"

At that moment, she felt the sensation of hot lead entering her body. She looked up at the sky, then felt her legs buckle under her as the ground flew up to meet her with a resounding thud. Then she saw a couple more bright flashes from the guns pointed at her.

For Delisha, everything became dark . . . frozen.

As Lufti struggled with the man who had him by the neck, he felt the sensation of blacking out. He watched his sister fall to the ground, following three gun blasts.

His fingers tightened around the cord attached to his explosive harness. His grip stiffened, pulling the string straight down.

The blast engulfed the Ahmed's residence, creating a huge crater where half of it had formerly stood, a crater that extended outward another twenty-five feet. The three cars parked in the driveway were transformed into bits and pieces.

Although Lufti had disintegrated, along with Siddiqui and the two men accompanying him, Delisha was lying unconscious fifty feet past the crater's imprint and still breathing.

Within minutes, police sirens blared throughout the Ahmed's neighborhood as its residents walked from their homes, astonished, to stare at the devastation at the end of the block. Fortunately, the Ahmed's next-door neighbors had left for the Christmas holidays. Their home was also partly destroyed by the impact of the explosives. Most of the homes on the block now had shattered windows.

Among the first cars to arrive, along with the police and ambulance, was Ridge Southerland, one arm in a cast and sling. His daughter, Madi, was driving.

An hour before, Madi had received a strange call from Delisha, advising her that she had not yet left for Islamabad, that the flights had been delayed. She also said that she had just noticed a copy of the "Plantation Ward Bulletin," containing the church announcements for that week, which indicated the ward choir was scheduled to sing Christmas carols that night in the food court of the Sawgrass Mills Mall—the same place Delisha knew Lufti would deploy his bombs. She had insisted frantically that Madi and her family stay away from the mall that night.

As Delisha attempted to extract a promise from Madi that she and her family would not go near the mall that night, Madi was convinced something was terribly wrong with Delisha. Immediately after hanging up the phone, she notified her father, who was filling out some reports at the Plantation Resident Agency of the FBI's Miami Division, while convalescing. He was putting in a few hours there while still on limited duty, writing a report covering his recollection of the events leading up to the demise of Buck Bowen. He had just finished the report on Ike Grimsley's apprehension and subsequent interview.

Ike Grimsley had survived Bowen's attack. Both of Bowen's bullets had been successfully removed. Grimsley would be ready to be tried in a couple of months. He had cooperated with the authorities and was sure to receive a reduced sentence for having provided information that would save thousands from death.

The phone rang once, and Agent Southerland had picked it up. He heard Madi's account of what Delisha had told her, specifically the warning that she and her family should not go near the

Sawgrass Mills Mall. Based upon Ridge's earlier suspicions that the Sawgrass Mills mall would be the target, it and a few other major shopping areas in South Florida had already been evacuated.

Ridge had his daughter come directly to the Plantation office to pick him up. Then he had immediately notified the Miami headquarters office; the local authorities in the Plantation/Sunrise area; and his supervisor, Denny Campo, at FBI headquarters that a planned assault on the Sawgrass Mills Mall had been confirmed. When Madi arrived fifteen minutes later, they instantly drove to the Ahmed residence and gasped when they saw the devastation. Upon seeing her friend lying in the field between the Ahmed house and the orange grove, being treated by paramedics, Madi broke into tears and ran toward her, with her father just steps behind. The medics were preparing Delisha to be put on a gurney for transportation to a waiting ambulance. Ridge and Madi got clearance to approach Delisha, once Ridge identified himself.

Madi ran her hand over Delisha's forehead, clearing off the sweat and grime, looking into her eyes. She saw some faint recognition. Delisha tried to muster up a little smile for her friends. Madi kissed her forehead tenderly. With the little strength she had, Delisha pulled Madi down to her and asked, "Lufti's gone, isn't he, Madi? Lufti's dead?"

Ridge had apprised Madi that witnesses had observed Lufti struggling with three men, apparently trying to prevent them from shooting at Delisha. They had seen him pull something dangling from his shirt that presumably detonated a massive explosion.

Madi nodded affirmatively to Delisha. "Yes, Delisha. Lufti's gone. He did all he could to save your life. He was a wonderful brother!"

Delisha's expression didn't change. She had prepared herself for the worst. As she was loaded onto a gurney and placed in the ambulance, she became motionless. Her eyes half closed. She looked up one more time at Madi and her father and spoke a few more words that were labored, yet deliberate.

"I'd always wanted to be a martyr. So did Lufti. Maybe now, finally, we will be . . . but for a righteous cause."

As Delisha's eyes closed, she was completely still. Her clenched right fist opened slightly, and a bright metal object rolled out onto the floor of the ambulance. Madi quickly picked it up. As she looked at it, she paused briefly, then showing it to her father, she broke into sobs.

It was Delisha's Young Womanhood Recognition medallion.

CHAPTER 34
TAKING THE LIMELIGHT

WASHINGTON, DC
DECEMBER 26

THE POST-CHRISTMAS PRESS CONFERENCE was attended by Chief of Staff Gifford Pipps, FBI Director Clarence Hagen, Press Secretary Jim Murray, and the vice president of the United States.

Pipps presented a brief rundown on the purpose of the conference, which was to announce the successful, coordinated arrests of eight individuals, suicide bombers that had attempted to slaughter thousands of US citizens.

Every major news outlet in the Washington, DC, area was present for what was sure to be the announcement of the most significant law enforcement coup in the history of America.

Director Hagen was first. He presented an abbreviated, concise report on the arrest of eight subjects without incident. In addition to those arrests, he announced the detention of ten additional subjects, anti-American extremists from the northwest part of the United States, who had transported explosives throughout the country to the suicide bombers. The director kept his release very short, taking no personal credit for the Bureau's success, then sat down without taking questions.

Next was the PR guy—Jim Murray. He had been prompted and prepared by Pipps. Murray gave a succinct, unexaggerated account of the monumental risks taken by FBI agents in corralling the suicide bombers, along with the people transporting explosives, before they could strike and harm American citizens. Wanting to please both the FBI and his boss, the US president, he emphasized the continuous planning and implementation of new and unique policies that reflected investigative techniques encouraged and endorsed by the president himself.

Supervisory Special Agent Denny Campo, who was watching the conference from a television in FBI Headquarters on Pennsylvania Avenue, cringed when he heard Murray's remarks, recalling the tribulations the administration had put him through as he had tried to implement the A Team concept.

Jim Murray was just getting wound up, but Pipps had allowed him only five minutes after which the vice president—subbing for the president, who was on a humanitarian mission in Africa—was to have the majority of the time.

"Ladies and gentlemen," Murray announced pompously, "the vice president of the United States."

The vice president strode briskly to the podium, raised an arm of welcome to his listeners, and began his remarks.

"Members of the press and news media, ladies and gentlemen, this is a great day in America. It's with the utmost pride that I approach this podium today. Never has there been a moment when I have felt so honored to be a part of this administration. Even from the very day he was elected, our president has focused on innovative, creative, and highly proactive programs for law enforcement. Through his leadership and under the guidance and direction of numerous members of this administration, a program was fostered and successfully developed to meet the terrorist threat that blossomed far before the Omaha tragedy. It is called the A Teams.

"Like all novel developments, there were numerous obstacles and challenges to bring it to fruition, but the president persisted in supporting the initiative carefully implemented with the concurrence and support of the FBI," he said, motioning in a patronizing gesture toward Director Hagen.

SSA Campo was fuming as the vice president continued stealing the credit for his, Campo's, brainchild. The vice president was clearly giving the president credit for saving the country. He was upset that nothing was being said about a courageous young woman who had stood up to the al-Qaeda and for doing so, had almost paid with her life, but in the process saved the lives of hundreds, maybe thousands, of Americans. He was angered by the fact no mention was being made of the innovative interviewing techniques and amazing people skills and power of persuasion deployed by Special Agents Jim Flynn, Ken Grogan, and Hank Duffin, the leadership of Joe Fredette, and the courage and suffering of Ridge Southerland.

The vice president continued. "These are ominous times for America . . . the flagship nation of the world, the last bastion of freedom and hope. A nation fraught with danger from the growing menace of international terrorism. These are times that call for leaders of sterling character and inspired direction. The kind of leadership demonstrated by this president."

When he's here, thought Campo.

"Folks, the calamities that could have occurred on December 24 would have been without precedent in the history of this country," the vice president stated. "Few leaders in the history of America have stepped forward in the face of such a daunting challenge as the Omaha bombing and these subsequent attempts to destroy Americans and have succeeded in achieving both protection and prosecution, as your president has done."

As the vice president continued heaping praise upon everyone except those who deserved it, SSA Campo turned off the television.

It's okay, he thought. *It's okay. Now that the president has seen the light, the power and potential of the FBI will finally be unleashed with the A Teams out ahead!*

CHAPTER 35
BUSINESS AS USUAL

WASHINGTON, DC
DECEMBER 27

SUPERVISORY SPECIAL AGENT DENNY Campo's facial expression was ecstatic as he welcomed in A2 Team for an assessment and overall critique of the OMAMALL case. All members were present with the exception of Agent Ridge Southerland, who was still recuperating and assigned to limited duty.

"What's the latest scoop on Southerland?" asked Joe Fredette with obvious concern.

"Yeah. What's up with the Ridge Man?" added Jim Flynn. "We've heard very little about how he's doing. What gives?"

"Easy guys, . . . easy!" responded Campo, happily. "With all this going on coordinating surveillances across America, along with the arrests of the other eight members of The Ten, who were *only* going to destroy the country, then trying to keep the Director updated and happy while I'm worrying about you guys out there—I've been busy, so maybe you didn't get *all* the news you wanted on a timely basis? So, what? You going to hang me out to dry? You know I can still take any one of you guys on *mano a mano*, so don't press your luck, okay?"

"Typical supervisor response," replied Ken Grogan, speaking under his breath to Flynn, with a smirk on his face.

"I heard that, you Georgia cracker meathead!" said Campo. "Okay, enough is enough! The bottom line is Ridge's doing fine—he's pulling some limited duty there at the Plantation Resident Agency out of Miami. Last night the only concern he had was for the Ahmed girl, who he's going to invite to move in with his family—"

"Oh yeah, that's Bishop Ridge! For sure," interrupted Grogan. "The one guy in the whole bloomin' organization that would adopt a suicide bomber!"

The room erupted with laughter.

"You guys may not believe this, but the Ridge Man says this one has all the traits of a good Mormon!" said Campo. "There's been a complete change of heart in this girl, according to Southerland."

"Maybe she decided to find religion after her brother went up in flames," speculated Grogan. "I mean that was something else. The kid pulls the string on himself and takes out three major al-Qaeda operatives here in God's Great Land, saving his sister in the process."

"Right," answered Flynn. "All in one fell swoop! Better there at the house than in that mall!"

Fredette was uneasy. It was obvious that he was still fretting. "All right . . . let's get back to Southerland. Are there any residual problems? When will he be ready to go?"

"Okay, Old Mother Hen," said Campo. "No, there are no residuals that will be permanent. His arm will be in a sling a couple more weeks, then he'll rehab maybe three or four more weeks, but he can work in the meantime, once he starts rehab. He'll get back in shape and will be reassigned to the team by no later than the end of February."

"Good thing," said Fredette, "because it looks like we're going to need him. All the intel Duffin and I have been picking up from the East Coast sources is that the Christmas Eve event was to be just the second installment of a planned sequence of attacks, the first of which was the Omaha bombing. According to one well-placed and reliable snitch, al-Qaeda is going to hit us hard around Easter in a big way . . . again from south of the border."

"Now that's hot data," Campo said, "real hot, because it corroborates what we're hearing back from a couple of arrestees of

The Ten who sang after they were busted. We're hearing that now they want to come after us on our religious holidays, starting with Easter . . . about a *hundred* of them!

"What a stroke of Irish luck that was!" added Duffin. "The one kid that gave it up in San Francisco told us that he'd spent almost a whole hour with the two skinheads that brought his bombs. They had been drinking beers . . . lots of them. He told the kid and his sister way too much about the attack next Easter. Like you said, Denny, they'll be coming like bees after the honey!"

"What do you mean, Duffin? Translate what you said. It's not time to make up games!" Campo insisted.

"No, it was just a thought while shaving," said Duffin. "Joe was right. There's a hundred of 'em coming, and not with Easter baskets."

Campo shook his head and looked up toward heaven, his eyes rolling. He knew he couldn't live with or without these guys.

"We still don't know for sure all the whos and wheres," Duffin continued, "but we know they're coming. God help us! The skinheads told the kids in Frisco that they knew the Mexicans at the border were going to make it easy for them."

Campo reported that the major consensus among the apprehended Patriots was that there had been major restructuring of the Mountain Patriots. Headquarters had been moved to an extremely isolated area near Joseph, Oregon, on the Imnaha River. Campo further advised that according to the arrestees, new leaders had come forth immediately to fill the vacuum in the Mountain Patriots created by two game-changing events: the death of Buck Bowen and Ike Grimsley going into the federal witness protection program. The same sources had revealed that new ties had been formed with key al-Qaeda operatives in the United States who replaced Abu Khan. Campo also stated that an alliance with a previously unknown Mexican cartel leader, now believed to be Carlos Quesada and his drug cartel, was in place that generated training sessions, documents for identification, and transportation for assisting al-Qaeda operatives to cross the border and attack Americans.

"It's like the whole bucket of worms is starting all over again," remarked Fredette. "These guys never give up!"

Fredette was right. Within a month's time, Rashid Siddiqui's assignment to develop "homegrown" suicide bombers within America had been delegated to a new imam—Abeer Akhtar. Confidential sources describe him as being even more militant than his predecessor.

Abu Khan's role in coordinating the terrorists' business in the United States was taken over by Tahir Babi and Parvaiz Hussain. They chose to operate out of New York City with part-time residence at a different luxury hotel in the Grand Cayman.

Bashir Sayed's involvement in coordinating the al-Qaeda actions from Islamabad was now very suspect, following the failure of The Ten to carry out their missions. Al-Qaeda replaced him with one of many terrorist operatives who could effectively assume that responsibility . . . a young jihadist by the name of Aadab Kauser. Kauser continued to work closely with the new leaders of the Mountain Patriots and with Carlos Quesada's organization in Mexico to carry out the planned Easter attacks.

With the new intelligence gleaned from reliable FBI sources, Campo knew all ten of the A Teams would have to be deployed immediately and tasked with the challenge of stopping The Hundred and others lined up behind them. He knew the administration would now be ready to back the Bureau in that effort. But he questioned if it was enough. He, like everyone else in the room, was absolutely convinced the terrorists would never stop and that their hate for America would never falter.

CHAPTER 36
THE STRUGGLE

PLANTATION, FLORIDA
NIGHT OF DECEMBER 27

DELISHA'S DELIRIUM HAD CONTINUED for three days. Once the two bullet fragments were removed, one from an area next to her heart and another from near her lungs, the doctors indicated somewhat tentatively, that there was some hope for recovery. As she lay motionless in the hospital, she recalled the advice that then Bishop Southerland had given her regarding her approach to overcoming adversity. "Substitute wonderful, happy thoughts for what pains you," he had suggested. "Think of those wonderful moments as a child or in your youth that were the most carefree and happy and allow them to drown out your pain and sorrow."

Why not? Delisha asked herself. The sedative had taken effect. She was warm and comfortable under the blankets of her reclining bed and was feeling no pain. She decided to follow Bishop Ridge Southerland's advice.

Her thoughts retreated back in time. She and Lufti were at the merry-go-round at the carnival shortly after moving to Florida. Lufti was six years old and she was five. Her parents were happy then. They knew they would have their children for almost two entire decades before they would have to give them up as a special gift to Allah. Besides that, all the major expenses of the Ahmed family would be taken care of through al-Qaeda funding. Like the other families of The Ten, the Ahmeds had the world by the tail.

Delisha recalled her father laughing happily, as he mounted her and Lufti on the horses while their mother looked on smiling. Each time she and Lufti made a complete circle on their horses past her parents, they would wave at them proudly as their mother snapped photos. Her father waved at them and made funny faces.

A smile formed on Delisha's face.

Next, she remembered watching the sumptuous cotton candy being spun from the machine at the carnival, spewing forth fibers of colored sugar webbing onto the paper cone funnels, forming a huge, mouth-watering bundle of sweet delight.

As the morphine continued to ply its soothing effect, Delisha continued, absorbed in fond recollection. There were the picnics in the many parks bordering the Atlantic Ocean on the sandy shores of South Florida near Las Olas Boulevard in Fort Lauderdale. Her father would help her and Lufti build large sand castles, while her mother would spread out a delicious lunch on a blanket with all the children's favorite goodies.

Once the lunch was devoured, everyone would lie down for a nap or just watch the waves come in. Often she and Lufti would giggle at their father, who would wade out in the water with their mother to wait for the waves to come in. He would roll up his pants past his knees, but it was never far enough to prevent his trousers from getting soaked. Delisha recalled her mother trying to modestly hold her dress down to keep the rushing water from pushing it up over her knees. She smiled a little more, recalling how her father always started splashing her mother and how her mother tried in vain to retaliate.

Yes, thought Delisha. *They were happy then . . . my parents. Those were the best days of my life! Probably for them too.*

Then Delisha recalled with sadness how her parents became more on edge and filled with apprehension as the years went by and she and Lufti became teenagers. Both became less happy. Now, for the first time, she understood! *No wonder they became more grumpy and irritable and unable to communicate well with us*, she thought. *They knew they were going to lose us. How would any parent feel?* she asked herself. Delisha was beginning to comprehend the turmoil that her parents must have experienced, once they had consented to sacrificing their children . . . even if it was for what they must have considered a just and holy cause. Delisha recalled the pain in her mother's face in the brief good-bye and how all her father could do was wave.

The pain returned.

Delisha pressed the button to summon the nurse. She was subsequently administered another dose of painkiller. Once she felt the soothing relief of the morphine coursing again through her blood stream, Delisha started drifting.

Lufti's face kept coming, first as a small child, then transitioning to a young adult. Delisha remembered his expression when he was being subdued by Siddiqui and his thugs. She envisioned him again in that choke hold, looking at her in desperation, wanting her to be far enough away from the impact of the catastrophe that he was about to create. It would end his life . . . but save hers.

Tears flowed. She worried about Lufti. *Where was he? Would she ever see him again?*

Suddenly, Lufti's image appeared directly in front of her. He smiled at her and appeared relaxed and content. He stood quietly next to Delisha's bed, looking directly into her eyes. He didn't utter a word but continued radiating the most pleasant smile.

At that moment, Delisha knew everything was okay with Lufti . . . and that she needn't worry any longer about her brother. Wherever he was, he was all right. Delisha recalled what the young missionaries, Elders Brown and Sterling had taught her regarding paradise, the place spirits go to after death to await the resurrection. Delisha knew Lufti was there, waiting for her.

She smiled.

* * * * *

Two more days passed as Delisha continued to experience bouts of severe pain, resulting from the procedure where the bullet fragments had been removed. Her suffering was intense during the time her flesh was healing. She was not administered any more morphine and was given less painkiller. Her thinking became more clear.

That's when the reality of her situation set in.

She was alone now. Her parents could never return to the United States without being arrested as accomplices to attempting to commit mass murder. Lufti was gone. She had no further means of support and no employment. Her home was demolished. She had no funds for furthering her education. If she did survive, how would she pay her medical bills? Where would she go to recuperate . . . and then, where would she live? Anticipating that her life would end on December 24, she had no need to do any planning. Indeed, her life was now in shambles.

Delisha felt disenfranchised from the future.

These thoughts were overpowering Delisha, as the pain again returned, along with an intense fever. She was fatigued, beaten down, and full of despair. The tank of happy thoughts and positive thinking had emptied.

It was just past midnight. Overcome with anguish, Delisha began wishing her life would end. She was convinced that she had no life and no purpose. She sank into a deep slumber, a sleep accompanied with a notion of oblivion—oblivion she hoped somehow might lead to her annihilation. Dark clouds formed on her horizon. They began encircling her. It was a darkness like none she had ever experienced. *Am I dying? I hope so!* she thought. *But why is death so dark and foreboding? Why must it be so awful?*

There were no answers for Delisha. But there was something else. Just a slim needle of light, miles and miles away, beginning to penetrate a miniscule portion of darkness far, far away on the horizon, barely perceptible. Coming a little closer . . . just barely closer, casting off a little more illumination.

What is this? Delisha asked herself. *That light is so small . . . yet so powerfully bright!*

Now the light became increasingly more present, and the bigger it got, the faster it moved into her room, filling it, magnifying its presence ten fold, then a hundred times that.

Delisha brought her hands in front of her face, now shielding herself from the expanding brightness. The huge ray of light appeared to suck in the darkness and the gloom from Delisha's room as well as from her soul, fattening itself with what it was consuming, becoming still bigger and bigger, until the hospital room was totally engrossed with the magnificent light.

Delisha felt the light permeate through her, saturating her mind and body. It was both warm and resplendent. As it continued to fill her soul, Delisha felt like she was partaking of an absolutely fulfilling, heartwarming feast with all the trimmings.

When the light reached what appeared to be its complete elucidation, an outline appeared within it—a countenance. The face was kind and bearded. The eyes were piercing, as they stared directly into Delisha's. The entire body materialized, cloaked in a white robe. The person was muscular, perfectly symmetrical. His palms were outstretched to her.

Delisha recognized this individual immediately, based upon her study of the Holy Bible. The Savior came as an answer to her prayers.

Delisha discerned the nail marks in the outstretched palms, wrists, and feet. Her heart filled with a warm assurance that she had felt at no other time in her life. All she desired was to be in the presence of this Glorious Being—forever!

A smile formed on her Visitor's lips, again filling Delisha with an ecstatic joy that surpassed anything she had ever felt or experienced.

As the image began to fade, Delisha fell into a deep sleep and slumbered pleasantly throughout the night. Her doubts vanished and her life changed forever.

She didn't wake up until shortly after ten the next morning. Her pain had gradually subsided some and her fever had broken. As she opened her eyes, she noticed she had visitors. Ridge Southerland was there with his arm in a sling, accompanied by Madi, who was holding a tall crystal vase, full of freshly cut flowers.

A third individual stepped out from behind Ridge . . . a dark-complected, handsome man in his mid-twenties. It was Rhett Brown, one of the young missionaries who five years before, had taught Delisha about Jesus Christ, trying to convince her that He was the Savior of the world and that He had established his church again on the earth through a living prophet. She recalled the discussions she'd had with Elder Brown about that and how she studied the Bible just to disprove him.

"Hi, Delisha. It's been a while. Wow, look at what you've been through!" Rhett smiled, sympathetically. "Bishop Southerland called me shortly after you went into the hospital. He asked me to come down and help give you a blessing. It looks like it's taken effect. You look great today."

Rhett noticed that Delisha had matured into a beautiful young woman since he had first met her in Florida. He had thought about her often since finishing his mission, but college and a part-time job had consumed most of his time and effort. Although he had never recontacted her personally, he had been in touch a few times with Ridge, who had encouraged him to apply for a special agent position with the FBI.

As Delisha became cautiously aware of a unique warmth radiating through her arm, she realized Rhett had taken her hand into his while talking to her. She felt something special. So did Rhett. It was something he had felt years before when he first met this pretty young Pakistani girl. He could not pursue that feeling as a missionary. It was different now. There she was—beautiful with soft olive-colored skin, and smiling at him! Rhett felt a need to see that situation transform into something more permanent.

Delisha was holding onto Madi with her other hand. She motioned Madi to lean down to her so she could kiss her friend on the forehead. Next, she motioned Ridge over and squeezed his hand.

Delisha addressed Rhett. "Elder Brown . . . uh . . . Rhett, tell me about Elder Sterling. Where is he and how is he?"

"Elder Sterling passed away, as he always knew he would, soon after he got home," answered Rhett. "It was about a year later, I think. He was in a hospital the last four months of his life. I visited him three times. Each time he asked about you and Lufti, wanting to know if I had heard anything. He really liked Lufti. Did you know that they had the same birthday?"

Delisha was amazed. "Lufti and I had no idea. He never mentioned it."

"He never wanted to interject himself with teaching the gospel," replied Rhett. "That was just Elder Sterling. But while we were teaching you and Lufti, he mentioned it to me all the time. He thought it was a good omen, I guess. Personally, I firmly believe that Elder Sterling and Lufti are now in touch with one another." Rhett smiled.

"I'm anxious to hear more about that,"said Delisha as she returned Rhett's smile.

"Delisha, your situation has been discussed with the United States Attorney's office," Ridge said. "You and Lufti prevented a disaster from occurring at that mall. Your case has been referred to the Victim Relief Coordinator, part of the US Attorney's office. Certain monetary reparations will be made for you as a victim of al-Qaeda terrorism. You'll receive substantial compensation for future living expenses and furtherance of your education for the coming few years. Meantime, my wife and I insist you live with us. I want you to know that we're not prepared to take no for an answer. Our oldest son, Charley, just left to serve a two-year church mission. You'll inherit his room."

Delisha's heart nearly jumped out of her body. Tears came freely as Madi embraced her again and pronounced her joy at the arrangement. "Delisha, I can't wait to have you in my house."

"We've made arrangements for a special memorial service at the church for Lufti, if we have your permission," Ridge continued. "All of his prior track and basketball teammates want to be there, along with some teachers and others who knew him."

Delisha couldn't believe all that was happening, especially in view of how she had felt just hours before. She continued weeping happily, breathing in the outpouring of love she was receiving.

"Another thing, Delisha," added Madi as she placed Delisha's Young Womanhood Recognition medallion around her neck. "I replaced the other chain this was attached to. It got pretty beat up during your . . . accident. So I bought you this one."

It all seemed like a wonderful, unbelievable dream to Delisha. *Should I pinch myself?* she wondered.

Another development eclipsed even the jubilation of all else that was happening. Delisha realized that Rhett Brown had never let go of her hand, nor had he taken his eyes off of her.

Delisha looked up at Rhett hopefully, suddenly feeling like no one else was there, except him.

MIKE MCPHETERS, raised in Ketchum, Idaho, served as a Special Agent of the FBI and a SWAT team member for over thirty years, while also serving four times as a Mormon bishop. He was decorated by the Bolivian government for his role in investigating the killing of two LDS missionaries in La Paz, Bolivia. He also investigated the James Hoffa murder, the D. B. Cooper hijacking, Rajneeshpuram (a commune founded in Central Oregon by a bhagwan from India), major narcotics distributors, and many other significant cases. Mike completed his undergraduate work at Brigham Young University and received Master of Business and Master of Public Administration degrees from City University in Bellevue, Washington.

Mike is a retired member of the "National Association of Legal Investigators," the world's premier private investigator association. He was a Certified Legal Investigator (CLI) with them before he retired. It's a board-certified position held only by approximately 120 investigators worldwide.

Currently, Mike is a lecturer for Norwegian Cruise Lines, Royal Caribbean Cruise Lines, and Celebrity Cruise Lines. He has lectured in over twenty countries. He and his wife, Judy, have five children and twenty-one grandchildren. They reside in Ivins, Utah.

Mike recently authored the bestselling book *Agent Bishop: True Stories from an FBI Agent Moonlighting as a Mormon Bishop* and *Cartels & Combinations*.

Visit www.MikeMcpheters.com for more information, or email Mike at mikem@gcpower.net for setting up speaking engagements or book signings.